Death on the Edge

– Douglas Binstead –

Printed and bound in England by www.printondemand-worldwide.com

http://www.fast-print.net/bookshop

Death on the Edge
Copyright © Douglas Binstead 2018

ISBN: 978-178456-630-2

All rights reserved

No part of this book may be reproduced in any form by photocopying or any electronic or mechanical means, including information storage or retrieval systems, without permission in writing from both the copyright owner and the publisher of the book.

The right of Douglas Binstead to be identified as the author of this work has been asserted by him in accordance with the Copyright, Designs and Patents Act 1988 and any subsequent amendments thereto.

A catalogue record for this book is available from the British Library

First published 2018 by
FASTPRINT PUBLISHING
Peterborough, England.

DEATH ON THE EDGE
BY
DOUGLAS BINSTEAD

AUTHOR'S NOTE

The events described at Pottery Cottage did actually take place between the 12 and the 14 January 1977 and William Hughes, the Morans, the Mintons and their neighbours were all real-life persons.

Otherwise the events portrayed in this book are fictitious, although some features are drawn from other cases known to the author. Those other cases are based on events that occurred in other places or at other times from those depicted here.

All the characters are fictitious, although again some of the characteristics of a few of them are drawn from persons known to the author. Those few persons were mostly, although not entirely, to be found in west Derbyshire at the time of or within a few years of the events described in this book.

CHAPTER ONE

January 12th

January the 12th, 1977. The first snow of the winter in the Peak District of Derbyshire had fallen and by daybreak lay heavily on the top of the escarpment of the long eastern gritstone edges, and on the jumble of boulders, millstones and paths to be found at the base of their fifteen miles of crags.

The body was found just before ten o'clock by two young male rock-climbers from Sheffield. It was half-submerged in the bracken below the escarpment known as Curbar Edge and about halfway along its length. It had clearly sustained severe head and pelvic injuries, but appeared to be that of a young woman. Her clothing, flared jeans and a thin sweater, seemed scarcely suitable apparel for outdoor activity on a cold winter's morning in the bleak crag and moorland country in that part of Derbyshire. She wore no headwear of any sort, but was wearing a pair of boots, readily identifiable as the type commonly worn by rock-climbers and known to them as 'PAs'.

One of the two climbers who had found the body hurried off along the rough track at the bottom of the crag to the village of Curbar, some two or three kilometres away, where he rang for the emergency services from a public phone box. Less than an hour later two police constables from Bakewell had reached the scene of the incident, closely followed by six members of the mountain rescue team from Buxton, including their team doctor. Their urgency was in vain, since it was soon apparent that this young woman was beyond help and had been dead for some time.

In the circumstances there was time for those who had gathered at the scene to consider how the unfortunate victim had come to grief. The mountain rescue men had no doubt that she had been climbing alone on the edge, probably on a route of average difficulty, and had fallen, possibly from a height of seventy or eighty feet above the ground, striking the exposed rocks and boulders at the foot of the crag, the momentum of the fall taking her below the path and into the bracken. Despite the fact that she was hardly dressed for rock-climbing on that day, that she was not wearing a helmet, and that there was no sign of a rope, never mind a climbing partner, her footwear clearly marked her out as a climber. It was by no means unusual in the mid-seventies for accomplished rock-climbers to climb 'solo' and many at that time did not bother with a helmet, taking the view that if they fell any distance a helmet was not likely to make any difference.

The police officers saw no reason to disagree with or challenge this reasoning and soon departed the scene, leaving the mountain rescue team to stretcher the body off the edge and to the ambulance that had arrived in the carpark at the southern end of the escarpment. The deceased was then transported to the mortuary to await post-mortem.

There was another more pressing reason for the police officers not to remain long at the scene. Their presence was required to assist in a major manhunt that had begun earlier that morning and which, by eleven o'clock, involved dozens of their fellow officers from north and west Derbyshire. William Thomas Hughes, a thirty-year old man from Preston, had been travelling to Chesterfield Magistrates' Court from Leicester prison to face charges of rape and wounding with intent. On the outskirts of Chesterfield he had overwhelmed and stabbed his prison guards with a seven-inch blade he had smuggled out of the prison and hijacked their car, driving off at speed in a westerly direction towards the Peak District. He was a desperate man with a history of criminal violence and the need to find and apprehend him was imperative. The death of a lone 'climber' on a Derbyshire crag was, at this time, of only passing interest to the constabulary.

★★★★★★★★★★★★★★★★★★★★★★★★★★

Just after one o'clock that afternoon the road through Chatsworth Park was almost entirely obliterated by a white carpet of snow. It had seen little traffic that day and the only clue to its course was the barbed wire fence on one side, liberally festooned with the corpses of dozens of moles, left to hang there by the prolific 'mole catchers' employed on the Chatsworth Estate. The dark colouring of the dead mammals stood out against the glistening white landscape.

Martin Tory, at the wheel of his rear-wheel-drive Ford Capri, was beginning to bitterly regret his decision to take the 'scenic' route back to his office in South Darley. His day as the duty prosecutor at Chesterfield Court had finished earlier than anticipated when the prisoner William Hughes and his escort had failed to arrive for the remand hearing, and it had become apparent that Hughes was now unlawfully at large. After a leisurely lunch at the Devonshire Arms at Baslow, it had seemed a sound idea to meander back through the park rather than follow the main road through Bakewell.

Martin, however, had not bargained for the fact that, on such a day, the public at large would tend to avoid the back road, and the need to try and locate the tarmac surface and to generally keep his vehicle off the verges, meant that his speed had been reduced almost to a crawl. His other pre-occupation was with the possible whereabouts of the escaped prisoner. His car radio, tuned to a local radio station, had told him that the car that Hughes had 'hijacked' had been recovered, having apparently ploughed into a dry-stone wall on Beeley Moor. Of Hughes there was no sign. Beeley

Moor was only a few miles from Martin's current location and in the lonely park and in his motoring predicament, he felt somewhat vulnerable and not a little apprehensive, since it occurred to him that a slow-moving vehicle might present a possible target for a desperate man. On another day, the complete absence of other persons in the park and the gently falling snow, would have been welcome, pleasant and even enchanting. That afternoon it was forbidding and ominous.

After what seemed like an eternity of nerve-shredding, painful progress, hunched over the steering-wheel, Martin suddenly became aware of a pair of headlights approaching him. The oncoming vehicle was moving at a confident pace and Martin pulled over as far as he dared to his nearside to let it pass. As it drew nearer he recognized the distinctive squat shape of a Land Rover, and then he saw, to his relief, that it bore on its side panels the equally conspicuous livery of the Chatsworth Estate. The Land Rover halted as it drew alongside Martin and the driver wound his window down. Martin did likewise. The man's appearance was reassuring – flat cap, craggy face, Barbour jacket. 'Alright, mate?' he enquired. Martin nodded uncertainly.

'Nice motor,' said the other driver. 'All right for picking up girls, but no bloody good for this weather. But take your time, follow my tracks, and you'll be okay.'

Martin gratefully murmured his thanks and set off with renewed confidence, now that he could drive in the deep, clear tyre-tracks left by the Land-Rover. Making faster progress, and meeting no other vehicles, it seemed that in no time he was pulling on to the main A6 at Rowsley. The busy trunk road was almost snow free.

Relieved of his earlier anxieties, Martin now allowed his mind to wander off on to thoughts of what awaited him back at the office. He knew that he had a number of files on his desk relating to serious criminal offences, including rape and grievous bodily harm, all awaiting his consideration and advice to the police. Although barely thirty, and with only four years of experience as a prosecutor, Martin was held in high esteem by his colleagues and the police force he served, and had quickly achieved promotion in the office of the County Prosecuting Solicitor to a rank where he routinely dealt with such cases. In a relatively short time he had forged close relationships with a number of senior local police officers and he strongly valued the mutual warm respect that had resulted. Some of his colleagues adopted a more 'arms's length' relationship with the officers they advised, and, if they thought a case should not be pursued because of insufficient evidence, they would say so, often quite bluntly, and move on to the next file. Martin, however, in the same circumstances preferred to look for ways the police might reinforce the evidence or pursue other lines of enquiry, and he would advise accordingly, rather than rejecting the case out of hand. This was an approach the police liked and respected.

One of the serious cases he had recently reviewed was that of the man who was now unlawfully at large – William Thomas Hughes. Martin mused that there was now likely to be a further file to consider for Hughes: if and when he was caught he would almost certainly face charges of escaping from lawful custody, and wounding with intent or even attempted murder. And who knows what other offences he might commit before he was apprehended? He would need to find shelter before nightfall. He was hardly going to be booking into a hotel or looking for accommodation at a pub. Some unsuspecting householder at one of the remote farms or dwellings on the edge of the moors was going to be opening his door to a man brandishing a knife and in no mood for pleasantries.

His thoughts were interrupted by the arrival of the side road off the A6, which he needed to take to get to his office. The road was still snow covered and required his full attention, particularly where the carriageway narrowed as it crossed the bridge over the river Derwent. The office carpark, which he reached shortly after, was almost empty of vehicles. No doubt, Martin thought, his lawyer colleagues were holed up in pubs or police stations across the county, and almost certainly the office staff had been sent home early. He parked gingerly and turned off the engine. The radio was tuned to a local station and as he was turning it off he was dimly aware of a newsreader referring to the discovery of a woman's body below Curbar Edge. Climbing accident, he thought, and put it out of his mind.

★★★★★★★★★★★★★★★★★★★★★★★★★★

The office staff at Brook, Hassop & Co., solicitors of Bakewell, had also been sent home by mid-afternoon that day. The partners had decided by two o'clock because of the adverse weather conditions, but more particularly the fact that a violent, escaped prisoner was abroad, that all employees should have the opportunity to travel home in daylight. Quite a few of them lived in rural locations to the east and south-east of the town and they needed no encouragement to leave the office and set off home as soon as possible.

For senior partner Bob Hassop, still sitting at his desk at three o'clock, it had been a frustrating day. His secretary Beverley had not turned up for work that morning and he had been obliged to deposit some of his increasing backlog of typing on the already hard-pressed secretaries of his two partners. And now the early finish to their working day meant that little headway had been made.

It was really time, Bob thought, that he should finally get rid of the wayward and unreliable Beverley. This was by no means the first time she had let the firm down. It was not the first time she had absented herself from work without leave or notice, or even the courtesy of a later phone call to say that she was ill or had to wait in for a tradesman to call. Anyway, Bob mused, it was more likely that she had gone off for a day's rock climbing, or, equally likely that she was with some man, taking advantage of the absence of her husband, whose work regularly took him well away from the area. It was common knowledge that Beverley was a free spirit, with little attachment to her marriage vows, and she made little attempt to conceal her frequent illicit liaisons with other males, both from Bakewell and beyond. Her husband was almost certainly aware of her activities, but, for whatever reason, seemed to condone them. Indeed, Bob reflected, whenever he had seen the two of them together, they seemed at ease in each other's company and came across as a happy and contented married couple.

The problem Bob faced with Beverley, however, was that he had never been able to bring himself to even chide her for her misdemeanours, let alone sack her.

Even though he might have intended to have been firm with her, he had found, again and again, that her particular brand of flirtatious charm was completely disarming, and every time he had shrunk from handing out even a mild rebuke. She was 'easy on the eye' and knew precisely how to massage the ego of her middle-aged, balding employer. According to his wife, he was 'putty in her hands' and he knew she was right in this assessment. It would be much easier if the girl was ever truculent or morose. Unfortunately she was always affable and cheerful, and gratuitously apologetic when she was in the wrong. Bob found it quite impossible, in these circumstances, to show any hint of anger or annoyance, and things would simply carry on as before. Another difficulty was that when she was at work, which, to be fair, she was more often than not, Beverley Simpson was a diligent and highly efficient secretary and Bob knew that he would be lucky to find a replacement who would come close to matching her very obvious qualities.

The sudden shrill ringing of the telephone in the outer office brought Bob out of his reverie. Immediately the realization dawned on him that he was the last person left in the building, and he hastened to answer the phone. The caller was his own wife and he quickly detected the concern in her voice. Why was he still at work? Didn't he know there was a violent escaped prisoner at large? Didn't he know what the weather was like? Daphne was a worrier at the best of times and Bob tried to reassure her by telling her he was about to leave the office and would be home very shortly. He knew that she wouldn't cease worrying until he actually entered the house. As he lived west of Bakewell at Ashford-in-the Water he somehow doubted that the escapee would turn up there, and his brand new Range Rover would be more than equal to the weather conditions. However, there was no more work going to be done that afternoon, so he might as well leave. He put on his overcoat, gathered up his keys and prepared to leave the building.

★★★★★★★★★★★★★★★★★★★★★★★★★★

Martin Tory, finding his workplace practically deserted, had stuffed a few files in his briefcase, and had left the building within minutes of having arrived there. Before he and Bob Hassop had left their respective offices, however, William Thomas Hughes had already found himself shelter for the night and, for the moment at least, no longer presented a danger to the public at large. For the inhabitants of Pottery Cottage, Eastmoor, however, tragedy was about to engulf them.

Having abandoned the crashed stolen car at Beeley, Hughes had set off across the moors on foot. Trudging for almost three hours through drifting snow and blizzard, in a generally north-easterly direction, he spotted a terraced row of cottages on the edge of the moor. These isolated dwellings were situated on the A619 at Eastmoor, a hamlet about four miles to the east of Baslow. At one end of the row stood Pottery Cottage, and Hughes, by now no doubt cold and hungry, decided that this was to be his resting place for the time being. Having picked up two axes that he had found outside the property, he silently entered the house.

Inside he came across the only two people who were home at that time – 72-year-old Arthur Minton and his 68-year-old wife Amy. Their daughter Gill Moran and her husband Richard were out at work, and their grand-daughter Sarah was still at school. Confronted by an armed man, the two pensioners, at that time anyway, were not going to involve themselves in any heroics. The same applied to Gill and Richard when they returned home later, both resolving to co-operate with Hughes rather than provoking him into violence. Ten-year-old Sarah, when she came in from school, was told that Hughes was a stranded motorist who was waiting for help, and, initially at least she was kept out of the way in her bedroom. She was shortly to be disabused of this notion, however, when Hughes decided to tie up all of his captives, using electrical flex and a washing line.

Up to this point the family had been entirely submissive. As he was being bound, however, Mr. Minton suddenly lost his composure and began shouting at Hughes. This proved to be a fatal mistake on his part. Hughes gagged the others and moved them upstairs to the bedrooms, but left Arthur downstairs on his own. Unbeknown to the others, he then silently murdered the old man, knifing him to death with a boning knife he had found in a kitchen drawer. This was the first act in the unspeakable tragedy that was to take place over the next forty-eight hours.

CHAPTER TWO

January 13th

The large-scale police search for William Thomas Hughes on the 12th January had drawn a complete blank. It was to fare no better on the following day. The weather proved to be a significant hindrance to the enterprise. Although the abandoned stolen car had been found at Beeley early on the first afternoon, enabling the immediate search to be focused on areas within a five-mile radius of the village, the continuous falling snow ensured that any footprints were quickly obliterated and dramatically slowed the progress of the bands of searching police officers. The weather prevented the use of helicopters on that first day, and the search dogs had failed to pick up any scent. The search area consisted of a mix of moorland, fields, woodland and small villages and settlements, and hundreds of scattered and isolated dwellings and farm buildings. The police were well aware that Hughes would almost certainly have found shelter in one of these buildings before nightfall and, bearing in mind his need for sustenance, it was equally certain that he would have insinuated himself or forced his way into an occupied dwelling. This created a further problem for the searching officers, since knocking on doors was likely to be an unfruitful and possibly even a dangerous activity. Hughes was hardly going to answer the door in person, and any member of a family being held hostage who was sent to do so was not likely to betray their captor in those circumstances, and any attempt on their part to 'give the game away' with a covert or coded message might seriously jeopardize the safety of the other hostages.

The snow had abated by early morning on the 13th January, and the day was clear and bright. With the new day, the police strategy changed. Instead of the massive manhunt of the previous day, it was decided that a waiting game was the right approach. At some point Hughes would have to break cover and waiting for him to do so was less likely to lead to civilian casualties, or so it was thought, and ultimately likely to be more productive. The police, however, reckoned without the deranged mind of their quarry.

★★★★★★★★★★★★★★★★★★★★★★★★★★

The 'deranged mind' was at work again on the morning of the 13th January and moved into overdrive. It was a Thursday and should have been a working day for members of the Pottery Cottage household and a school day for Sarah. Hughes' first actions that morning were clearly designed to create an impression of normality. He released Gill's gag and asked her to contact her place of work and Sarah's school and to inform them that both she and the girl were sick and would not be attending. Gill also informed Hughes that a truck driver would be calling that morning in order to clean the septic tank at Pottery Cottage. Gill was released to greet the man when he called and to deal with him while he conducted the cleaning operation. Hughes made it quite clear to her that serious consequences for her family would follow if she did not co-operate. He need not have worried. Such was the depth of her fear that she coped with the event without raising the slightest suspicion in the mind of the tradesman that all was not well.

It was during the time of her 'freedom' that Gill briefly glimpsed her father lying on the floor covered by a coat. Hughes told her that the old man was 'asleep' and that he had covered him with the coat 'to keep him warm'. To perpetuate the charade of normality, Hughes then asked Gill to drive into Chesterfield and buy newspapers and cigarettes for him. Gill readily complied, still believing that he intended to do the family no harm if they continued to co-operate. Had she known, however, what evil Hughes had already perpetrated and of the further foul and depraved act that was to be carried out in her absence, she would surely have gone to the authorities?

Whilst Gill was out running his errand, Hughes took the opportunity to conceal Arthur Minton's body in an annexe. It is believed that he then carried out, for no obvious reason, what was surely the cruellest, vilest and most depraved act in the entire tragedy of the Pottery Cottage affair. While her mother was out, while her grandfather lay dead, and while her father and grandmother were bound and gagged upstairs, Hughes went to the bedroom where little Sarah was held and calmly and silently slit her throat using the same knife with which he had butchered Arthur.

★★★★★★★★★★★★★★★★★★★★★★★★★★★

Only a few miles away, in the mortuary in Chesterfield, away from the glare of publicity, a hospital pathologist was conducting a post-mortem examination on the body of the female recovered from below Curbar Edge. The only other persons present were a technician and a young police constable, who, to his chagrin, had been removed from the excitement of the hunt for William Thomas Hughes. As far as the youthful pathologist was concerned, this was just another routine examination and he conducted it in as perfunctory a manner as his sense of professional duty would permit. He had been informed of the circumstances in which the body had been found and the injuries spoke for themselves. Anyone, qualified or not, would be able to ascertain the cause of death, and it didn't require the expertise of a forensic pathologist to assist him in reaching a conclusion. Nonetheless he went through the motions of external and internal examination of the corpse. There was nothing remarkable about the internal organs, there was no sign of sexual trauma, and the bodily injuries were entirely consistent with a fall from seventy or eighty feet on to a bed of rocks and boulders. This was the body of a healthy young woman in her early thirties who had met with an unfortunate accident.

The only question that remained to be answered was 'who was she'? There were no clues as to her identity in her clothing or on her body. There was no wallet, purse or bank card. There were no name tags in her clothing. She wore no wedding ring or indeed any jewellery at all. No-one as yet had reported a missing person that matched her description. No anxious husband or relative had turned up at a police station to report concerns about a wife or daughter who had not come home for tea.

There were other ways to identify the deceased. Blood samples were taken and these might lead somewhere if the woman had been through surgery in the past. There was no indication on the body, however, that this was the case. There were no operation scars and it seemed clear that the deceased had not been through childbirth. There were, however, conspicuous tattoos on each shoulder, which would assist identification by someone who knew her intimately. Her fingerprints were taken, but these would not help unless she had a criminal record. The only other possibility was identification from dental records. In this instance, however, the traumatic injuries to the head had obliterated and fragmented the contents of the mouth and it was simply impossible to ascertain whether the deceased had had dental work in the past. Unless the fingerprints came up trumps, this was a case of 'identity unknown', what the Americans would call a 'Jane Doe'. Until there was an identification the coroner could not allow the body to be released for disposal.

★★★★★★★★★★★★★★★★★★★★★★★★★★★

Sitting behind his desk in his Bakewell office, Bob Hassop's normal composed and patient demeanour was being sorely tested. For the second successive day his errant secretary had failed to turn up for work. She really would have to go. Distasteful as it would be, he would find her and deliver the message himself. The chief clerk was able to find a telephone number for her and Bob rang the number himself. His call was unanswered and there was no answering machine to field it.

As he sat considering his next move, one guilty thought intruded on his annoyance. What if Beverley was in fact not absent without leave but was ill? What if she was lying in bed and too sick to come downstairs and answer the phone? Bob realised that it was quite possible that her husband was away on one of his frequent business trips, leaving Beverley alone in the house. There were no children of the marriage. If she was indeed ill and incapacitated would anyone have known? He summoned his articled clerk.

Michael Donald was a thin, mousy-haired young man of twenty-two, with an incipient moustache and a sallow complexion still bearing the vestiges of teenage acne. He had been Bob's articled clerk for six months and was still very much in awe of him. But then he was in awe of most of the people at Brook, Hassop & Co., both the lawyers and the unqualified staff. Even the clerical staff made him feel inferior, and they, sensing his lack of confidence, were not slow to treat him as the callow youth he appeared to them to be. His particular tormentor was Vera, the head of the admin department, who would never miss an opportunity to rib him about his youthful appearance and lack of girlfriends, and in a way which often left him feeling embarrassed and humiliated. Vera was a large, Junoesque woman of thirty-five, with exaggerated curves and an impossibly large bosom. It was at least some consolation to Michael that the other women in the office, whether out of jealousy of her physical attributes or otherwise, were given to making cruel or ribald remarks about Vera behind her back. The shared jibe, which never failed to amuse them, was 'Vera's tits entered the room, followed, but not very closely, by Vera'. Michael suspected that Vera would be mortified if she ever learnt of how the others joked at her expense, and he secretly hoped that one day she might find out.

He now knocked timidly on Bob's office door and waited for the command to enter. His principal, he noted, looked worried and not a little flustered. This was unusual as Bob rarely showed his emotions, or not to his subordinates anyway. But on this occasion his normal inscrutability was absent and he was clearly concerned about something. Michael was soon to learn the cause of his concern.

'Michael, am I right in thinking that you know where Beverley lives?' Bob asked.

Like the rest of the office staff, Michael knew that Beverley had something of a reputation. Surely Bob didn't think that he, Michael, had had a 'fling' with Beverley? For a moment he felt flattered and felt himself blushing. But then he remembered that he had, at Bob's request, recently given Beverley a lift home during a very heavy downpour, at a time when her husband had had the family car.

'Yes, I do, ' he replied. (He hadn't yet worked out whether he should be calling his principal 'Bob', 'Mr. Hassop' or even 'Sir', so tended to avoid calling him anything at all).

Bob explained his concerns to his articled clerk and asked him if he would call at the house to see if there was 'any sign of life'. This came across to Michael as an 'order' rather than as a 'request' and he wondered if it was in fact within the remit of his employment as an articled clerk to check on the whereabouts or welfare of missing secretaries, not that he was going to demur. It was not that unusual for Bob to send him on errands that had little or no connection with work – he had, for example, been despatched on more than one occasion to buy flowers for Mrs. Hassop or to find a birthday present for her. Basically, although Michael was supposed to be 'learning the trade' and being prepared to sit the solicitors' exams in due course, he had learnt precious little from Bob in the time he had been with the firm. Bob didn't really seem to know what to do with him and seemed to rely on his partners to show Michael 'the ropes'. He tended to give him only the odd menial task or to treat him as a 'go for' – 'go for this' or 'go for that'. So the current direction to go to Beverley's house and check up on her scarcely came as a surprise to Michael.

Michael really had no objection to the task. Beverley was one of the only two people at Brook, Hassop & Co. that he got on with. In fact his feelings for her went deeper than merely 'liking' or 'getting on with her'. He was quite infatuated with her. He knew about her reputation for 'playing the field', despite her marital status, but he cared not at all. In fact, in his eyes, her promiscuity only increased the appeal whilst underlining the unattainability. He secretly cherished wild desires of having a relationship with her. He knew, however, that there was no chance of this, even if he could have summoned up the courage to ask her out. Despite the fact that she was a secretary and he was, in theory at least, on the way to becoming a solicitor, he knew she was out of his league. In her presence he always felt overawed, diminished by her elegance and easy-going charm. She was always warm and affectionate towards him, but she just made him feel awkward and inadequate. She was quite simply out of his reach.

As he headed towards the office car park, Michael was intercepted in the corridor by Kevin Malcolm. Kevin was the junior partner in the firm, dealing with crime and the county court business. He was the other person at work with whom he felt he had any sort of rapport. Kevin was in his early thirties, recently married to a clerk in the office of the County Prosecuting Solicitor, where Kevin himself had worked before he joined Brook, Hassop & Co. He had built up a thriving criminal practice and he had gone out of his way to encourage Michael to become involved in his work. Unlike others at the firm, and the solicitors in particular, Kevin always treated Michael as an equal, often sought his views on cases and, on the surface at least, always gave the impression of taking these seriously. He took Michael to court, involved him in conferences with clients and barristers, and, more recently, allowed him to draft written instructions to counsel. He acted as the mentor and coach that Bob Hassop should have been but was not.

Kevin greeted Michael warmly. 'Fancy a trip to Buxton court?' he asked. 'One of my regulars is in custody on a rape charge.'

Michael explained that he was running an errand for the senior partner. When he outlined the nature of his task Kevin didn't speak but silently shook his head. Not the sort of job the articled clerk should be asked to undertake, he thought.

'Okay, catch up with you later,' he said, and retreated to his office to pick up his file for court.

Michael carried on to the car park and got into his

battered VW Beetle. He would have liked to go to Buxton, but his slight regret at missing this opportunity was outweighed by his concern for Beverley's welfare and the hope that he might be able to do her a service. If she was lying ill in bed, she might need some shopping doing, or a hot drink, he mused.

Although Michael had only taken Beverley home on the one occasion, the location of her house and how to get there was imprinted on his mind, and in no time at all he was pulling up outside her modern semi-detached dwelling in the quiet cul-de-sac on the southern edge of Bakewell. Despite the heavy snowfall of the previous day, the roads were by now fairly clear and it took him less than ten minutes to reach his destination. There was no car parked on the drive, but this did not mean that there would be no-one at home. Michael knew that the Simpsons were a one-car family and Beverley's husband was frequently away as his job took him all over the north of England.

Michael rang the doorbell twice. There was no response. He noticed that none of the curtains at the front of the house were drawn. He decided to check round the back. Peering through the kitchen window, he saw that there were no dirty dishes in the sink. The back door was locked and, again, the curtains in the rear bedrooms were not drawn. It seemed unlikely, therefore, that Beverley was a bed-bound invalid. All the indications were that there was no-one at home.

He returned to the front of the house, and as a precaution rang the doorbell once more, with the same result. He looked up and down the road and toyed with the thought of knocking on a neighbour's door to enquire if he or she might know of Beverley's whereabouts. He quickly abandoned that idea. There was no sign of life in any of the neighbouring dwellings. No twitching curtains. Michael's activity at the house seemed to have gone entirely unnoticed. But then this was the sort of road where, in all probability, most of the houses stood empty during working hours on a weekday. Most of the occupants would be thirty- or forty-somethings with no, or school-age, children, and both spouses out at work. But it was also the sort of road where people 'kept themselves to themselves' and would have little interest in or awareness of the comings-and-goings of neighbours. Michael reflected that he could have forcibly entered Beverley's home and walked out to his car with the television set and the stereogram without attracting the slightest suspicion or even being noticed. House-to-house enquiries by the police after a burglary in this neighbourhood would be a complete waste of time.

He drove back to the office and reported his findings, or lack of findings, to Bob Hassop. Bob sadly shrugged his shoulders and asked his managing clerk to put in motion the process of obtaining a temporary replacement typist from the recruitment agency, and advertising for a permanent replacement for Beverley.

No-one in the office, it seemed, had become aware of the discovery of the body a few miles away below Curbar Edge. This was, however, scarcely surprising, given that the local news had been dominated for the last 24 hours by the activities of a violent escaped prisoner and the failure to apprehend him.

★★★★★★★★★★★★★★★★★★★★★★★★★★★

At Pottery Cottage, William Hughes was continuing to lull the family into some sense of security. When Gill returned from Chesterfield, he assured her that all the other family members were safe and well but that he was keeping them apart from each other to prevent them conspiring to escape. He brought Richard downstairs temporarily and instructed him to telephone his place of work and report sick. A few hours later he carried both Richard and his mother-in-law downstairs and ordered Gill to cook toast and soup for them all. He even made a show of taking bowls of soup to Sarah and Arthur in a cynical ploy to convince the others that the girl and her grandfather were alive and well. Their 'co-operation' even extended to sitting down with Hughes that evening and playing cards with him. At this stage, they all believed that keeping their captor 'happy' was the key to ensuring the safety of all the family.

As evening drew on, the snow started to fall again outside. Hughes then outlined his immediate plans to the three adults. When the snow relented, he told them, he would take Richard's car and drive to Sutton-in-Ashfield, just over the border into Nottinghamshire, taking Gill with him as a hostage. He would, however, he said, release her as soon as he was well away from the area. The intention was to meet a criminal associate in Sutton-in-Ashfield, a man who owed him money. The money he was owed, he went on, would finance his continuing life on the run.

The pair set off in the car and did travel to Sutton-in-Ashfield. Hughes, however, did not release Gill Moran, and although he went into a café, ostensibly to meet the 'friend', it seems that he did not retrieve the money he was owed. Indeed, he drove back to Pottery Cottage, with Gill still a hostage, arriving there at about 2 o'clock in the morning. Gill pleaded with him to allow her to see her daughter. Not surprisingly the request was refused, she was bound and gagged again, and the three surviving hostages were moved to the bedroom in which Hughes was to sleep that night, 'so he could keep an eye on them'.

As they entered the third day of their 'imprisonment', Gill, Richard and Amy were still unaware of the terrible fate that had befallen Arthur and Sarah …

CHAPTER THREE

January 14th

The Friday morning dawned cold but bright. There had been no snowfall since the previous evening and traffic was flowing freely on the treated major roads. Snow, however, still lay heavily on the side roads and to a depth of several inches on the driveway of Pottery Cottage. Keen as ever to create an impression of normality and a sense that all was well, Hughes went outside with a shovel and cleared a path to the road. He also had an ulterior motive, however, as he required Richard and Gill to drive into Chesterfield to purchase supplies for his own impending journey of escape. It was hardly necessary to warn them of the penalty for non-co-operation or for alerting the authorities, but nonetheless Hughes chose to remind them before they left that if they went to the police he would kill Sarah and Gill's parents. His remarkable and extraordinarily callous parting words to them were, 'while you're out, buy a nice present for Sarah.'

As directed, Gill and Richard drove to Chesterfield and in a supermarket bought tinned food, cigarettes, and a camping gas stove for Hughes. The car was filled up with petrol, again at Hughes' behest. On the way home, in a final heart-wrenching gesture, they stopped at a book store and bought their daughter a collection of Enid Blyton stories.

Back at Pottery Cottage the façade of normality was still in place. On returning the Morans found Gill's mother at the home of the Newmans at the other end of the terrace, carrying out her weekly cleaning duties for them. The Newmans were out that day and Hughes had insisted that Amy undertook her normal routine, presumably so as not to arouse any suspicions among the neighbours that anything was amiss.

Come the evening and Hughes was still not ready to take his leave. Such was his skill in covering his tracks and creating an impression of normality, that none of the three surviving members had yet any inkling that Sarah and Arthur were dead, and neither Richard nor Amy had any reason to believe that they were living the last day of their respective lives. They all sat down to eat an evening meal cooked by Amy.

Hughes had one more pressing need before he could leave – money. He ascertained from Richard that there was cash to be had at the plastics factory where Richard was a director. At six o'clock, Richard drove Hughes to his place of work in Chesterfield. When they arrived the night shift had just begun, and Richard told a colleague that he was 'working late'.

The colleague later told the police that it appeared that Richard wanted to say something more, but decided against it. Richard then brought Gill and Hughes into his office, where Hughes carried out a search and retrieved £210 from Richard's desk. The three of them then returned to Pottery Cottage.

Back at the house, Richard was again bound and gagged and Hughes then packed the car with the provisions that had been purchased earlier. Prior to his departure he informed Richard and Gill that he was once again taking the latter with him as a hostage but reiterated his previous promise that he would release her once he was well away from Pottery Cottage. Hughes then drove off, with Gill as a passenger, but before he had travelled two miles, he abruptly decided to turn round and drive back to the house. He told Gill that he wanted to change into one of Richard's suits, and also pick up a road atlas. His real intentions, however, were very different ...

★★★★★★★★★★★★★★★★★★★★★★★★★★

All day the police had been waiting patiently for Hughes to show himself or for some intelligence or report as to his whereabouts. In the meantime, all appropriate preparations had been made – they were ready to set up roadblocks wherever they would be required, an armed response unit was on standby, and tracker dogs and their handlers were ready to go into action at a moment's notice.

In Chesterfield 'Jane Doe' still lay on a slab in the

mortuary, still unidentified. All the methods of establishing identity that had been tried thus far had drawn a blank. By Friday evening no-one had come forward to report a missing wife, daughter or sister. At this point the police were making only very low-key enquiries about her identity. There were greater priorities for the constabulary.

At Matlock police station that afternoon, Detective Sergeant Alan Woodman was sat at his desk. He was stocky, late thirties, with a rather 'lived-in' face. Even in the depths of winter he wore a short-sleeved shirt, exposing powerful forearms. He had the physique of a prop-forward, which he had been, and he was still a prolific hitter of sixes for the first eleven of Ambergate cricket club. He showed only mild interest when a sudden death report appeared on his desk. A female rock-climber, no rope, no climbing partner, no helmet, ill-clad, falling to her death. Must have had a death wish! He slid the report into his out-tray.

★★★★★★★★★★★★★★★★★★★★★★★★★★

It was close to seven o'clock when Hughes got back to Pottery Cottage. He told Gill to wait in the car. She believed he meant to change into a suit and pick up a road atlas. He then went into the house on his own. But the last instalment in this horrifying saga was about to begin …

On this Friday evening, on the last day of his life, William Hughes retrieved the same knife from the kitchen that he had used to butcher Arthur and

Sarah. It is believed that he then went upstairs to the bedroom where Amy had been incarcerated. As there were no living witnesses to the exact sequence of events, the order in which things happened can only be presumed or inferred. It seems highly likely from subsequent events that, in Hughes' absence, Amy had managed to release herself from her bindings. What is certain is that Hughes violently slashed her across the throat with the knife.

On the last day of his life, in an adjoining bedroom, Richard Moran almost certainly heard the sounds of Hughes murdering his mother-in-law, and, no doubt in a horrific and awful moment of realisation, knew that all Hughes' promises, implied at least, that no-one would be hurt were empty and malicious. He knew for sure that it would be his turn next and it is apparent that he made a desperate attempt to escape by hobbling towards the front door of the house. His efforts were entirely in vain as Hughes caught up with him and stabbed him repeatedly in the back until he lay still.

By now Hughes would have been covered in the blood of his victims, but he still had the presence of mind not to betray himself to Gill. Opening a window he shouted to her that he was 'just going to check on Sarah and your dad.' Even in the wake of two frenzied killings, he had the self-composure to act in a way that was perpetuating the cynical charade that all was well, and it was convincing enough to still reassure Gill. She turned off the car engine, 'to save fuel', and sat and waited for Hughes to return to the car.

Five minutes or so later Hughes re-emerged from the house, having washed and put on clean clothes. He was ready to depart from Pottery Cottage for the last time. Unfortunately for him, there was to be a hitch. The car would not start. It seems that a faulty alternator had caused the battery to go flat. Hughes, now, for the first time in front of any of his captives, lost his temper, and cursing loudly, ordered Gill to go and seek help from her next-door neighbours. The delay that resulted and the events that immediately followed, although too late to save the lives of Gill's family, were instrumental in preventing Hughes making an effective escape, and may, possibly, have saved Gill's own life.

The occupants of the adjoining cottage, the Newmans, were up to this point totally unaware of the tragic events that had been unfolding in the Moran household. But this was about to end. When Len Newman opened his front door to Gill Moran's knock, he could sense immediately that something was very much amiss. Gill had reached breaking point and her face and demeanour betrayed her state of mind. 'Where's Richard?' asked Mr. Newman. 'He's been tied up,' was the reply. Before Len could make further inquiry, he and Gill heard a plaintive cry from the open first-floor window of Pottery Cottage – 'Len, for God's sake help us'. The mortally wounded Amy Minton had remarkably managed to drag herself to the same window that Hughes had opened in order to shout to

Gill a little earlier, and she was now desperately trying to climb out of the window.

The Newmans, by now, realised that it was up to them to summon help and they urgently made for their car (they had no telephone in the house) and frantically drove away to look for assistance. Hughes was still trying to start Richard's car, and Gill decided she had no option but to get in beside him. Although she had heard Amy's shouts, she had not seen her mother at the window and still had no reason to believe that she was injured, let alone fatally wounded. As the Newmans drove off, however, and to her utter horror, she saw a face at the driver's window of the car in which she was sitting. Amy had fallen from the upstairs window and, in the last moments of her life, despite gaping wounds to her neck, she had crawled through the snow to her son's car. It was an astonishing effort of will on the part of this 68-year old lady, but it robbed her of her remaining strength, and she slid to the ground dead.

Gill was now paralysed with fear. She knew, for the first time, and beyond any doubt, that Hughes had murdered her husband, both her parents, and her 10-year old daughter. She didn't try to resist as Hughes dragged her bodily from the car, having already pulled her mother's body away from the vehicle. He then physically propelled his numb and terror-stricken passenger along the snowbound road to a cottage occupied by Ronald Frost, a mechanic by trade.

Hughes' own composure had not deserted him, and when Mr. Frost answered the door he was politely asked if he could help to start the vehicle in which Hughes intended to make his escape. The unsuspecting Ronald Frost agreed to come back to the car with Hughes and see if he could render assistance. Frost's wife, Madge, had come to the door as well, and whilst Hughes and Madge's husband were engaged in conversation, Gill quietly whispered to Madge, 'Help me.' Unlike her husband, Madge was not deceived. She had recognised Hughes from coverage of the case on local television, and she quickly realised that Gill was a hostage. When Ronald left with Gill and Hughes to go up the road to the car, she went to her phone and dialled 999. At more or less the same time the Newmans were making the same call from the home of another neighbour …

Ronald had succeeded in starting Richard Moran's Chrysler saloon car and Hughes, still with Gill as his captive passenger, wasted no time in speeding off westwards along the A519 towards Baslow. Before he had departed, however, the police had been alerted by Madge Frost and the Newmans as to his whereabouts and officers were busily setting up road-blocks all over the county. As it was, by driving at dangerous speeds, Hughes soon drew attention to himself and before long he was being pursued by an unmarked police car. This vehicle managed to overtake the Chrysler and forced it to swerve to avoid a collision and to hit a wall. This brought the pursued car to a halt and the two police officers ran towards it. They stopped dead in their tracks, however, when they saw that Hughes was holding an axe to the head of his female passenger.

'Back off or I'll kill her,' Hughes screamed at the officers. They had no option but to obey and then to comply with his request to hand over the keys to the unmarked Morris Marina. The officers were then left standing at the side of the road as Hughes once more sped off, still with his hostage.

As the stolen police vehicle now approached the Derbyshire/Cheshire border, the net was closing on Hughes. Thus far he had managed to evade the roadblocks, often by taking minor roads, but this had slowed his progress as many of these roads had not been gritted and were still badly affected by snow and ice. The police, out in large numbers across the county, were now tracking and anticipating the movements of the Morris Marina. Just over the border into Cheshire, at the village of Rainow, Hughes was suddenly confronted by a bus parked across the carriageway. He swerved to try and avoid it but only succeeded in once again colliding with a wall. Armed officers quickly converged on the vehicle but held back when they saw that Hughes was brandishing the axe and threatening to kill his passenger. There now followed a thirty-minute standoff, with Hughes shouting threats and demanding a fresh vehicle and safe passage with his hostage. Finally his patience ran out, and shouting, 'Your time's up,' he swung the axe at Gill, gashing her forehead with the blow. He was prevented from swinging the axe again, however, by the intervention of a courageous police superintendent, Peter Howse, who launched himself into the car and grappled with Hughes. This presented an opportunity to other armed officers present to end the matter once and for all. Four shots were fired at Hughes from close distance, the first hitting him in the head, then two hitting his torso, but it was only the final shot, which pierced his heart, that stopped his struggling and finished his life.

Hughes' traumatised passenger was then assisted from the vehicle and transported to a nearby hospital for treatment for her facial injury. At the hospital, police officers were obliged to confirm her worst suspicions – that the other four members of her family were dead. Her physical injury was entirely negligible compared with the indescribable damage that had been inflicted on her mental state. Months and years of anguish and counselling lay ahead for her. It was difficult to believe that she would ever completely recover from the nightmare of the last forty-eight hours and her unimaginable and unbearable loss.

★★★★★★★★★★★★★★★★★★★★★★★★★★★

At 10 o'clock that same night, Pottery Cottage and its immediate surroundings were bathed in bright light. Police officers and scenes of crime technicians swarmed over the house, the garden and the road outside. A lighting system had been rigged up outside to facilitate their work, and all the interior lights blazed.

The whole area had been cordoned off with police

tapes. It was a crime scene.

Although clearly horrific crimes had been committed, no-one present was in any doubt as to the identity of the perpetrator, nor were they in any doubt that there would never be any criminal prosecution. The hunted man was not going to surrender and none of the 'hunters' were going to have any qualms about shooting him, particularly when he was armed and had a hostage.

The pursuit of William Thomas Hughes was only ever going to end one way.

The posse of police officers and a trio of ambulances had arrived at Pottery Cottage at about 9.45 pm, approximately forty minutes after the frantic phone call from the Newmans. No-one was prepared for the scene of carnage that greeted them when they arrived at the scene. They found the body of Amy Minton in the garden, and the butchered corpses of Richard Moran, Arthur Minton and young Sarah Moran inside the house. The older officers and the paramedics were accustomed to coming across dead bodies, including those horribly disfigured in road traffic accidents, but the like of this they had never encountered before and would never encounter again. It was a scene beyond their comprehension. For the youngest of their number, a police woman in her early twenties, it was simply too much. At the sight of the body of the child, she was overcome by hysteria, and had to be gently led away by a colleague to sit in a police vehicle. For hours she would be totally inconsolable, and would be off work for weeks. All those present would be offered, and would accept, counselling in the days that followed.

★★★★★★★★★★★★★★★★★★★★★★★★★★★

At the same time as the emergency services were arriving at Pottery Cottage, a man called Richard Simpson was presenting himself at the front desk of Bakewell police station. The station was almost deserted, most of its regular inhabitants being involved in the on-going manhunt. The sergeant behind the desk was one of the only two officers remaining. This was a job he had not undertaken since he was a constable, and his resentment at his 'demotion' clearly showed as he uttered a gruff 'Good evening,' to the unwelcome visitor. His attitude, however, quickly changed to a business-like concern as the man in front of him outlined the reason for his attendance at the police station.

He had returned home at about 8 o'clock that night, Richard Simpson explained, after being away on a business trip since the Wednesday morning. He had expected to find his wife at home when he got back, but she was not there and it appeared she had not been in the house since he had last seen her on that morning two days ago. There were two days' worth of milk still on the doorstep, and two days' newspapers on the mat inside the front door. The bed did not appear to have been slept in since his departure, and there was no sign of any cooking or cleaning having been done.

He went on to tell his listener that he had said goodbye to his wife on the Wednesday morning and left in his car to travel to the north-east on a sales trip.

He was the northern area sales manager for his firm. Beverley, his wife, had told him that she planned to go rock-climbing that day and he assumed, as she had no car of her own, that she would be picked up by a climbing partner. This was not unusual, and he also assumed that she had arranged a day off from work for this purpose. She would sometimes not come home at night after being out during the day. This was not unusual, said Richard – it was part of her lifestyle and he was used to it. But, as far as he could recall, she had never been away from home for more than one night. And now he had seen a short entry in the *Derbyshire Times* that day about a lone female being found dead below Curbar Edge, apparently having fallen while climbing. He had a dreadful feeling that the unidentified body was that of his wife.

Having established a brief description of Beverley Simpson from Richard, the sergeant was thinking along the same lines. Although all the news had been about the Hughes affair, he was aware of the discovery at Curbar Edge. He decided that it was now the time to involve his inspector, the only other person in the police station at that time.

Inspector Tyzack was sat in his office when his sergeant brought in Richard Simpson and relayed the latter's story to him. Jim Tyzack was an avuncular man with twenty-years service in the police force behind him, and he quickly grasped that Richard Simpson was the person who would be able to identify the body that still lay on the mortuary slab in Chesterfield. Nonetheless, his experience and training led him to make some attempt at least to try and assure Richard that this was not necessarily the case. There may be all sorts of reasons why Beverley had not come home, he said. He knew, however, that his words sounded hollow and unconvincing. He asked a few further questions to supplement the initial interview conducted by the sergeant. Did Richard know the identity of the proposed climbing partner? Did he know where she was going to climb? Richard, however, was not familiar with or very interested in his wife's rock-climbing activities and had no answers to these questions.

The inspector realised that there were other questions that he could have asked.

Why was Beverley apparently climbing on her own? How would she have got back from Curbar? He was a little surprised that Richard himself didn't ask the first question. But this was neither the time or the place for him, the inspector, to be asking these questions or for him to be challenging Richard's failure to ask them. The priority was to get Beverley identified as the deceased, if that was the case, or eliminate her from enquiries if not. He informed Richard that he would have to be taken to Chesterfield for these purposes. Richard nodded quietly but said nothing. The inspector had noted that throughout their meeting

Richard was pale but seemed quite composed.

Taking Richard through to Chesterfield was a task that the inspector decided he would have to carry out himself, as there was basically no-one else to do it. The sergeant would have to be left in sole charge of the police station. He dissuaded Richard from driving himself and they set off on the 12-mile trip to Chesterfield.

Inspector Tyzack was very accustomed to supervising the identification of dead bodies by next-of-kin or other close relatives. In his experience the reactions he witnessed were varied. Some people became hysterical and needed to be carefully restrained, some just cried and were inconsolable, some were passive and unemotional. Richard Simpson was definitely in the last category. On being asked if the body that he was shown was that of his wife, he nodded, closed his eyes briefly, and turned away.

On the journey back to Bakewell, the inspector found his passenger to be withdrawn and uncommunicative, and quickly deciding that trying to converse with him was inappropriate, he left Richard to his own thoughts. He did, however, feel compelled to ask one question: Did Richard have anyone to be with him that night? No, said Richard, but he would contact his sister in Derby and he would arrange to go to her or ask her to come to him. Until then he would be alright, he said. Back at the police station, Richard insisted on driving his own car home. As he lived minutes away, the inspector didn't attempt to dissuade him, gauging that he was not the sort of man to do anything stupid or reckless on the journey home. There was a brief conversation before they parted about when the coroner might release the body, and about the need for Richard to make a statement for the inquest, he being the next-of-kin and possibly the last person to have seen Beverley alive. Nothing, however, would happen before Monday. It was going to be a busy time for the coroner.

CHAPTER FOUR

January 17th

Following the shooting of William Hughes and the discovery of the four bodies at Pottery Cottage, a sense of shock and horror engulfed the inhabitants of north-east Derbyshire and the Peak District. The snow, for the moment at least, had ceased to fall, but the days were dark and overcast and the gloom seemed to reflect the collective state of mind. The four bodies now joined that of Beverley Simpson in the morgue, but little public attention was focused on the latter, her fate being totally eclipsed by the tragedy that had befallen the Moran family.

In some quarters, however, Beverley's death was keenly felt; and in some quarters it was about to attract renewed interest.

At Hassop, Brook & Co. in Bakewell, the senior partner was experiencing profound feelings of guilt. Bob Hassop had learnt of his secretary's fate on the Saturday morning when his junior partner, Kevin

Malcolm, had rung him at home. Kevin himself had picked up the news from local radio earlier that day and had immediately contacted his partners and Bob's articled clerk. Although he knew that really he had no cause to reproach himself, Bob's conscience was deeply troubled by the thought that he had roundly cursed Beverley's 'fecklessness' and 'discourtesy' at a time when she was lying dead in the snow.

He was still in possession of her home phone number and, not without some trepidation, he rang it that afternoon. His call was answered by a woman, who identified herself as Richard Simpson's sister. She informed Bob that her brother did not wish to take any calls at that time, and Bob should ring again in 'a day or two'.

Michael, the articled clerk, had no pangs of guilt, but he was devastated by the news. He knew that he meant nothing to Beverley, but he felt a deep personal loss. He was also experiencing a mixture of sadness and anger that such a radiant and vibrant life should be expunged by, what seemed to him, a stupid and senseless accident.

Some of the office staff had heard the news over the weekend; others received it on the Monday morning with complete disbelief. Not a lot of work was done that morning as they sat and reminisced and exchanged memories of Beverley. No-one chastised them for this or sought to discourage them. At lunchtime they all trooped off to the pub to drink to 'absent friends'.

★★★★★★★★★★★★★★★★★★★★★★★★★

There was not much work done that morning either at the South Darley offices of the County Prosecuting Solicitor. Three-quarters of the lawyers were out at court, but those who weren't sat round a table in the common room with most of the rest of the staff and 'chewed the fat' for the best part of an hour. There had never previously been such sensational developments to occupy their thoughts and their conversation. The 'Hughes affair' was the main topic for discussion, but the matter of Beverley Simpson was not far behind.

Beverley had been known to a good few of the lawyers and other staff, if not in person, at least by reputation. The local 'legal' grapevine was the source of much of the information about her, but a good deal more came courtesy of the senior typist, Deborah, who was married to Kevin Malcolm, the junior partner at Brook, Hassop & Co. It was Deborah who had brought the news about Beverley's demise to the office that morning, having been put in the picture by her husband, but most of the staff had already picked it up from local radio and television over the weekend. The 'information', true or false, was that Beverley Simpson was, or had been, a woman who had 'slept around', and wasn't particularly fussy about her choice of sexual partners, although she had a penchant for police officers, and senior police officers at that. What was of particular interest to those present was that it was widely believed that one of her paramours had been no less a person than the Deputy County

Prosecuting Solicitor, Ronnie Fox. Needless to say, he was not present during the discussion that morning.

Martin Tory was present but made no contribution to the conversation. He didn't care much for what he regarded as scurrilous talk and unsubstantiated rumours. The fact that the lady in question was now dead made it even more unpalatable, to his mind, that her reputation should be shredded in this fashion.

However, he supposed it was inevitable that there would be such prurient interest in the woman and her 'reputation', given the nature of the rumours and the one in particular regarding their absent superior, Ronnie Fox.

He didn't care much for Ronnie Fox, who he saw as a philandering, idle waster.

No doubt the rumours about him and Beverley Simpson were not entirely unfounded, but it was still wrong to talk about the man behind his back, however much he was deserving of disrespect.

Neither did he care much for Deborah Malcolm, who was very much at the forefront of the animated conversation that was taking place. Deborah was thirtyish, blonde, slender and very elegant. She gave the impression of being much more than a typist, an impression she almost certainly deliberately set out to create. She dressed expensively and she was always immaculately made up and manicured. Her speech was refined, without even a hint of a local accent. To the uninformed observer coming to the office she could easily be mistaken for one of the lawyers or even a visiting dignitary, and she would work hard to sustain that impression. Martin regarded her as a snob and a social climber, who had 'set her cap' at Kevin Malcolm when he was one of the lawyers in the office, not, he was certain, out of love or affection, but so that she could present herself as a solicitor's wife. And so that had come to pass when she and Kevin were married some six months previously.

There was, however, another side to Deborah Malcolm, as Martin had discovered three months before. He had come back to the office late one afternoon and noticed that Ronnie Fox's MG soft-top was still in the car-park, although most of the staff had left. This was unusual in itself as the deputy was rarely to be found in the office at that time of day, his invariable practice being to arrange his day so that at its end he was as close as possible to his home in south Derbyshire. Martin had been waiting to see Fox, to discuss a case, for several days, and he decided that he would catch him now, otherwise it might be a week or so before he saw him again.

The top corridor of the office block was quiet as he approached Fox's office but he detected movement from within that office itself. It was not the practice to await an invitation to enter anyone's office, and after knocking once, Martin opened the door. What he saw within, however, caused him to mutter a hurried apology and beat a hasty retreat. In the second or two that the interior of the room was visible to him, he was nonetheless able to form a clear picture of what was taking place. The blonde woman lying on her back on Fox's large desk was unmistakably Deborah Malcolm. The male kneeling astride her was unmistakably Ronnie Fox. Both appeared to be fully clothed, although Martin had sufficient time to glimpse a pair of black silk knickers on the floor, which certainly did not belong to Fox.

In a state of shock, Martin half walked, half ran back along the corridor, got back into his car and headed for home. In his rush to leave he neglected to pick up the files he had intended to take away with him. He started to drive in something of a haze, and had to make a supreme effort to revive his concentration as he pulled into the traffic on the main A6. He was a serious and even quite intense individual, but as a prosecutor it was impossible not to become broad-minded about the seamy side of life. Nonetheless, he was shaken to the core and appalled by what he had just witnessed. His principal disgust was reserved for Deborah Malcolm – newly married, and to a man he regarded as a friend and whose wedding he had attended.

The following day he made a conscious effort to avoid Deborah, and, thankfully, Fox was nowhere to be seen. He toyed with the idea of informing Kevin Malcolm. Kevin had been his mentor at the CPS when he joined a few years ago, and he held him in great respect, even now when they were regular courtroom opponents and had 'crossed swords' in court on more than one occasion, sometimes quite heatedly. He decided, however, to consult a colleague before doing anything precipitate, and a day or two later he managed to arrange a lunchtime drink with Roger Duddon. Roger, who was on the same level as Martin in the office hierarchy, was someone in whom he often confided, but was also someone who always knew what was going on in the office and could be relied on, Martin felt, to give him sound and appropriate advice.

They met on a Friday lunchtime in the Three Stags in South Darley. This was the closest pub to the office, but one that tended not to be frequented by CPS personnel. In fact Martin and Roger had the lounge bar to themselves. Martin outlined the events he had witnessed to his colleague, leaving no doubt, he was sure, as to the nature of what he'd seen. If he had expected a reaction of shock and horror from Roger, however, he was disappointed. All he got was a knowing smile and a slight shake of the head.

'You're behind the times, Martin,' he was told. 'He's been shagging her for months, and before you ask, before and after her honeymoon, and probably during as well!'

Martin was astonished. 'I had no idea,' he said.

'Then you wouldn't know either,' Roger went on, 'that Fox wasn't the only one.

One or two of our colleagues have had the treatment as well. She's a raving nymphomaniac.'

'Well, she hasn't tried it on with me,' said Martin. 'What about you?'

'Yes, but I wasn't interested. She's bad news. She probably hasn't come on to you because she would realise she was wasting her time.'

'What about the chief?' Martin asked.

'No, I don't think so. Even Deborah draws the line somewhere.'

Martin thought for a moment in silence. Then he asked, 'Do you think Kevin knows about all this?'

'He must suspect at least. He's nobody's fool. He probably had a good idea before he married her, and knew what he was getting into.'

Martin shook his head. 'So why did he marry her?'

'Well, good question. But then he's no oil painting, was getting on a bit, and was probably flattered that an attractive bird was interested in him, let alone was prepared to marry him. He maybe thought she would change once the ink was dry on the marriage certificate. Fond hope!'

'I suppose there's no point in telling him what's going on then?'

'No, I don't think you'd be telling him anything he didn't know already'.

'And incidentally,' Roger continued, 'don't have any sympathy for Fox. He's had women all over the county. There's a probation officer in Derby now, there was a secretary in Bakewell before that, and it's rumoured that he even had a fling not so long ago with a magistrate on the bench at Ilkeston.'

'But isn't he living with his partner in Ashbourne?' asked Martin.

'Yes, but so what! He can't keep it in his trousers. He's even made a play for young Becky.'

Martin knew this was a reference to one of the junior typists. Becky was about twenty-three, and was everything Deborah wasn't: she was polite, respectful, personable, with no 'airs and graces'. But he could see why Fox might be interested in her – she was full-bodied and curvaceous, although she would probably have to watch her weight in due course. Thinking back, Martin had heard Fox refer to her as a 'ripe peach'.

'I hope she's managed to resist him.'

'So far, I think,' said Roger, 'but give him time.'

Martin left the pub that lunchtime a wiser but a sadder man. He had had no idea that so much was going on beneath the surface in the office in which he had worked for more than four years. He could only suppose that he had been so absorbed in his casework and preparation for court that he had missed all the signs of the illicit sexual activity going on around him. On one level he was appalled by all this activity. But he was also intrigued as to how and why these liaisons had arisen and developed.

Now, three months later, he sat listening to Deborah Malcolm sounding off about the lifestyle of a dead woman, and her alleged association with Ronnie Fox. The wretched woman was now adding hypocrisy to the list of her unattractive features! Well, it was time to put a stop to it. Exercising his undoubted authority, he ordered the assembled company back to work and headed back to his own office.

Sat at his own desk, Martin retrieved the William Hughes file from his cabinet. He made a file entry recording the death of the accused and left it in his in-tray. All he needed now was the official notification of the death, and then the case could be closed.

★★★★★★★★★★★★★★★★★★★★★★★★★★★

That afternoon, Detective Sergeant Alan Woodman was sat at his desk in Matlock Police Station when he was brought written information that the body found below Curbar Edge had now been formally identified by her husband as Beverley Simpson of Bakewell. This news made him sit up. He recognized the name as one that had come to his attention previously, not in relation to any criminal activity but for other reasons. In his job, Alan received lots of pieces of information from many sources, some of which might be classed as 'intelligence', some as gossip or 'tittle-tattle'. The former was important to his work, the latter, by and large, was not, but, nonetheless, he mentally filed it away in case it ever became so. The information that had come his way about Beverley Simpson was firmly in the second category, but was nevertheless of some interest to him.

Beverley Simpson he knew as a married woman with scant respect for her marital vows, a husband who was often absent, and a woman, moreover, who had a penchant for affairs with police officers, and senior police officers in particular. Indeed, one piece of information he had received, from what he regarded as a fairly reliable source, was that Beverley had for a while been involved with his own boss, the head of Derbyshire CID. CID officers tended to have irregular, and often long, working hours, and this state of affairs was not always conducive to a stable and successful marriage. Alan's own marriage had foundered because his wife would not put up with his working arrangements. He was aware that probably fifty per cent of his colleagues in CID had failed or failing marriages behind them. It didn't help, either, that there was an established culture amongst the same officers of after-work drinking, something that was regarded as almost 'de rigueur' in those circles. It was scarcely surprising then that marital harmony was often at a premium.

A woman like Beverley Simpson, who would not have been looking for a permanent relationship, and who would not be critical of her lovers' lifestyles, would often be a draw for officers, and indeed others, who wanted a largely 'no-strings' relationship, without the stresses and commitment of a marriage – either instead of or as an adjunct to their permanent relationship. Alan had never met the woman, nor had he ever had any desire to do so. She might have been an attractive proposition to some, but in his eyes she was little better than a whore. In any event, her 'whoring', or however one described her lifestyle, was now over.

Of more immediate interest to Alan at this time, however, was the knowledge that Beverley had some reputation for making enemies as well as 'friends'. He had acquired information that there had been would-be 'suitors' that she had rejected, and occasionally in acrimonious circumstances. It was quite possible that there were men out there who bore her ill-will, and who might have harboured thoughts of revenge.

Thoughtfully, Alan now sifted through his out-tray and retrieved the sudden death report he had discarded a few days before. He now began to read it with renewed interest and with attention to detail.

He read the report twice, and made a number of notes. He then made a telephone call to a friend in Chesterfield. The friend, he knew, was a keen rock-climber and climbed regularly on the gritstone edges of the Peak District. The information he was able to provide to Alan only served to increase his growing unease about the circumstances of the death, if not the conclusion in the report that death was the result of a fall from the rock face. Consulting his notes, and reflecting on what his friend had told him, he now compiled, in writing, a number of points which he felt should have been dealt with in a police investigation, but which had not been, largely, it seemed, because any investigation of the death had been superficial or non-existent. No doubt this was because the event had been overshadowed by the search for William Hughes and the police having had much bigger fish to fry. To complete the picture he also rang Inspector Tyzack at Bakewell police station, the officer who had been present when Richard Simpson had identified his wife and who was also in possession of the latter's account of the circumstances in which he had last seen Beverley.

It seemed to Alan that there were a number of very pertinent questions about Beverley's death that needed to be answered:

1) How had Beverley got to Curbar Edge that morning? She had no car, and public transport to such a location was almost non-existent. Her husband believed she was going to be picked up by a climbing partner. If so, who was he or she, and, as Beverley appeared to have been climbing alone, what had happened to this third party?

2) If the deceased was climbing alone, how was she going to get back to her home? She had no money in her possession when her body was found and, in any event, as already stated, public transport was a non-starter.

3) Why was she climbing alone, when it appeared that she must have set off with a climbing partner? Was this something she did often? If so, did she often climb without a helmet?

4) Why was she so scantily dressed on what was probably the coldest day of the year so far?

5) Why did she not have any outer clothing or non-climbing shoes to change into once she had finished her climbing activity? There was no sign of a rucksack or bag containing such garments and footwear. Unless of course she was expecting to be picked up in the car park at the southern end of the crag, and, if so, by whom?

It might have been tempting to many to 'let sleeping dogs lie' but this was not an option for Alan Woodman. In any event, these were questions which the widower would almost certainly be asking, not to mention the coroner at an inquest. There needed to be an investigation.

Alan thought first of contacting his immediate superior, Detective Inspector Bill Moore, who was based at Alfreton police station. Really there should be no question of his not doing this before embarking on an investigation which might possibly disturb the inference that death had resulted from a fall in an accident. However, it occurred to Alan that informing his superior at this point might have unwanted results. Bill Moore would almost certainly in turn inform the overall head of CID, Detective Chief Superintendent Fred Gorringe. Given the latter's rumoured previous connection with the deceased, it was quite conceivable that he would find a reason to veto an investigation that might include inquiries about Beverley Simpson's background and lifestyle. Alan therefore decided to instigate inquiries on his own initiative and tell Bill later. It was a risky course of action, but Bill Moore had known Alan a long time and Alan knew that his detective inspector trusted his judgment and would not be too concerned, particularly if the investigation yielded positive results.

Alan decided to share his concerns with the two detective constables stationed at Bakewell, and get them to do the 'legwork'. He knew that, now the Hughes manhunt was over, they would have the present capacity to carry out the necessary inquiries. He rang Bakewell police station and left a message for DC Ian Forrester. He should come to Matlock police station in the morning and bring DC John Murdoch with him …

CHAPTER FIVE

January 21st (Morning and afternoon)

For the best part of three days Detective Constables Forrester and Murdoch had been busily and diligently pursuing the inquiries allocated to them by Detective Sergeant Woodman. He had explained to them his concerns surrounding the death of Beverley Simpson; both of them had no difficulty in sharing those concerns, and neither needed any encouragement to start investigating the matter.

Their investigation, initially at least, was targeted at identifying and questioning previous boyfriends of the deceased, and also regular and occasional climbing partners. Of particular interest were those who could be regarded as unsuccessful or rejected 'suitors', especially if they were also persons who had climbed with her. Wider inquiries were also made to try and establish if anyone had seen Beverley on the morning of 12 January. A brief visit was also made to the home of Richard Simpson. The deceased's husband was involved in organising the funeral, the coroner having now released the body, and appeared surprised that there were ongoing inquiries into the circumstances of her death. He admitted, however, that he had made the assumption that Beverley had been climbing with a partner, but had been too pre-occupied thus far to make any inquiries of his own or learn any further particulars concerning her death. The officers did not want to intrude too much on his time at this stage, but considered that he would have to be seen again at a later time, as there were questions that needed to be put to him.

As far as tracking down former or current boyfriends was concerned, the staff at Brook, Hassop & Co. were seen, although none of them had any names to offer. Her life, in that respect, they said was something of a 'closed book'. They all knew that she had had numerous affairs, but she had never revealed the identity of any of her lovers. Where they could assist, however, was in pointing the officers in the direction of pubs she had been known to frequent, and also a climbing club in Chesterfield of which she had professed membership.

Visiting the pubs in the locality proved to be a fruitful source of information for the officers. Beverley seemed to have been well-known in three or four pubs, and landlords and bar staff are invariably well-informed about their regular customers and their romantic involvements. Very soon the investigators had a number of names, and at least sufficient detail about others to be able to identify them with further inquiry. These were men who had been seen in the deceased's company over the last six or nine months, or, in some instances, men who it was strongly rumoured were 'involved' with her. The two officers were aware of her reputation but were quite staggered by the number of names and descriptions they were getting. And these did not include the names of police officers or other 'worthies' who were, presumably, more discreet about their association with Beverley. If the information was anything like true and accurate, the woman had a habit that amounted to an addiction.

Inquiries with the secretary and chairman of the climbing club in Chesterfield, however, produced no further names. Beverley, they said, was a member of the club in name only: she had rarely attended meetings, had never joined members on their regular weekend trips to North Wales or the Lake District, or indeed mid-week evening visits to local crags and outcrops. It appeared that whoever her regular climbing partners were, they were not members of this club. The officers considered that perhaps Richard Simpson might have some information to provide in this respect, but this was not the time to be quizzing him about the identities of climbing associates.

The two detective constables then set about tracking down and interviewing the men whose identities or descriptions they had been given in the pubs. Their local knowledge simplified this task for them, as some of the persons were known to them and others they could identify from the information they had been given. They were both conscious of the fact that there were almost certainly other names they had not been given but which were known to them. They decided that this area was too sensitive for them to be exploring at this stage, and would require the involvement of an officer of higher rank than themselves.

Over a couple of days they saw nine or ten men, all of whom lived in Bakewell or within a radius of five or six miles of the town. These persons were, perhaps unsurprisingly, not particularly forthcoming. One or two denied knowing Beverley. Some admitted that they had 'socialised' with her, once or twice, but no more than that. Only two were prepared to acknowledge that they had actually slept with her, and then on no more than three occasions: they both said this was because she was 'up for it' and neither had been desirous of anything more than casual sex. The picture the officers were getting was that there was no-one here that had harboured any hankering for any sort of more permanent relationship with Beverley Simpson, and no-one that had any resentment towards her. The impression gleaned, indeed, was that she was seen as a warm-hearted 'good-time girl', and was well-liked and popular.

The two officers also asked their uniform colleagues, whose duties included patrolling the area between Curbar and Froggatt, to make inquiries of motorists using the car parks at either end of the Curbar Edge escarpment as to whether they might have seen a woman of Beverley's description on the early morning of 12 January. It was likely that she would have had to set off from one of these points to access the edge and reach the place on the crag where her body had been found. By the morning of 21 January, however, these inquiries had so far drawn a blank.

Just as DCs Forrester and Murdoch suspected that their investigation was going nowhere, they had a 'lucky break'. In fact it was two 'lucky breaks' in quick succession.

On the Friday morning, 21 January, they visited the home of John Carswell, a farm near Stoney Middleton, some nine or ten miles north of Bakewell. Mr. Carswell was the last name they had turned up as a possible previous paramour of the deceased. He proved to be considerably more open about his involvement with Beverley than many of the other men interviewed. Yes, he had known her well and for some years. They were good friends and often had a drink together when his business took him into Bakewell. But their relationship had never progressed further than this, quite simply because he did not want it to go any further. Beverley's husband was also a long-standing friend and he 'would not dream' of jeopardising their friendship by making advances to his wife.

The officers found his account perfectly believable. But this was not the end of what he had to offer. He went on to tell the DCs that he had been part of the local farming fraternity for a good many years and knew most of the people who farmed in the Peak and that part of West Derbyshire. One man he knew well, David Hersey, farmed at Wardlow Mires, about four or five miles to the west towards Tideswell. He had seen David recently at a farm sale and afterwards they had a couple of pints in a nearby pub. David knew that John was a friend of Beverley Simpson; he knew her too through his regular dealings with Brook, Hassop & Co., who were his solicitors. David had disclosed to John Carswell that he had serious concerns for the welfare of one of his young farm-hands, a nineteen-year-old youth called Rex, who had been behaving strangely recently. About four months ago Rex, who was as he put it 'a climber of rock', had taken to climbing regularly with a woman, some years older than himself, from Bakewell. It hadn't taken David long to find out that this was Beverley Simpson.

David had gone on to tell his listener that it had become apparent after a week or so of Rex's association with Beverley, that the young man's interest in her had developed beyond that of just as a climbing partner. David's information, it seemed, came from his other employees who worked with Rex on a daily basis. Sadly for Rex, his passion for Beverley was not requited. Equally sadly, it seemed, despite the lack of response from her, Rex quickly became infatuated with the older woman. His workmates, mainly older and wiser, had urged him to forget her and move on. He was wasting his time, they told him. She was too old for him and would never be interested in him 'in that way'. Their advice, however, had fallen on deaf ears. The love-struck youth had begun to bombard her with flowers and presents. One evening he had followed her to a pub in Bakewell, where she had humiliated him in front of her friends, referring to him as 'a schoolboy'. She had made it plain that their climbing partnership was at an end.

The impact on Rex of this rejection was profound. He had become morose, uncommunicative, and even tearful. His workmates, who had been initially sympathetic, soon tired of his moods, and began to quite pointedly ignore him. David himself, having become aware of the situation, had spoken to Rex, but, as he freely admitted, he had absolutely no skills as a counsellor, and his attempts to 'pour oil on troubled waters' seemed only make things worse. The youth appeared to be in the depths of despair, and David was now seriously worried about his mental state.

All this was of great interest to the officers. A recent climbing partner of the deceased, and a rejected lover to boot! This was potentially 'dynamite'. Thanking John Carswell for his invaluable assistance, they returned to their car, intent on making the Hersey farm at Wardlow Mires their next stop.

★★★★★★★★★★★★★★★★★★★★★★★★★★

At the same time as DCs Forrester and Murdoch were on their way to Stoney Middleton to see John Carswell, Alan Woodman was being summoned to the front desk at Matlock police station, where he had been told that he had a visitor with information to impart about the 'dead climber'.

The 'visitor' introduced himself as Trevor Birt from Sheffield, and said that he had been earlier to Bakewell police station, where the desk sergeant had pointed him in the direction of DS Woodman at Matlock. A few minutes later, now ensconced in an interview room, Mr. Birt began to tell his story.

He was a friend, he said, of the two climbers who had found the body below Curbar Edge just over a week ago. They were all in the same climbing club in Sheffield. He, however, had not climbed for several weeks as he had been in hospital in Halifax following a fall while climbing in the quarry at Heptonstall, near Hebden Bridge. He had sustained broken bones in the small of his back and had only just been discharged from the hospital. On 12 of January it had been his intention to watch his friends climbing on Curbar Edge. He had travelled to the area separately, in his own vehicle, and had arrived in the car park at the southern end of the escarpment ahead of the other two men. In fact, as it turned out, he was there a good hour before them, he having got there at about 8.30 am. The car park, he said, was fairly empty at this time. Indeed he was surprised there was anyone there at all, as it was a cold morning and snow lay quite heavily on the ground.

About half-an-hour after his arrival, he became aware of a dark or 'bluey-green' van at the far end of the car park. He hadn't seen it drive into the car park, but it wasn't there when he got there. The vehicle was partially obscured by another car parked alongside it, so he couldn't identify the make or model, and anyway he had no reason to pay it much attention. Within a minute or two he saw two people at the rear of the van: a slim young man and a woman. They began to unload a rope and climbing gear from the back of the van and pile it into rucksacks. He couldn't describe the two people in any greater detail. They were some distance away and he had removed his spectacles when he had ceased driving. Indeed, he was only dimly aware that the pair were male and female, and were young or youngish. After a while the two of them left the vehicle and moved off in the direction of Curbar Edge.

Mr. Birt then went on to tell the officer that he had begun to experience discomfort in his back and made the decision not to wait any longer for his friends. It was not the sort of day, anyway, to be hanging around watching other people climb. He set off to drive home and never met up with his companions that morning. He had, however, caught up with them on the following Saturday in a pub in Sheffield, when they had told him of their discovery of the body. None of them were particularly surprised by the fact that the woman had been climbing alone and without a helmet, as this was far from uncommon in climbing circles, and especially on the Derbyshire gritstone edges. What had puzzled them, however, was the fact that the deceased had been so scantily dressed on such a cold day.

Trevor had thought no more about the incident at Curbar that weekend. The following Monday he read in the local paper that the body had been identified, but the name of the deceased meant nothing to him. He would probably have thought no more about the event at all, had it not been for a chance telephone conversation on the Thursday evening with a friend in a Chesterfield mountaineering club. The friend told him about the police making enquiries about Beverley Simpson's climbing partners and who, if anyone, might have been teamed up with her on the morning of her death. Trevor then began to wonder if there might have been a possible connection between the deceased and the couple he had seen with the green van in the car park that morning. He recalled his discussions with his friends about the woman's inadequate clothing. Were the police thinking that there was more to the incident than met the eye? Was it perhaps not an 'accident' but something more sinister? It was time, he decided, to share what he had seen with the police, even if it might have no bearing on their investigations.

Alan thanked Trevor Birt for his visit and his information, and, without giving anything away, told him that it had been 'very useful'. Only he knew, in fact, how useful it might prove to be. He made arrangements for Trevor to make a witness statement and bade him goodbye. He then set about trying to contact his two detective constables.

★★★★★★★★★★★★★★★★★★★★★★★★★★

As they reached their car parked in John Carswell's yard, the two officers heard their radio crackling. The voice of their detective sergeant then came on the line. He told them about the information he had just received from Trevor Birt; they, in turn, related the account of John Carswell. Alan instructed them to let him know immediately if anything came out of their visit to Rex's place of work. He would make sure that he was available to receive their call.

It took the two officers less than fifteen minutes to travel to Wardlow Mires and locate the David Hersey farm. They found the man himself in the farmyard. A large, cheery individual in his forties. His countenance, however, clouded over when they told him they were making inquiries into the circumstances of Beverley Simpson's death, and needed to speak to Rex as an identified former climbing partner of the deceased. He nodded gravely and told them that Rex was out in the fields but he expected him to return at any time.

'A word to the wise,' he continued, 'Rex is a good lad, but he's not a "full shilling" and he's not been himself lately either.'

The officers knew that 'not a full shilling' was Derbyshire-speak to describe someone whose mental state could range from having learning difficulties to simply being slow-witted, or, at worst, being mentally retarded.

'Was he working the Wednesday before last?' asked

DC Forrester.

'I'll have to check the paperwork,' replied the farmer, 'although I know he did have some time off last week.'

He disappeared into the farmhouse and emerged a minute later with a sheaf of timesheets.

'He was off last Tuesday and Wednesday,' he told the detectives.

While they were waiting for Rex to appear, DC Murdoch glanced around the farmyard. His attention was drawn to a vehicle parked just inside the entrance to a barn. Closer examination revealed it to be an old navy-blue mini-van, battered and not a little rusty in places.

'Whose is the van?' he asked Mr. Hersey.

'It belongs to Rex. He bought it off one of the other lads for a tenner. He uses it for carrying his climbing gear about. Here he is.'

At this point a youth in his late teens appeared in the farmyard. He was slight in stature, gaunt, and the officers noticed that, even before they had identified themselves, he had a somewhat haunted look about him. The officers told him who they were and why they were there. Mr. Hersey then excused himself and went into the farmhouse.

'Are you Rex?' DC Forrester asked the youth.

'Yes, Rex Maitland,' was the reply. His voice cracked as he spoke, and he coughed, seemingly to cover his embarrassment.

'Did you know Beverley Simpson?' asked DC Murdoch.

'Yes ... I did. I ... er ... know she's dead.'

DC Murdoch continued to question him. 'How did you know her?'

'I used to go climbing with her.'

'When was the last time you climbed with her?'

'Er ... about a month ago'

'Any reason you haven't climbed with her since?' asked DC Forrester.

'No, don't know why really.'

'Where were you the Wednesday before last, the 12th of January?'

'At work, I think.'

'Sure about that?'

The youth was silent for a moment or two, then said, 'Yes, because I was off the first two days of the week.'

DC Murdoch then asked him about the blue van in the yard. He agreed it was his. He was asked if he had any objection to the officers having a look in it. He looked unsure but then nodded his assent. He took the keys out of his pocket and handed them to DC Forrester.

As they opened the rear doors of the van the first

item that the officers noticed was an orange frameless cylindrical rucksack that lay on the floor just inside the doors. Beyond that was a jumble of climbing gear, ropes, waterproofs, boots and other paraphernalia.

'Is this all your stuff?' he was asked.

'Yes, except the rucksack,' indicating the item just inside the doors. 'That's Beverley's.'

'Why have you got it?'

'She left it last time I climbed with her.'

'Have you been climbing since?'

'Yes, a few times.'

'Then is there any reason,' inquired DC Murdoch, 'why it isn't under the rest of your gear, instead of being loose at the back of the van?'

Up to this point, although Rex had been hesitant with his replies to questions, he had provided answers. Now, however, he dropped his head, and appeared to be struggling for a response. Eventually he raised his head. 'I'd been keeping it separate, so I could give it back to her when I saw her next.'

'From what we've heard there wasn't going to be a next time,' said DC Forrester. 'Hadn't she told you that she wasn't going to climb with you again?'

This time there was no reply at all.

The officers decided not to ask further questions at this stage, but completed their search of the van.

They found nothing else of significance but seized the orange rucksack. Rex was allowed to go off and have his lunch in the farmhouse kitchen, and the officers retired to their vehicle to discuss their findings and communicate with their superior.

Back in the car cigarettes were lit and the two officers talked. Both of them had no doubt that Rex Maitland was concealing the truth about a number of matters. He was lying about his whereabouts on Wednesday 12 January. His explanation about the position of the orange rucksack in his van was quite unconvincing. He hadn't disclosed that the reason for the demise of the climbing partnership with Beverley was that she had rejected his romantic overtures. He owned a van which corresponded, to a degree at least, with that seen by Trevor Birt on the fateful morning in the car park at Curbar Edge. He had a motive for wishing her harm, which could easily extend to pushing her off a crag, particularly given his possible mental instability. The two officers were still very much conscious of and preoccupied with the events of the previous week and the horrendous psychopathic conduct of William Hughes. There was no evidence that Rex Maitland suffered from this sort of mental disorder, but the case of Hughes highlighted how those with mental abnormality could behave in certain circumstances.

Both officers realised that one sticking point in any theory that Beverley's death was non-accidental and that Rex was involved, was that the evidence suggested that Beverley had terminated her climbing relationship with him, so why, therefore, would she be apparently resuming their partnership on the morning in question? They had answers for that: Beverley needed a lift, and possibly a climbing partner, and Rex was available. She was perhaps prepared to overlook his infatuation for her in the interests of her passion for climbing, if he promised to bury his feelings for her in the interests of their mutual enthusiasm for their sport?

They both knew that they needed to give Rex an intensive grilling in a police station situation, but the question was did they have enough to arrest him on suspicion of murder? Both felt they had sufficient reason to suspect him of that offence, but they needed the endorsement and support of their detective sergeant. The radio call to Matlock police station was made.

Alan Woodman listened carefully to what his detectives had uncovered at the Hersey farm and an account of the conversation with Rex Maitland; also their arguments for justifying his arrest. He wasn't entirely convinced by those arguments, but they were the men on the spot and he trusted their instincts. Somewhat reluctantly he agreed to the course of action they were proposing. He would later have cause to regret his decision.

A few minutes later, now in handcuffs, Rex was being bundled gently into the rear seat of the officers' vehicle. DC Murdoch sat down next to him. Rex hadn't resisted in any way but he had reacted angrily, and then tearfully, when he had been informed that he was being arrested on suspicion of the murder of Beverley Simpson. After being cautioned by DC Forrester that he needn't say anything but that anything he did say might be used in evidence, he exclaimed 'I didn't do it! I loved her! Why would I kill her?'

David Hersey had witnessed the arrest. He hadn't said anything because he was very pro-police and he felt that the officers must have had good reason to do what they had done. Furthermore, given the way that Rex had been behaving lately, it hadn't come as a complete surprise to him. After the officers had departed with their prisoner, however, his concerns for the welfare of the youth arose again. He was little more than a boy, he reflected, probably educationally sub-normal, and he was likely to feel scared and vulnerable. He made a phone call to his solicitors, Brook, Hassop & Co., and asked to speak to Bob Hassop. Bob was with a client, but when David explained what his call was about, he was put through to Kevin Malcolm. He told Kevin what had happened and asked him if he could 'help'. Kevin was taken very much by surprise, because, like most people, he had believed that Beverley's death was just a tragic accident, and he was astounded to hear that the police were conducting a murder inquiry, and, indeed, that they had actually made an arrest. Nonetheless, he told David, he couldn't just go down to the police station and demand to see the prisoner. Rex would need to ask for the servicers of a solicitor. Anyway, he went on, because Rex was to be questioned about the death of a member of the firm's staff, he doubted whether it was ethical or appropriate for him to represent Rex at the police station.

David put the phone down. It seemed there was nothing he could do to help the young man, or not at this stage, anyway. He was certain, however, that Rex would not be left for long without the services of a solicitor. If Rex didn't ask for a solicitor, then surely the police would insist he had one, given the seriousness of his predicament. David's confidence in this regard, however, would prove to be misplaced.

CHAPTER SIX

January 21st (Evening)

Before DCs Forrester and Murdoch had left the farm at Wardlow Mires, it had begun to snow, and snow heavily. Well before they reached Bakewell, driving conditions on the A623 and then the A619, had become hazardous and the journey took longer than it normally would. On arriving at Bakewell police station they were made aware that the A6 beyond the town had become impassable, thus preventing their onward drive to Matlock police station, whence the prisoner would usually have been taken. The facilities for detaining and interviewing accused persons, and the cell accommodation in particular, were much superior at Matlock, but they would have to make do with what there was at Bakewell. The combination of the adverse weather conditions and the inability to get to Matlock police station was to have unfortunate consequences for the investigation.

At Bakewell police station Rex Maitland was 'booked

in' and then left in a cell whilst the two officers went for refreshment in the station canteen. In theory the cell was 'heated' but it was less than effective, and before the officers returned to see him Rex was already feeling cold and uncomfortable. When they returned, he was made aware that he had the right to consult with a solicitor before he was interviewed, and arrangements could be made for one to attend the police station. He was told that this would take a little time.

'Why do I need a solicitor?' he asked. 'I've done nothing wrong. Do you think I need one?'

'It's entirely up to you,' DC Murdoch told him.

'I just want to get it over with. I don't want to wait for a solicitor.'

Rex was then told that his clothes were going to be seized 'for forensic examination' and he would be allowed to contact a relative or friend to bring him a change of clothes. He rang his mother at home in Tideswell. His mother was divorced and had no car, but he hoped that her live-in boyfriend would bring her to Bakewell in his vehicle. The response he got was that there was no way in which the boyfriend would attempt to drive the fifteen miles to Bakewell in the present weather conditions, and Rex would have to 'do without' a change of clothes. The officers told Rex that they would try to find him some suitable clothing, but in the meantime he would have to make do with a blanket.

At 4.30 pm, sat on a plastic chair in a spartan windowless room, wrapped in a blanket, Rex was cautioned by the two detectives, who then commenced to interview him about the offence for which he had been arrested, the murder of Beverley Simpson ...

By 4.30 pm that afternoon, Alan Woodman knew that interviews with the suspect would be taking place at Bakewell police station rather than at Matlock. He would have preferred to have been available for discussion with the two officers but he would have to make do with telephone updates. He had no intention of going home that evening and told his subordinates that he would be available 'as long as necessary'. He had also now put his detective inspector in the picture. As he had anticipated, Bill Moore was not unduly disturbed that Alan had acted on his own initiative and instigated the investigation, but asked that he be regularly updated. Alan realised that Detective Chief Superintendent Fred Gorringe would also have been informed by late afternoon of the events, but, with a suspect in custody, it would be too late for him to put a stop to the investigation.

★★★★★★★★★★★★★★★★★★★★★★★★★★★

Back at Bakewell the first interview with Rex Maitland was in progress. Initially the officers asked him routine questions about his age, schooling, domestic situation, and his work record. They learnt that he was nineteen years old, born and brought up locally, had been to primary and secondary school in Bakewell, leaving at sixteen without any academic qualifications. He confirmed that he had had learning difficulties and was barely literate or numerate. He had managed to find work on David Hersey's farm within weeks of leaving school. He had often, as a younger teenager volunteered there to help at harvest-time. He enjoyed the work and had no aspirations to pursue any other career. He still lived at home with his mother and her current boyfriend. His father had deserted the family some ten years previously. He didn't much like his mother's boyfriend, and he thought the feeling was probably mutual. He had older siblings but they had all married and left home.

He was then asked about his interests outside work. He had only one, he said, rock-climbing. He had been introduced to the sport on a school trip to an outdoor pursuits centre in Buxton when he was fifteen, and had found that he had an aptitude for climbing on rock. He and one or two like-minded friends had managed to borrow equipment from the same centre in Buxton and had started to climb regularly on the gritstone edges and other crags in Derbyshire. They had persuaded the older brother of one of their number, who had access to a vehicle, to climb with them and this solved the transport problem. They had also climbed in the Lake District and North Wales over the last three years. Rex said that he had passed his driving test twelve months ago and had acquired an old minivan. He still climbed frequently with the same group of friends.

Having hopefully put him at ease, the officers then

went on to explore with him his relationship with Beverley Simpson. He had met her, he said, in the Lovers' Leap café in Stoney Middleton, which was routinely frequented by those who had been climbing on the nearby roadside crag. This was about six months ago. She was on the lookout for a new regular climbing partner and he had 'offered his services'. She took him up on his offer and they began to meet most weeks to climb locally. She was a very fine climber, he said, and had climbed to a higher standard than he had himself. Soon she was pushing him to climb to her standard.

The officers' agreed strategy was to keep the questioning fairly neutral in this first interview, hoping to lull Rex into a false sense of security. Their questions remained open ones, and they did not at this stage seek to challenge his replies. He was asked if he ever wanted Beverley to be more than just a climbing partner. They had to clarify this by asking Rex if he 'fancied her' and had he asked her out for a drink or a meal on occasions other than meetings purely for climbing. He shook his head. No, he liked her but didn't think of her 'in that way'. He had never asked her out and they had never even had a drink together after climbing.

He was asked again about his whereabouts on the morning of her death, 12 January. He reiterated that he was at work. He was sure of that because he had seen a film in Sheffield on the second of his days off and the last showing was on the Tuesday. The film he said was *The Omen*.

What about the orange rucksack, he was asked? He confirmed that the loose rucksack found in the back of his van belonged to Beverley. It had been in the van since he last climbed with her, about a month ago. He had been climbing since and had thrown his own climbing gear in the back of the van. It had initially been piled on top of the rucksack, but then he had pulled it out so it was available to give back to its owner when next he saw her. He was expecting to climb with her again in the near future.

At this point the officers stopped the interview. Rex was asked if he wanted food or refreshment, but he replied that he didn't feel at all like eating. He did, however, receive a mug of tea in his cell, to which he had been returned. The cell was now much colder than the interview room had been and he was shivering under his blanket. He was told that a check would be made to see if any clothing had been found for him. Half an hour later a uniform officer appeared in his cell with a T-shirt and a pair of overalls. This clothing didn't make him feel much warmer, so he was allowed to keep the blanket as well.

It was almost 7.30 pm when Rex was brought out of the cell and returned to the interview room. DCs Forrester and Murdoch then embarked on the second interview of their suspect. He wasn't asked again at this time if he wanted to consult with a solicitor. He was, however, cautioned once more at the commencement of the interview. The caution reminded him that he was under no obligation to say anything to the interviewers, but that anything he did say might be used in evidence. Although Rex was to claim later that he didn't really understand what the caution meant, when asked now by the officers if he realised what it meant he replied that he did.

In this second interview, the officers were altogether more confrontational, challenging his assertions and making use of closed questions. First of all he was asked again about his relationship with Beverley. He insisted that they were just climbing partners and he had never aspired to be anything else.

'But we have evidence that you did want more than just a climbing partnership,' DC Forrester told Rex, 'and that you asked her a few times to go out with you as a "girlfriend". Isn't that right?'

No, no – I didn't want that!' he exclaimed. 'I didn't feel that way about her.'

'Can we remind you what you said to us when you were arrested,' said DC Murdoch. 'Your exact words were "I loved her", and that's why you wouldn't have killed her.'

'But I didn't mean that I loved her in that way!'

'So what did you mean by "I loved her"?'

Rex shook his head and looked down at the table. He made no reply. This was to become a repeated reaction throughout the interview.

'We also have evidence, Rex,' said DC Forrester, 'that

she turned you down, but you didn't accept that, and bombarded her with flowers and presents.'

No reply.

'And that on one occasion you followed her to a pub and she humiliated you by referring to you as a "schoolboy" in front of other people.'

'No, that never happened.'

'Isn't it right,' DC Murdoch put to him, 'that because you kept pestering her to go out with you, she told you that she wouldn't climb with you anymore?'

'No.'

'Then why did she terminate your climbing partnership? Why didn't she want to climb with you any longer?'

He looked at the table and made no reply.

The officers then told Rex they were going to ask him about his movements on Wednesday 12 January. They put in front of him his work timesheets for all that week. They had been given these by David Hersey. He agreed that these showed that he had worked on the Monday, the Thursday and the Friday; but that the absence of any timesheets for the intervening two days meant that he had not been at work then.

'You have told us more than once, Rex,' said DC Murdoch, 'that you were at work on the Wednesday. That is clearly not the case.'

'I must be mistaken.'

'But it was only last week. How could you be mistaken about the days you worked and didn't work?'

Again, a shake of the head and he looked down. No reply.

'So what did you do on that Wednesday?'

'That must have been the day I went to the cinema.'

'To see *The Omen*?'

'Yes'.

'Rex,' said DC Forrester, 'when you were in your cell before this interview started, I checked with the cinemas in Sheffield. None of them were showing *The Omen* that week.'

Again Rex had no reply to this, but shook his head and looked down at the table.

Now the interviewers turned again to the finding of the orange rucksack in his van. 'When were you going to return the rucksack to Beverley?' they asked.

'I was going to contact her to arrange another day's climbing.'

'But she had told you that she didn't want to climb with you again,' DC Forrester reminded him. 'Why would she change her mind?'

'Because there were times when she didn't have anyone to climb with and, anyway, she trusted me as a climbing partner, and you need to climb with someone you trust.'

'So she would have been prepared to put aside whatever differences that there were between you, so that she could have a trustworthy climbing partner?'

'Yes.'

'In fact,' said DC Murdoch, 'isn't it right that you had arranged to climb with her on Wednesday the 12th January? And that you had arranged to pick her up in your van that morning?'

'No, not that day.'

'So where were you then day?' asked DC Forrester, 'because you certainly weren't at the cinema in Sheffield, were you?'

'I was. I must have got the film wrong.'

'So what film was it?'

'I can't remember now.'

'Why not? It's only nine days ago. Are you seriously suggesting that you went to Sheffield to see a film and that you can't now remember what film it was?'

There was more silence and staring down at the table.

DC Murdoch asked him: 'Did she ever climb alone?'

'I don't know. Maybe.'

'Had you ever seen her not wear a helmet when climbing?'

'Not when she was with me.'

'Alright,' DC Forrester continued, 'this is what really

happened that day. You had contacted Beverley, she agreed to climb with you that day, and you went to pick her up that morning in Bakewell in your van. It was quite early, certainly before nine o'clock. Her husband had gone when you got to her house. You drove up to Curbar Edge and parked in the car park at the Baslow end of the edge.'

Rex was rapidly shaking his head as the officer was speaking.

DC Forrester went on: 'At the car park you got changed, and walked along the top of the edge with your gear and rope, until you got to about halfway along it. At this point I believe you came on to her. I'm not suggesting that you tried to grope her, but maybe tried to kiss her. She resisted and pushed you away. You lost your temper and pushed her off the edge of the cliff.'

Rex was now sobbing violently. 'No, I didn't. I wouldn't do that to her.'

'Isn't it right that you had very strong feelings for her? In fact, you were infatuated with her. Do you understand what I mean by "infatuated"?'.

He nodded between his sobs.

'So,' said DC Murdoch, 'you were infatuated with this young woman?'

He nodded again. He was now weeping profusely.

'We're going to take a break here,' said DC Forrester. 'You're in a bit of a state.

But we will continue with this interview in half an hour or so.'

Rex was taken back to his cold cell. The officers went to the canteen for tea and cigarettes. Both of them felt they were close to 'getting a result', as they put it. One more push and they would have a confession. They phoned Alan Woodman and updated him with their progress.

★★★★★★★★★★★★★★★★★★★★★★★★★★

The interview resumed at 9.10 pm. The officers were hoping for a swift conclusion, but they were to be disappointed. It soon became apparent to them that they had probably made a tactical error by stopping the interview when Rex was at a low ebb. They should have pressed for a confession when he was at his most vulnerable. Now, he was still tearful and shivering under his blanket, but instead of answering the questions, he lapsed into a sullen silence, his only response being the repeated shaking of his head.

DC Forrester carried on where he had left off, putting it to Rex that, having pushed Beverley off the crag, he had picked up her rucksack containing her helmet, the rest of her clothing and her shoes, and hurriedly made his way back to his van. His intention, it was suggested, was to make it appear that she had been climbing alone and had fallen. He was asked what he had done with the contents of her rucksack. Where had he disposed of them?

At one point Rex appeared to be falling asleep, and

he had to be shaken by the shoulder to rouse him. The officers reluctantly decided that the interview was going nowhere and they would have to call it a day. Rex was returned once more to his cell and the officers retired again to the canteen.

In the canteen they considered the situation. They both had felt from the outset that the death of Beverley Simpson had been no accident. They were both now quite convinced that they 'had their man'. But equally they knew that the evidence they had against him, although it had been enough to justify his arrest, was not sufficient to enable them to charge him with murder. He probably had a motive for killing her, he had lied more than once, and he had not come up with a cogent alibi for the morning of 12 January. He owned a blue van, and a bluey-green van had been seen in the Curbar Edge car park at the material time. A man and a woman had unloaded climbing gear from the vehicle and headed off to the crag. Unfortunately they were very aware from what they had been told, that the witness Trevor Birt had not been in any sort of position where he could identify these persons, or even the make and model of the van. It might be a coincidence but it was no more than that. It was a long way from being conclusive.

What they needed, and needed desperately, was a 'confession'. They felt they had come close, but perhaps now the moment had passed? They didn't think there was much point in having another interview that evening, but perhaps a night in the cell might concentrate the mind of the prisoner? They would have another go at him in the morning. However, if there was no confession then, he would have to be released without charge.

As they sat musing over their tea and cigarettes, Police Constable Ernie Trousdale breezed into the canteen. 'Evening, lads. What's new?' He sat down at their table and cadged a cigarette from DC Murdoch. The new arrival already knew about Rex Maitland and his arrest, and the circumstances of Beverley Simpson's death, but the two detectives told him how the interviews had progressed, or not progressed.

Ernie Trousdale had been a police officer for more than twenty years, and most of his service had been spent in Bakewell. As far as he was concerned, he knew everyone worth knowing in the town, and also those not worth knowing. He was a freemason and was on first-name terms with magistrates, councillors and other local 'worthies'. He knew all the local tradesmen and they knew him. But more than this, he knew all the local 'villains and ne'er-do-wells' and their families. Many of those who had been in trouble with the law he had known since they were at school. He prided himself on always having his 'ear to the ground', more so than DCs Forrester and Murdoch, who were also local officers but hadn't been in the town for anything like as long as Ernie Trousdale.

Ernie knew Rex Maitland, had known him as schoolboy, and knew his family. He also knew all about Beverley Simpson and he had known everything there was to know about her various boyfriends and 'one-night-stands'. There was, indeed, very little that happened in Bakewell that passed him by.

He listened intently as the other two officers recounted the detail of the interviews, and the present state of the evidence. When they had finished, he sat back, drew on his cigarette and nodded sagely.

'Listen,' he said, 'I know this little bastard very well. I knew his father just as well. His father was a violent sod, and young Rex is out of the same mould, even if he has avoided getting into trouble so far. He may be a skinny little devil, but, mark my words, it was only going to be a matter of time before he did someone some damage. He's not a full shilling, and he's unhinged. He's been coming on to Beverley for some time, and he wasn't suited when she gave him the bum's rush. He was pestering her and she has humiliated him on one occasion in front of a pub full of people. I'm telling you he will have done it.'

He thought for a moment and looked at his watch. 'Why don't you give me fifteen or twenty minutes with him. I know how to press his buttons. He might tell me something that he wasn't ready to tell you.'

The other two looked at each other.

'Can't do any harm, I suppose,' said Murdoch.

'Absolutely nothing to lose,' said Forrester.

And so it was, that at 10.15 pm that Friday night, Rex Maitland was, for the last time that day, brought from his cell to the interview room, but this time to be confronted by a new face, albeit a familiar one.

★★★★★★★★★★★★★★★★★★★★★★★★★★

What was said in that twenty-minute interview conducted by PC Trousdale was to be recounted by Rex Maitland's solicitor when Rex appeared in court three days later. Or at least Rex's version of what took place. Ernie Trousdale's account was somewhat different. Suffice it to say that at just after 10.35 pm, DCs Forrester and Murdoch were summoned back to the interview room. They were met outside the door by Ernie Trousdale. 'He's coughed to the murder,' he told them, 'and now he wants to make a statement.'

The two officers looked at each other in surprise. How had a uniform officer succeeded where they, experienced detectives, had failed? However, they didn't want to 'look a gift horse in the mouth', and they entered the interview room. Rex appeared to be more composed than previously, although it was apparent that he was struggling to stay awake.

'Okay Rex,' DC Murdoch said to him. 'I believe you now want to make a statement about what you said to PC Trousdale. About your involvement in Beverley Simpson's death. Is that right?'

Rex nodded wearily. DC Forrester then took a form out of the drawer of the desk. The form was headed 'Voluntary Statement'. Rex was asked if he wanted to write the statement himself, or did he want one of the officers to write it?

'You write it, my spelling isn't very good,' he replied.

Over the next thirty minutes the statement was written down by DC Murdoch. It should have been at Rex's dictation, but he seemed unable to find the words so the officers, and PC Trousdale, who remained in the room, prompted him and suggested appropriate phrases and terminology. On two occasions Rex had to be shaken by the shoulder to keep him from drifting into sleep.

Before the commencement of the statement, Rex was cautioned that he didn't have to say anything and that anything he did say might be used in evidence. He had to sign a clause at the top of the form to the effect that he had been cautioned and that the statement was being made of his 'own free will' and that he wanted someone to write it for him. After the statement had been written, he further signed it as being a 'true' account. Prior to this it had been read over to him by DC Forrester as follows:

'I met Beverley Simpson about six months ago in the Lovers' Leap café in Stoney Middleton. She was a rock climber like me, and we agreed that we would meet to climb together. After this we climbed together on a number of occasions on various gritstone edges and crags in the Derbyshire Peak District. After a while I realised that I was attracted to her as a woman, even though she was more than twelve years older than me. I asked her if she would go out with me socially, for a drink or a meal. She made it clear that she did not want to do this. I would not take no for an answer and

I kept asking her to go out with me. She continued to reject me. I became obsessed with her and began sending her flowers and buying her presents. About five weeks ago she told me that she didn't want our climbing partnership to continue. I still wouldn't accept the situation and on one occasion I followed her to a pub in Bakewell one night. She rounded on me and told me I was a "schoolboy". This was in front of a pub full of people and I felt totally humiliated. I felt very depressed but also very angry at the way she had treated me.

I still didn't want to give up and about ten days ago I rang her at work and asked if she would climb with me again. I promised that I wouldn't press her to go out with me anymore and that our relationship would just be about climbing. She seemed to accept this and I got the impression that she was keen to resume our climbing partnership. We agreed to go to Curbar the next day and I said I would pick her up the following morning at her home in Bakewell.

The next day was a Wednesday, 12th January, and I drove to her house, arriving at about 8.15 am. Her husband had already left to go on a business trip. We drove to Curbar Edge and I parked my minivan in the car park at the eastern end of the escarpment. There were only a few vehicles in the car park at this time. It was quite cold and there was a lot of snow on the ground. We got our gear together and set off walking along the top of the edge. We were going to do a route about halfway along the crag. We were going to abseil down to the foot of the climb.

When we got to the place where we were going to descend, we changed into our climbing shoes. Beverley was wearing her usual pair of PAs. I don't know why but I was suddenly overcome with a feeling of desire for her. She had been very friendly and chatty up to this point and I must have misread the signals. I really thought she would respond if I tried to kiss her. I put my hands on her shoulders and tried to pull her towards me. She shouted "get off me, you little bastard" and pushed me away. I saw red and something snapped inside me. I went back towards her and roughly pushed her backwards. I knew we were close to the edge of the top of the cliff at this point. She gave a cry and fell back over the edge. I looked over and saw that she had fallen into the boulders, some eighty to a hundred feet below. She was not moving.

I was in a state of terror and panic. For a few minutes I couldn't move. I looked round and saw that there was no-one else in the vicinity. Still in panic I grabbed her rucksack, stuffed her ordinary shoes inside, and headed off quickly back the way I'd come. Back at the car I threw everything in the back and drove away.

Later I disposed of her shoes, her fleece, her helmet and her cagoule at the tip. I don't know why, but I kept her empty rucksack in the back of the van. I think I wanted something to remember her by.

I have lied to the police and I am very sorry about that. I am devastated by what I have done and I shall never get over it.'

Before he was returned to his cell for the last time that day, Rex Maitland was taken to the charge-room and charged by DC Forrester with the murder of Beverley Simpson.

It was 11.30 pm.

CHAPTER SEVEN

January 24th

Shortly after 10.00 am on Monday 24 January, Alan Woodman found himself sitting behind Martin Tory in Bakewell Magistrates' Court. He had still been sitting behind his desk, nursing a large whisky, when DC Forrester rang him at 11.30 on the Friday night to deliver the news about Maitland's confession statement. In these circumstances he could only endorse the decision to charge Rex with the murder of Beverley Simpson. The detective hadn't given him a lot of information, and in particular he hadn't told Alan of the intervention and involvement of PC Trousdale.

Rex had been kept in custody at Bakewell police station over the weekend, and was now, on the Monday morning, to be put before a specially convened court in Bakewell town hall. DCs Forrester and Murdoch, having clocked up many hours of overtime in the previous ten days or so, firstly with the hunt for

William Hughes and then with the Beverley Simpson investigation, were now off for a couple of days. DC Murdoch, however, had prepared a typed report on the Maitland case, which would accompany the prisoner to court and furnish the prosecutor with the information necessary to apply to the court for Rex to be remanded in custody for the next few days. The report was brief, and again made no reference to the interview that had been conducted by Ernie Trousdale.

Martin Tory was the prosecutor that morning. He'd had time to read the report and wasn't expecting any difficulty in persuading the magistrate to keep Rex in custody. Rex was brought into court in handcuffs, escorted by two burly police constables. He was also accompanied by Paul Hargreaves, a solicitor from a firm in Chesterfield. Rex had been advised, after he had been charged, that he would need the services of a solicitor from that point, and the police had put him in touch with Paul Hargreaves, who was an experienced criminal practitioner. Inspector Tyzack had suggested to Rex that it would probably be appropriate that he be represented by a solicitor from outside Bakewell, given that Beverley was probably known to the local solicitors, as Bob Hasssop's secretary, if for no other reason.

The magistrate came into court. Rex recognised him as his old headmaster from his primary school in Bakewell. Martin rose to his feet, outlined the brief circumstances of the case, including the fact that the prisoner had made a statement admitting the charge, and asked for Rex to be remanded in custody to Leicester prison until he could appear before the court again the following Friday.

Paul Hargreaves then stood up to respond on behalf of Rex. He wasn't instructed to make an application for bail that day, he told the magistrate, but he was putting the court and the prosecution 'on notice' that he would be making such an application at the next hearing. He then set out, in some detail, why there would be an application for bail on the Friday, and why, he said, his client would, in due course, be pleading 'Not Guilty' to the charge of murder. What he then went on to tell the court was to be uncomfortable hearing for both Martin Tory and Alan Woodman.

He had had a lengthy conference before court with Rex Maitland, the solicitor said, and he had been disturbed by what he had been told by his client. Rex Maitland, he continued, had been detained at Bakewell police station for eight hours before he had been charged, and during that time he had spent at least half of this period in a poorly heated cell and with inadequate clothing. At least some of this time he had been provided with no outer clothing, his garments having been seized for forensic examination, and had had only a blanket to keep out the cold. This on an evening when the temperature outside was barely above freezing point. He had been at work since 5.30 that morning, had received almost no refreshment during his stay in custody, and by the time of his 'so-called confession' he was cold, hungry and very tired. The worst aspect of the whole affair, however, the solicitor went on to say, was the 'highly irregular' intervention of Police Constable Trousdale, who had nothing to do with the investigation, and should not have been allowed the opportunity to interview the prisoner. This 'maverick', moreover, had gone on to offer a series of threats and inducements to the accused, which had succeeded in 'forcing' him into making a false confession.

Hargreaves had not yet finished. He had every confidence, he said, that the 'confession' would not be allowed in evidence because it had been obtained by oppression and inducement. As he understood the case against his client, the rest of the evidence against him was inconclusive and insufficient to prove his guilt. The accused was adamant that he had not killed Beverley Simpson and was nowhere near her at the evident time of her death.

If the magistrate had been listening to Paul Hargreaves, nothing of what he had said appeared to have registered with him. Almost before the solicitor had sat down, Rex was being sternly told that he was being remanded in custody until the following Friday. He was then quickly removed from the courtroom by the two police escorts.

Martin Tory had been somewhat shaken by Hargreaves' address to the court. He was used to defence practitioners making extravagant claims for their clients at this stage of the proceedings, and he and his colleagues used to joke that if they had been given a pound for every occasion that solicitors, when making applications for bail, had told the court that their client would be pleading 'Not Guilty', and yet, when it came to it, the client had pleaded 'Guilty', then they would all be very wealthy men. But this seemed to him to be rather different. Paul Hargreaves was attacking the case at a time when he wasn't even making an application for bail, and, indeed, with such an apparently strong belief in the truth of what he had been told by the client. Paul was as guilty as any other defence solicitor in making cynical statements about the case at this juncture but somehow this was different. If there was a grain of truth in what he had been saying, then the prosecution was in trouble.

As he got up to leave the courtroom, Paul leaned over to the prosecutor. 'I think you'd better have a good look at this one, Martin,' he told him. 'I don't think it's a "kosher" investigation'. He spoke loudly enough for Alan Woodman to have been included in his remarks.

Alan had also been disturbed by the solicitor's comments to the court. He was hard-bitten and experienced and accustomed to the blandishments and hyperbole of defence practitioners like Paul Hargreaves, but there had been some observations made that had left him feeling uneasy, an uneasiness that he had also felt when agreeing to Maitland's arrest. As soon as Hargreaves had departed, he turned to Martin. 'I think you and I will need to have a crack about this case, Martin,' he said, 'and before the next hearing. I'll gather up the evidence and I'll give you a bell.'

Martin nodded. 'The sooner the better, I think,' he replied.

★★★★★★★★★★★★★★★★★★★★★★★★★★★

Back in his office, later that morning, Alan Woodman reflected on what he had heard in court. What caused him most concern and unease was the reference to the involvement of PC Trousdale. He had known Ernie Trousdale for some years. He was a man he instinctively loathed and mistrusted.

He knew Trousdale as an 'old-fashioned copper'. In some instances this might amount to a compliment. In this case, however, as far as Alan was concerned, it was a euphemism for 'dinosaur'. Ernie Trousdale had been a police officer for close on twenty-five years, and had grown up with the culture that suspects in custody were 'pond-life', were not there to be treated with kid-gloves, or any sort of respect. Officers of that ilk were not averse to using violence, physical or psychological, to obtain confessions if their instinct told them that the prisoner was guilty; nor were they strangers to the use of threats or inducements to obtain the same result. They would never admit to such improprieties, of course, because that would lead to any confession being excluded from evidence as having been obtained by oppression or other means that would render it as not having been made 'voluntarily'. But it had gone on, and still went on. Alan was afraid that what Paul Hargreaves had said about PC Trousdale may have had the ring of truth.

Ernie Trousdale, Alan was aware, was also a freemason. At the masonic lodge he would fraternise with a lot of local 'worthies'. He was on first-name terms with councillors, magistrates and also some senior police officers. Alan was totally hostile to the idea of police officers being freemasons. He believed it could lead to corruption, or could influence the way in which an officer carried out his duties. From his own knowledge, he was aware of one or two senior officers in the force who could only have achieved their exalted rank through their masonic connections. Ernie Trousdale was only a police constable, but he had always loudly proclaimed that he never aspired to higher rank because being a constable was where 'real policing' was done. His lowly status, however, did not stop him using his masonic connections to 'have a word in the ear' of senior officers if he felt he had been badly treated by his immediate non-masonic superiors. Alan was always careful in his dealings with Trousdale and resented that he had to be thus.

Two or three years ago, Trousdale had been prosecuted for an offence of driving without due care and attention, following a road accident he had been involved in whilst driving his own private vehicle. He had denied the offence and his trial had been held at Bakewell Magistrates' Court. The trial shouldn't have been there anyway, given that Ernie was well-known to the local magistrates, but this was nothing unusual in Bakewell Court. There was a rumour circulating at the time that Ernie had arranged to be loitering at the entrance to the court building when the chairman of the bench arrived. The two knew each other well and the story went that the chairman said to Ernie 'what are you here for,' to which Ernie replied 'I'm facing a trumped-up driving charge.' At the trial he was found 'Not Guilty'.

The story might have been apocryphal, but, on the other hand, it might not, and there was no surprise that the prosecution failed!

Alan decided that he needed to have a close look at whatever entries PC Trousdale had made in his pocket notebook about his dealings with Rex Maitland, and as soon as possible. He also needed to quickly gather in all the available evidence in the case. He left a message for PC Forrester to make sure that he submitted to him by Thursday morning all witness statements that had been taken in the investigation, together with Maitland's confession statement and copies of all the pocket book entries made by officers who had been involved in the case up to that point. He then made provisional arrangements to meet with Martin Tory on the Thursday afternoon.

CHAPTER EIGHT

January 27th

Beverley Simpson's funeral had taken place on the 26th of January, on a cold and wet afternoon at Bakewell church. There was a very large attendance, numbers swelled no doubt by the realisation by then that Beverley had possibly not died in an accident but may have been murdered. Brook, Hassop & Co. had closed its doors for the day at lunchtime and all the office staff were present at the ceremony. As well as family members, there were also a significant number of local townspeople, members of the climbing fraternity and one or two police officers. Alan Woodman, who was in attendance, noted that those present did not include Ronnie Fox or Detective Chief Superintendent Fred Gorringe.

The principal mourner of course was Richard Simpson. DC Ian Forrester had spoken to him a few days before to inform him that someone had been charged with his wife's murder. Although he had been made aware before that that there was an ongoing investigation into Beverley's death, he had appeared to be quite shaken by the news that it was no longer regarded as an accident. Alan Woodman, however, had not approached Richard after the funeral. The last thing he wanted to tell him now was that the case against the alleged murderer was under review.

★★★★★★★★★★★★★★★★★★★★★★★★★★

By the date of Beverley's funeral, those of the Moran family had also taken place in Chesterfield. The body of William Hughes had already been cremated at Brimington crematorium, Chesterfield. Arrangements had been made by his family to have him buried in Boythorpe cemetery in Chesterfield. His grave had been dug. The locals were having none of it, however, and the trench was filled in by a group of them before the funeral could take place.

★★★★★★★★★★★★★★★★★★★★★★★★★★

On the morning following the funeral he had attended, Alan Woodman was presented by DC Murdoch with the evidence that had been gathered thus far in the case against Rex Maitland. The file included the post mortem report, witness statements from the climbers who had found the body, police officers and mountain rescue personnel who had been at the scene of the death, Inspector Tyzack, John Carswell, David Hersey, various persons who had been interviewed as previous 'boyfriends' or climbing associates of Beverley, Trevor Birt, Rex's 'confession' statement, and the pocket-notebook entries made by the two CID officers and PC Ernie Trousdale. He shut his office door, lit a cigarette, and sat down and began to read.

Two hours later, Alan closed the file and sat back in his chair. The feeling of unease that had been with him ever since he endorsed the arrest of Rex Maitland was as strong as ever. Much of the evidence he already knew about. As far as the rest was concerned, on paper it completed the jigsaw and the whole added up to a strong case against the prisoner. There was evidence of a motive for the killing, circumstantial evidence at least of presence close to the scene at the material time, evidence of lies told, lack of an alibi, and, above all, a confession to the crime. What troubled Alan, however, was not what was present, but what was missing, and what he knew or suspected he was not being told. What concerned him most was the content of PC Trousdale's notebook, and why Rex, after denying his guilt during hours of interviews with two experienced detectives, had suddenly 'rolled over' and confessed after twenty minutes in the company of a uniform police constable.

Trousdale's notebook contained the details of the 'interview' he had conducted with Rex Maitland. The tone of the conversation was noticeably 'matey' and conspiratorial. Alan saw immediately that at no stage had Rex been cautioned by the officer, as if the interview was intended to be no more than a 'cosy chat' between two old friends. It began with Rex being offered a cigarette, which he accepted. According to PC Trousdale the conversation then went like this:

TROUSDALE: We've known each other a good few years, haven't we, Rex.

MAITLAND: Yes.

TROUSDALE: Since you were running around in short pants.

MAITLAND: Yes, Ernie.

TROUSDALE: I sorted things out for you when you were getting bullied at school, didn't I?

MAITLAND: Aye, you did.

TROUSDALE: We've always been good mates, you and me.

MAITLAND: Yes, we have.

TROUSDALE: You know you can trust me, don't you.

MAITLAND: Yes, I do.

TROUSDALE: That Beverley Simpson, I've known her a good while as well. She was bad news. A tart and a 'prick-teaser'. You know that now, Rex, don't you?

MAITLAND: I know now, yes.

TROUSDALE: I would put money on it that she led you on and then pushed you away.

MAITLAND: She did

TROUSDALE: She treated you like shit in front of a

pub full of customers. She treated you like you were no better than something on the bottom of her shoe, didn't she?

MAITLAND: She did, the bitch.

TROUSDALE: You see, Rex, if I'd been in your shoes I would have lost it with her too. I'd have given her a good hiding. She deserved it.

According to the notebook entry, at this point Rex was silent and looked down at the table.

TROUSDALE: You must be a saint, Rex, because even after she had treated you like shit you asked her to go climbing with you again. That's right, isn't it?

Rex was silent again, but after a few seconds he nodded.

TROUSDALE: That Wednesday morning you went out of your way to go and pick her up and you took her out to Curbar Edge. Yes?

Rex nodded again.

TROUSDALE: I think what happened there was that you thought that you were back in favour with her, and on the cliff top you misread the signals and went to try and kiss her. Am I right?

Again the nod came.

TROUSDALE: But the cow had led you on again and told you to get off, didn't she?

More nods.

TROUSDALE: And in that split second, and no-one can blame you for this, you pushed her in anger. Unfortunately she was close to the edge of the cliff and she went over. I think that's how it happened, didn't it Rex?

There was a short period of silence, then Rex, still looking down at the table, nodded again.

TROUSDALE: Listen, Rex, what you did was entirely understandable. She might be dead but you're a victim in this too. As your friend I can help you and make sure that any punishment you might get is reduced. I can tell the judge that you're a good lad, that you don't have a violent bone in your body, and that you've been led on by a no-good tart. Do you understand what I am saying?

Rex nodded silently again.

TROUSDALE: We'll need to get all this down on paper, Rex, so my advice to you is to make a statement about what we've just discussed. Are you happy to do that? If so, I'll get the other two lads back and they can take a statement from you.

MAITLAND: OK, Ernie.

There was nothing in the interview, Alan mused, that corresponded with the lurid description applied to it by Paul Hargreaves in court a few days ago. But then this was only PC Trousdale's version of it, and Alan suspected it was probably well short of what actually went on. There were no threats made, but even in the Trousdale account there was what seemed to

Alan to be an 'inducement' made to the prisoner. The implication that he, PC Trousdale, could influence the sentence passed by 'having a quiet word with the judge' was surely a statement calculated to push Rex into making an admission of guilt, with the promise of a lighter sentence if he did so. Alan decided he would need to get Martin Tory's 'take' on that.

But this was only part of the problem, Alan realised. The absence of a caution at the commencement of the 'chat' was also a serious issue. It meant that Rex could argue, or at least his barrister could, that he believed that he was involved in no more than an informal conversation with the officer, and that whatever he said could not be used against him in court. Whilst Rex may have gone on to make a written statement to other officers, which included admissions of guilt, and after he had been properly cautioned that anything he said in that statement might be used as evidence against him, the 'impropriety' of what had gone before might well taint the admissibility of that statement. The Trousdale interview was, in short, a potential minefield that could affect the whole case against Rex Maitland.

But even this was not the end of the difficulties. Leaving aside the maverick activities of PC Trousdale, there was the issue of the entire circumstances of Maitland's time in police detention. Alan had very much in mind that it had been reported to him that Rex's employer had provided the information that the youth was 'not a full shilling'. The implication was that he probably had learning difficulties and could be seen as 'a vulnerable adult'. He should probably have been handled 'with kid gloves' by the police at Bakewell police station. In particular, it seemed to Alan, it simply wasn't enough to have asked him once, at the beginning of his detention period, whether he wanted the services of a solicitor. Apart from anything else, he should have been reminded several times during the eight hours of his detention that he was entitled to have a solicitor present and, indeed, how a legal representative could assist him.

Alan had also been made aware that for almost the entire eight hours, Rex had had no outer clothing and, surely, sitting for long periods in a cold cell or a poorly heated interview room in the depths of winter was almost certainly going to be perceived, at best, as oppressive and, at worst, as inhuman and degrading. It may have been an unfortunate combination of circumstances that had led to Rex being held at a police station with inferior facilities and without serviceable clothing, but this was not going to help the case. At the end of the day a young and vulnerable man was held in custody and interviewed in quite unacceptable conditions, effectively deprived of the services of a solicitor, probably deprived also of adequate rest and refreshment, not cautioned when he should have been, and probably led into making a confession by an improper inducement from a police officer.

Alan Woodman had little doubt that the net result of all this was that at the trial the judge would not allow the prosecution to use the confession statement made by Rex. The jury would not be told that Rex had admitted his guilt, firstly to PC Trousdale, and then in a written statement made to two other officers.

If the 'confessions' were out of the equation, what was the remaining evidence and was it sufficient to justify carrying on with the prosecution? There was some evidence of 'motive'. Rex was the owner of a blue van and such a vehicle had been seen in the car park by Curbar Edge at what could be the material time, and, moreover, a young man and a woman had been observed with the vehicle, unloading climbing equipment, and had then moved off towards the crag area. Rex had told lies about his movements that day and had failed to come up with a credible alibi. Beverley's rucksack was found in the back of his van and he had provided an unconvincing explanation for having it and for where it had been lying in the vehicle.

That, however, mused Alan, was the case at its highest. The evidence about the blue van could be dismissed as no more than coincidence. Blue vans were hardly uncommon, and Trevor Birt could barely describe, let alone identify, the occupants of the van he had seen that morning. Maitland might have some other reason for lying about his movements, other than the need to conceal a criminal act. The evidence about the rucksack was useful but hardly compelling. It seemed to Alan that what the totality of the evidence amounted to was no more than a case of 'suspicion'. It surely wasn't going to be enough to allow a jury to find Rex guilty of murder. Even a prosecutor as robust and as positive as Martin Tory wasn't going to want to take this case to court ...

★★★★★★★★★★★★★★★★★★★★★★★★★★★

Alan Woodman was right about the view that Martin Tory would have on the evidence. That afternoon Martin spent an hour and a half studying the material that Alan handed to him, whilst Alan took himself off for tea and cigarettes and a visit to the office of a CPS lawyer in the same building to discuss another case. When he returned, Martin had just completed his reading and his face betrayed his feelings about the case.

'I don't think it's a runner,' he said to Alan, 'or at least, not as it stands.'

Alan nodded. 'I agree,' was his instant response.

Between them they analysed and dissected the evidence. In particular Martin confirmed Alan's worst fears about the 'confessions'. The intervention of Ernie Trousdale, he felt, was not only highly irregular but also extremely likely to be fatal to the admissibility of the confession statement that followed it. Like Alan, he was suspicious and uneasy about the veracity of that officer's account of his interview with Rex, and, even if it was accurate, there was an obvious inducement offered to the prisoner to make a full written confession when the 'official' investigators took over the proceedings again. There was also the issue of Rex not being cautioned by Trousdale before he made admissions of guilt to him, an omission which would almost inevitably undermine the integrity of those admissions.

Martin had also been made aware by Alan of the circumstances in which Rex had been detained – the lack of outer clothing, the inadequate heating, the lack of refreshment, and the fact that he was almost certainly highly fatigued after a long day at work and then eight hours at the police station. To cap it all, there was the situation of a probably vulnerable young man effectively being deprived of the opportunity to acquire the services of a solicitor. In order for Maitland's 'confessions' to be admitted in evidence in a trial, the prosecution had to show that they were made 'voluntarily' and not as a result of oppression or inducement. Martin had not come across a case in his career where there was such a combination of circumstances as in this one, a combination that, in his view, would make it a certainty that the confession evidence would be excluded at the trial. Alan did not demur.

Martin also confirmed that his view was that the rest of the available evidence fell well short of being sufficient to provide a 51% chance of conviction, the standard that the evidence had to reach if the case was to be pursued. His conclusions about that evidence matched those of the officer.

Did the police think they had got the 'right man' inquired Martin. Certainly the two detective constables did, was Alan's response, and they had been closer to the case and the prisoner than anyone else. Whilst he himself had kept an open mind on the subject, he was prepared to trust the other officers' instincts as to whether Rex Maitland was guilty of killing Beverley Simpson.

Martin's own instinct, in a case of this seriousness, and where the police believed they had 'got the right man', was always to look for ways to rescue the case, to see if the evidence could be improved, rather than just 'throwing in the towel'.

'Is there any prospect of more evidence?' he asked Alan.

Alan looked doubtful. 'It's not promising, but we could but try,' was his rejoinder.

Martin thought for a few moments. 'Well, what I would suggest,' he said after the pause, 'is that we don't kick the case into touch just yet. But we could take the immediate pressure off by withdrawing the objections to bail when Maitland is before the court tomorrow.'

Alan nodded. 'Sounds good to me. Will the court buy that, given that it's a murder charge and that it was only a week ago that we were wanting him in custody?'

'I think I can persuade the magistrates,' said Martin, 'and the defence are hardly going to object! Then it's over to you to see if you can come up with anything else. But I think we will need to nail this down one way or another before he gets sent to the Crown Court. So you've probably got six or eight weeks at most.'

On this note Alan took his leave. He felt some relief, firstly that Martin Tory shared his views on the case, but secondly that there was going to be a bit of breathing space before anything irrevocable took place. He knew, however, that he faced a difficult conversation with DCs Forrester and Murdoch, and possibly also his Detective Inspector, Bill Moore. He would also need to speak to Richard Simpson, to break it to him that the person alleged to have murdered his wife, was about to be released on bail ...

CHAPTER NINE

January 28th

Alan found Richard Simpson at home just after 9.30 on the morning of Friday the 28th January. Rex Maitland was due to be produced in court later that morning and Alan didn't want Richard to be taken by surprise if and when he learned that the prosecution had withdrawn their objections to the accused having bail. As it was, Richard had arranged his business affairs so that he could attend Bakewell court that day, so he would have witnessed this occurrence first-hand. As tactfully as he could, Alan explained to Richard that the case was under review, that there were some problems with the evidence, and that it had been decided, in the circumstances, that the prosecution would no longer object to Rex having bail.

Richard was bemused. Why were there problems when Maitland had only been charged a few days ago? What were the problems? Alan had to tell him that he couldn't divulge what the difficulties were, and that he couldn't discuss the evidence with him. Apart from any other considerations, Richard was a potential witness. He made it clear, however, that the case wasn't being dropped, and that the investigation was continuing.

Richard was anxious to know what 'the investigation was continuing' meant. Were the police looking for more evidence? Was this just against Rex Maitland or were there other suspects? Again, Alan couldn't go into any detail but Richard should be aware that the police had to keep an open mind, and that if the investigation led in other directions, then they had to pursue the inquiry wherever it led them.

Richard was disconcerted. Was it possible, he wanted to know, that Maitland was not the murderer? That the police had arrested the wrong man? And that someone else might be arrested in due course? All Alan could say in response was that the police had to 'keep an open mind'. He realised that this was not very reassuring, but, he stressed, surely Richard would want to be as certain as the police that the right man ended up in the dock? That might still be Maitland.

As Alan took his leave of the widower, he was very aware that Richard was not at all happy about the developments. He knew, too, that Richard was not being fooled by the platitudes he was being fed, and that he was intelligent enough to realise that the implication of what he was being told was that the case against Rex Maitland was ultimately going to be ditched.

Half an hour later Alan was having no easier a conversation with DC Forrester and DC Murdoch. He outlined his own views on the 'confessions' made by Maitland, the involvement of PC Trousdale, and the circumstances in which Rex had been detained at Bakewell police station, and also made it clear that Martin Tory was in complete agreement with him. He made it plain that there had been really no alternative but to carry out the interviews with the prisoner in conditions that were less than ideal at the police station – Rex was in custody following arrest, and short of releasing him normal procedures had to follow. But the existence of those conditions in themselves, as a background against which the interviews took place, may well have been fatal to the admissibility of the 'confessions', even if there had been no other pitfalls. Alan could not disguise, however, that the interviewing officers had made mistakes. They should have made greater efforts to ensure that the prisoner was aware of the assistance a solicitor could provide, and to remind him far more often that he could avail himself of those services. And they should never have let Trousdale intervene in the investigation.

Whilst the officers were duly respectful to their superior, and whilst they did not raise any counter-argument, their body language spoke volumes. They were patently very unhappy with the message they were being given. They were only partially appeased by being told that the case was not being dropped out of hand. They agreed to carry on with the investigation, and in particular to seek further evidence against Maitland, if that evidence existed. The reality was, however, that both seriously doubted that any more evidence would be forthcoming.

To crown a difficult morning, Alan had also had to break the news about the case to his Detective Inspector. Bill Moore had been completely persuaded by the views of Alan and the CPS lawyer, Martin Tory, but had expressed annoyance and irritation about the shortcomings of the interviewing officers. In particular, he vented his spleen about the decision to allow the intervention of the person he referred to as 'that arse'ole Trousdale'. He made it plain that it was important that the investigation continued and with increased momentum, whether it be directed at securing more evidence against Maitland or, indeed, looking at other possible suspects. Alan knew that Fred Gorringe would be briefed by Bill, and he suspected that the head of CID would view the current state of affairs with even less equanimity.

★★★★★★★★★★★★★★★★★★★★★★★★★★★

Over at court, Martin Tory was having a much easier ride than Alan. As he awaited the arrival of the prisoner, Martin had spoken outside the courtroom to Rex Maitland's solicitor Paul Hargreaves. When told about the decision to withdraw the objections to Rex having bail, the solicitor expressed no surprise and simply gave a knowing smile.

'Well, that's a start,' he said. 'Are the magistrates going

to buy it?'

'I don't see why not,' replied Martin. 'There's some good reasons why he should be bailed, now that the dust has settled.'

'What sort of bail conditions are you looking for?' asked Paul.

'Oh, I don't see the need for anything onerous – live with his mother, report to Bakewell police station a couple of times a week, surrender his passport, if he has one.'

'I'll check about the passport,' Paul responded, 'but I'd be amazed if he had one. I don't think he's ever been to Derby, let alone the Costa del Sol!'

A few minutes later, Rex was brought into court, handcuffed to a burly police constable. He had been brought earlier that morning from Leicester prison, by prison officers in a taxi, but heavily shackled. No-one was taking any chances following the escapade involving the late William Hughes.

Martin, with some trepidation, then rose to address the man and two women on the bench. He began by telling them that the prosecution now felt that Rex could be safely released on bail, subject to suitable conditions. There were some raised eyebrows, but the magistrates listened in respectful silence to Martin's explanation for the 'u-turn' being made by the prosecution. The prisoner had been in custody for a week, Martin told them, and in that time the prosecution had been able to carefully assess the pros and cons of whether he could be safely released on bail. The conclusion had been reached, and this was one with which the police entirely agreed, that Maitland could be bailed, providing he was prepared to abide by appropriate conditions. Rex Maitland, Martin continued, was a young man, nineteen years of age, and without any previous convictions whatsoever. The alleged offence, although clearly very serious, had been directed at a particular person and in very specific circumstances. It was felt that there was no likelihood of further offences being committed, and particularly not of the type alleged. He was a local man with strong local ties and he was not expected to abscond. In any event, he would agree to report regularly to the police station so that his movements could be monitored, and he would also agree not to apply for any passport or travel documents (it had been established, as Paul Hargreaves had predicted, that he had no passport). Nor was it felt that there was any danger of his intimidating witnesses as the ones on whose evidence the case mainly rested were all police officers.

Martin made no reference to the weaknesses in and difficulties with the evidence. This was not the time for that sort of disclosure, and, in any event, it was at least arguable that bail might not have been opposed even if the evidence had been strong. A Crown Court judge might well have 'read between the lines', Martin thought, and realised exactly why the prosecution were back-pedalling, but this probably was not the case with these lay magistrates. As Martin had hoped, the magistrates did indeed 'buy it'. They merely looked at each other, had a brief whispered discussion, and the chairman then announced that bail would be granted subject to the conditions that Martin had mooted in his earlier conversation with Paul Hargreaves.

Martin was relieved that the situation was indeed made easier by the conduct of Paul Hargreaves. There were no outraged references this time to the irregularities in the police investigation and the 'appalling' conditions in which Maitland had been held. In fact the solicitor was positively complimentary about the stance taken by the prosecutor and 'endorsed' everything he had said.

Following the hearing, Rex was escorted back across the road to have his belongings restored to him and to be released. He was now adequately dressed, his mother and her partner having relented and visited him in Leicester prison bringing spare clothing. He had to sign a bail notice before he was actually released, acknowledging that he had to comply with the bail conditions set by the magistrates. This presented him with no difficulty, as the conditions were not oppressive and didn't prevent him going back to work or restrict his movements. His solicitor had explained to him that he suspected that the real reason why the prosecution had not objected to his release on bail was that they knew that their case was now weak. Rex felt quite light-hearted as he travelled back home as a passenger in his mother's partner's car. He would have been less sanguine, however, if he could have foreseen what other problems lay ahead for him ...

★★★★★★★★★★★★★★★★★★★★★★★★★★★

Martin Tory had other cases to deal with at court that morning and it was early afternoon before he was able to set off back to South Darley. He had enjoyed a convivial hour after court in the back bar of the Wheatsheaf Hotel in Bakewell, in the company of some of the magistrates, the Clerk to the Justices, and one or two local solicitors, including Kevin Malcolm. He was relieved that the magistrates hadn't tried to quiz him about the Maitland case, but Kevin had quietly and subtly probed him about why the prosecution had changed tack on the issue of bail. Martin gave nothing away, he thought, but he realised that he wasn't fooling an experienced hand like Kevin.

On the drive back, the roads were now clear of snow and the weather was much brighter than it had been for much of the previous two weeks, but there was no warmth in the sun and the temperature wasn't much above freezing point. Martin knew that he would have to brief his boss on what had happened in the Maitland case. Thus far he had spoken to no-one in the office about the developments over the last twenty-four hours, although it would have been widely known that Rex had been charged. He needed to get his superior's backing for the stance he had taken over bail, and, even more importantly, for the potential abandonment of the case if the ongoing police investigation didn't turn up any further material evidence. He hoped that the Chief Prosecuting Solicitor, Robin Caulfield, would be available when he got back. The last thing he wanted was to speak to his deputy. Ronnie Fox had been in the pub at lunchtime but he had managed to avoid being drawn into conversation with him. Ronnie tended to gravitate to Bakewell on a Friday, liking the 'crack' in the Wheatsheaf and then to buy a couple of pork pies in a local butcher's shop. But then, more often than not, he wouldn't return to the office but, instead, wend his way homewards, no doubt via one or two hostelries on the way.

Martin was relieved to find, on his arrival back at South Darley, that Ronnie had indeed not returned, but that Robin Caulfield was sitting at his desk. This description was not strictly accurate, as Caulfield was lying back in his chair with his feet up on the desk, engrossed in a magazine advertising foreign holidays. There appeared to be nothing else of note on the desk, and certainly no files or other work-related paperwork. This was nothing new in Martin's experience. Caulfield had long since ceased appearing in court, the general consensus amongst his lawyers being that, having been absent from court for so long, he had 'lost his bottle'. Certainly he studiously avoided making himself available for court, even contriving feeble excuses for not going when a substitute was being sought for a prosecutor who had fallen sick at short notice. Martin didn't understand how he filled his time, since, other than the occasional meeting at County Council headquarters in Matlock, there seemed to be nothing else to engage his attention. It was well-known, however, that at about 12.15 every day he would leave the office and spend at least two hours in the Sycamore Inn in Matlock, which was a regular 'watering-hole' for the CPS lawyers and local court staff. It never ceased to amaze Martin that neither Caulfield nor Fox, or indeed many senior police officers, paid any regard whatsoever to the drink-driving laws. He himself was always scrupulously careful when it came to drinking before he was required to drive – that lunchtime he had drunk but two halves of bitter, whilst he had observed Fox consuming at least three pints.

Caulfield greeted Martin, but instead of enquiring as to the reason for his visit, proceeded to launch into an account of his plans for his holiday in the summer, and why he had decided to change his holiday destination from his usual haunt of Grand Canaria to Tuscany. Martin sat patiently and listened politely while his boss regaled him with his views on the relative merits of Spanish and Italian resorts and why he had now opted for the latter. Eventually Caulfield tossed the magazine to one side and turned his attention and the conversation to more immediate matters:

'How's the murder going?' he asked.

'It isn't,' replied Martin and he went on to outline the difficulties with the case and the stance that had been taken on the question of bail for the accused.

Whatever flaws Robin Caulfield had as a chief prosecuting solicitor, he had a razor-sharp mind and was a first-rate lawyer. He very quickly assimilated the detail of what he was being told and, when Martin had finished his account, he was immediately ready with his own succinct appraisal of the case and the situation facing the police and the prosecution:

'Yes, it's a bummer,' he said. 'The confessions are going to get thrown out by the judge, and the rest of the evidence doesn't stand on its own.'

He agreed that withdrawing objections to bail had been the right course to take, and this would provide a breathing space and take the immediate heat off the prosecution. He cautioned, however, that the police should not be given too much time to come up with any further evidence against Maitland. If necessary the case against him should be withdrawn in three or four weeks' time. He pointed out that this would not prevent the case being resurrected later if further material evidence came to light. Martin could see the wisdom of this, and indeed he had already come to much the same conclusion himself. He thanked his boss for his input and, making his excuses, he quickly left Caulfield's office, before he could be subjected to a further discourse on summer holidays.

CHAPTER TEN

February 3rd

February ushered in a period of dry, warmer weather. The snow was a fading memory. There were cold nights but sunlit days in flawless blue skies. Spring seemed at hand.

Matching the brighter weather, there seemed to be a time of optimism abroad. No-one now spoke of the events at Pottery Cottage, and the newspapers had moved on to reporting more mundane matters. The tragedy, it seemed, had been obliterated from the collective memory. It had been buried along with the cremation of the bodies of the Moran family and that of William Hughes. The lone survivor of Hughes' murderous activities, Gill Moran, had slipped quietly away and her present whereabouts were unknown.

There was a lull too in the news coverage of the Beverley Simpson case. A man had been charged with her murder and was awaiting committal to the Crown Court. This was the cue for the media to enter a period of silence until they could feast themselves on the grisly details that would emerge in the trial.

Under the surface, however, Detective Constables Murdoch and Forrester were beavering away in their ongoing investigation, while Detective Sergeant Woodman and prosecutor Martin Tory anxiously awaited developments, one eye on the clock as time ticked by. Then, suddenly and unexpectedly, a series of events occurred that shattered the calm that had settled on the case, and catapulted the investigation into new and uncharted territory.

★★★★★★★★★★★★★★★★★★★★★★★★★★

On the Monday following Rex Maitland's release on bail, the investigating police officers, obeying their instruction to seek further evidence, had contacted the media in the various parts of Derbyshire and also in Sheffield. As it was a murder inquiry, they had little difficulty in persuading the local newspapers, radio and TV to publish or broadcast an appeal for information and assistance. The gist of the appeal was a request for anyone who had been in the car park adjacent to Curbar Edge between 7.00 am and 11.00 am on Wednesday the 12th January to contact the police. The request was worded in such a way that it invited anyone who had been there to come forward, whether or not they felt that they had information to give. In fact no reference was made to the fact that this was in connection with the death of a young woman, although by this time it would have been well-known that a body had been recovered at that location, and now, of course, that a man had been charged with her murder. It was, indeed, hoped and expected by the officers that, knowing that a man had been charged, would mean that persons would not be deterred from contacting the police, not fearing that they might come under suspicion if they did so.

Two or three days after the appeal went out, there was a positive result, albeit not one that the officers had been expecting, or indeed one that they welcomed. On the morning of the 3rd of February, DC Forrester took a phone call from a police constable at Buxton police station. The constable told him that he had been contacted by a young couple, who lived locally, who had disclosed that they had been in the car park in question on the morning of the 12th January and were willing to be interviewed. Arrangements were then made for the couple to attend the police station at Buxton that afternoon, and DCs Forrester and Murdoch made their way there from Bakewell.

Chris and Jenny Jackson, it turned out, had been climbing on Curbar Edge on the 12th January, travelling there from Buxton and parking in the car park close to the Edge at about 8.45 am. Once there, they had unloaded their climbing gear from the back of their vehicle, piled it into rucksacks, and set off to the crag. There had been a few other cars and vans in the car park when they arrived but they had not taken any notice of these and were not aware whether there had been persons in or with these vehicles. They had then walked along the top of the escarpment, almost to the far end of Curbar Edge, where they had spent about three hours climbing. They had not encountered any other climbers on the crag-top path, and had not been aware of any below or actually engaged in climbing. Other climbers or walkers, however, did pass them at various times later in the morning.

The most important part of their information, however, came out when they were asked to describe their vehicle. It was, they said, a dark green Morris van.

This information was a body-blow to the two detectives. It was very plain that this was the vehicle that Trevor Birt had seen in the car park at about 9.00 o'clock that morning, and that the Jacksons were the young couple he had witnessed unloading climbing equipment from the rear of the van. It was patently not Rex Maitland and Beverley Simpson that he had seen.

The two officers drove back to Bakewell knowing that the case against Maitland was now probably dead in the water. Worse news was to come, although it was to prove not altogether unrewarding.

★★★★★★★★★★★★★★★★★★★★★★★★★★

At much the same time as DCs Forrester and Murdoch were travelling to Buxton police station, Alan Woodman was engaged in quite a long telephone call with a Detective Sergeant Hopkins from Sheffield police. DS Hopkins told Alan that he was investigating a serious sexual assault that occurred in a rural area, north-west of the city, on the 12th January. He had seen the Curbar Edge murder case appeal in the Sheffield press and it had occurred to him that there might be something here that might be of interest to him. He had picked up details of the Rex Maitland case on the police grapevine, knew that the accused had been released on bail, and when he also learnt that Derbyshire police were appealing for assistance and information, he put two and two together and came to the correct conclusion that the case was not a strong one. He had contacted Bakewell police station, and in the absence of the two DCs, he had been put on to Alan Woodman at Matlock.

DS Hopkins then told his story, a story that, although it sent a shiver down Alan's spine, also tended to confirm his growing suspicions that his team had got the wrong man.

The Sheffield officer recounted how, on the early afternoon of the 12th January, Sheffield police had received an emergency telephone call from a public phone box from a woman clearly in some distress. A police patrol car had been despatched to the village of High Bradfield, seven miles out of the city, and here, sat on the snow-covered grass verge outside the red phone box, the police officers had found an eighteen-year old Sheffield university student, Annette Collins. The girl was dishevelled and weeping uncontrollably. The officers managed to ascertain from her that she had been attacked and a violent attempt made to rape her. She was conveyed back to Sheffield and taken initially to the Royal Hallamshire hospital. It turned out that she had no physical injuries, but was severely traumatised by her experience.

It was some hours later before Annette could tell the detectives who interviewed her exactly what had taken place. By this time she had recovered a good deal of her composure and was able to give a coherent account of her experience.

The previous evening, she said, she had been in a local nightclub with friends, and late on in the night she had met and fallen into conversation with a young man whose name she thought was 'Reg', although she couldn't be sure of this as they never really got to the point of exchanging names. He told her that he was a farmer from West Derbyshire. Annette wasn't altogether convinced by this as he seemed too young and 'a bit slow'. She was nonetheless attracted to him and they danced and he bought her several drinks. 'Reg' had told her that his van was parked in a multi-storey car park in the city, but by the small hours of the morning it was apparent to her that he would have been well over the blood-alcohol limit for driving and she invited him to 'crash out' on the sofa in her student flat, which was within walking distance of the nightclub. He readily accepted the offer.

The rest of the night, she said, was uneventful. Her flatmates were in when they got back, but the young man's conduct was 'impeccable'. They sat drinking coffee for half an hour and when she finally announced that she was going to bed, he simply bade her 'goodnight' and, apart from a chaste kiss on the cheek, he made no attempts at intimacy.

In the morning Annette had no lectures and Reg said that he was not working that day. He suggested to her that they could go for a drive out into the country and perhaps have a pub lunch. She had no reservations about going out with him in his van and happily went along with his suggestion.

'Reg' drove them out into the rural area north-west of Sheffield, and they stopped for a drink and a sandwich at The Old Horns Inn, in, what she now knew to be, the village of High Bradfield. He was, she said, good company, 'chatty' and solicitous for her comfort. She had no concerns therefore when he proposed a walk to a local crag, a crag he said where he had often climbed. He could show her the rock routes he had scaled, and, if she was interested, he might on a future occasion take her up some of the easier ones. Annette was keen to see where he had climbed, although, as a southerner, she had very little awareness of a sport which largely took place in northern England. They drove a few hundred yards from the pub, parked up, and set off through woodland until they reached a gritstone crag overlooking a reservoir. She was to learn later that the crag was known as Agden Rocher.

They walked along the foot of the crag and 'Reg' pointed out to her the various climbs. She remembered that one was called Campsite Crack, and another The Flying Dutchman. It was a cold day, there was snow on the ground, and they saw no other people – either climbers or pedestrians. They came across a boulder adjacent to the footpath and sat down to smoke. 'Reg' considerately took off his pea jacket and laid it down on the rock for her to sit on. They sat for a few minutes in companionable silence, smoking and looking at the view across the reservoir. Annette felt very much at ease and when 'Reg' put an arm round her shoulders, she made no attempt to shrug him off. Nor did she make any attempt to resist when he bent to kiss her on the lips, and in fact she reciprocated when he drew away. Then she realised he had undone the top button of her jeans and was pulling down the zip. She felt no immediate panic as she felt she may have encouraged him to be adventurous, but moved his hand away with a gentle request to desist – 'No, not here,' were the words she used.

It was at this point, however, Annette said, that his mood suddenly and abruptly altered. He became angry, then violent, pulling roughly at her jeans, and before she knew it he had pulled them over her hips and removed them altogether. She now began to struggle and lash out with her fists, but this didn't seem to deter him. He seemed like a man on a frenzied mission. She realised she was shouting and screaming. But there was no-one to hear her. Despite her struggle, he managed to pull her knickers downwards, tearing the fabric in the process. Then he was trying to force her legs apart with one hand, the other pulling off his own jeans and briefs. She was conscious of the fact that his penis, now exposed, was erect. Despite his slight stature, he was stronger than her and she knew she was losing the unequal struggle. She managed, however, to free one hand and struck him as hard as she could in the face. In that instant he relaxed his grip on her and with a huge physical effort she succeeded in rolling out from under his body and staggering to her feet. She had just time to grab her jeans from the floor and, leaving her knickers behind, she fled blindly off along the footpath.

In a minute or two she realised that he was not following her and she paused briefly to put her jeans back on. She was aware also that she was running in the direction from whence they had come earlier, and shortly she came across the parked blue minivan belonging to her assailant. She didn't stop but ran on into the village where they had visited the pub, dimly aware that she had seen a telephone box in that vicinity.

As the phone box came into sight she thought she heard the sound of a car engine to her rear and she quickly dived into a convenient front garden and behind a hedge. She was right to do so because a few seconds later, through the foliage, she saw the minivan drive past. To her relief she saw that it was travelling at speed, as if the driver were anxious to get away from the area.

The adrenalin rush that had accompanied her through the escape now abruptly dissipated and she began to shake and the tears started to flow. She forced herself into the phone box and dialled 999…

It was plain to Alan Woodman that, if the man DS Hopkins was describing were not Rex Maitland, it was an extraordinary coincidence. All the indications were there – a 'farmer', slow of speech, late teens, the minivan, a rock-climber. Add to that Maitland's early attempt at an alibi which put him in Sheffield at the material time, and he was very much fitting the bill as Annette Collins' assailant. Alan would normally have been a little reluctant to impart details of a serious criminal case he was investigating to an officer of another force, but in this instance he decided he would not hold back and he gave DS Hopkins all the information he had about Rex Maitland and the evidence against him, including its weaknesses, particularly the dubious 'confession'. The Sheffield officer was audibly excited.

'It's got to be our man!' he exclaimed. 'I'd stake my mortgage on it.'

Alan didn't seek to discourage him. He told DS Hopkins where he could find Maitland.

★★★★★★★★★★★★★★★★★★★★★★★★★★★

Events now moved on at a furious pace. That same evening Rex Maitland was arrested at his home address. He had been at home since his release, as his employer, David Hersey, had contacted him to strongly advise him that he should not return to work just yet as one or two of the other farm hands had been exhibiting strong feelings about working with a 'murderer'. They were, of course, ignoring the fact that Rex had not been convicted of anything and may never be convicted of anything, but they would hardly be alone in feeling that way. Many people locally would already have assumed Maitland was guilty, simply by virtue of the fact that the police had charged him with Beverley Simpson's murder.

The following day he was interviewed by detectives in Sheffield and, initially at least, strongly denied the offence. He agreed, however, to stand on an identification parade. He was picked out by Annette Collins as her attacker, and by one of her flatmates as being the man who had slept on their sofa on the night of the 11th January. Interviewed again, he now made a full and frank admission of being that person and that he had forcibly tried to have sexual intercourse with Annette without her consent. In a later phone conversation with Alan Woodman, DS Hopkins rather smugly pointed out that the confession was made in the presence of a solicitor, in a warm police station, after refreshment and rest, and without meddling by 'third parties'. Alan winced at these remarks, but could not think of a suitable response.

And so it was that Rex Maitland was charged with attempting to rape Annette Collins on the 12th January 1977. He was remanded in custody by Sheffield Magistrates, and he would remain in custody until sentenced for that offence.

Rex now had his alibi for the murder of Beverley Simpson, but it was not the kind of alibi he would have wanted.

CHAPTER ELEVEN

February 14th

Alan Woodman broke the news of Rex Maitland's new charge to the other members of his team on the same day that the event took place. It came as a bombshell to DCs Forrester and Murdoch, although they were already reconciled to the idea that the case against Rex was going to be dropped. They had been convinced of his guilt and it shook them to realise that their instincts had been so wrong. The compensating factor was that, had Maitland not been charged with Beverley Simpson's murder and had the case not run into difficulties, then he would probably not have been apprehended for what was, after all, a very serious offence in itself.

Detective Inspector Bill Moore was quite philosophical about it all.

'Out of the fire and into the frying pan,' was his quip to Alan Woodman on hearing the news. 'At least we know where we stand now,' he went on, 'and the investigation can proceed with a clean sheet of paper.'

Martin Tory was equally relaxed about the revelations. 'That's two big cases in a month that have gone west. Think of the work it's saved us,' was his jovial observation to Alan. Normally he would have felt disheartened by such developments, but there was really no cause for despair here. One of the defendants, William Hughes, was dead and Maitland was locked up for attempted rape in Sheffield, thus sparing Derbyshire CPS the agonising decision of whether or not to pursue a dodgy murder case. It was therefore in a light-hearted mood that he rang Paul Hargreaves to inform him that the murder charge against his client was going to be withdrawn.

'There's good news and there's bad news,' he told the solicitor.

Well, I know what the good news is going to be, and I already know about the bad news as I sat in on Maitland's interviews in Sheffield,' was the rejoinder.

Martin informed Paul that he would confirm in writing that the murder charge would be withdrawn at the next hearing, and he would write to the court to the same effect. Paul agreed to inform his client that he would no longer be facing the murder charge, although in the circumstances, 'it would hardly come as a surprise!'

Shortly after this telephone conversation, Ronnie Fox appeared in Martin's office. His normal breezy demeanour was missing and he appeared to be a little troubled.

'I gather we've kicked Maitland's case into touch?' he said.

Martin was surprised that Fox already knew this, particularly as it hadn't really happened yet. On the other hand, perhaps he shouldn't be surprised as the man had contacts all over the place and probably Fred Gorringe had put him in the picture.

'Yes, he's got the perfect alibi. He was picked out on an ID parade by the victim of an attempt rape, committed on the same day as the murder. She was with him all morning and he's coughed to that offence.'

So I suppose the murder investigation goes on? Is anyone else in the frame for that?' Fox asked.

'Well, the view is that it is a murder and not an accident, but as far as I'm aware there aren't any other suspects at the moment.'

Fox nodded and left the room. No doubt he and a few others would now be looking over their shoulder, thought Martin, as the investigators might well be widening the net to look at Beverley Simpson's more distinguished ex-paramours.

★★★★★★★★★★★★★★★★★★★★★★★★★★

On the morning of Valentine's day, Alan Woodman was sitting at his desk, pondering an investigation in a case that was absolutely nothing to do with that of the death of Beverley Simpson. He had resigned himself to probably having heard the last of it, not really expecting his investigative team to come across any new suspects. The trail was starting to go cold. Not for the first time in the history of that matter, however, there was to be another twist in the tail.

At 10.30 am the phone rang. It was Bill Moore, calling from his office at Alfreton police station. There were to be no opening pleasantries, no 'good morning', none of the usual banter that Bill usually began with. Just a sharp command:

'You'd better get your arse over here asap, Alan. There's someone and something you need to see.'

Alan didn't stop to ask questions, but ran down the stairs to the car park, got into his car and headed for Alfreton. On the journey he tried to think if he had dropped a 'clanger' and was in for a bollocking. He dismissed that possibility, however, as Bill Moore knew about all the developments in the Maitland case and, if he had wanted to take him to task about those events, then he would have already done so. No, this was something very different and Alan had a shrewd idea that it was to do with the Simpson murder, but something very new.

He found Bill Moore sat at his desk, but it was the other occupant of his office that caused Alan to raise his eyebrows. Sat on the other side of the desk was a man Alan had not seen for four or five years. Jim Donegani, although he had finished his police service as a uniform sergeant, had not had a distinguished career with Derbyshire Constabulary. He had had more than one brush with the authorities, had allowed his messy divorce to intrude unnecessarily upon his work, and had at one time been suspected of and investigated for an offence of receiving stolen goods. Somehow, in his 25-year career, he had avoided both disciplinary and criminal proceedings, but it was a complete mystery to Alan how he had achieved a belated promotion to sergeant. Unless, of course, like Ernie Trousdale, he too was a member of the Masonic Brotherhood. Alan didn't know if this was the case, but he wouldn't have been surprised to find that it was so.

On his retirement from the police service, Donegani had followed the path taken by a good many ex-police officers, and had taken employment as a private investigator. Eventually he had used his pension lump sum to set up on his own account as a 'private eye' in an office in Derby. He was, thought Alan, typical of the public's perception of a 'gumshoe': lank, greasy hair, badly shaven, shiny suit, and shabby mackintosh. No doubt most of his income came from snooping on errant husbands, or wives, to acquire evidence of adultery. Hardly a very lucrative existence, but it presumably went to supplement his police pension.

'Sit down, Alan,' said Bill Moore, 'and listen to what Jim's already told me.'

In quite an animated fashion, Donegani launched into his story. A couple of days ago, he said, he had received a visit at his office from David and Wendy Driver. He had known David for some years and he had known that he had a daughter living in Bakewell. What Donegani hadn't known before this visit was that the daughter was none other than the recently deceased Beverley Simpson. It seemed that, at Beverley's funeral, the Drivers had sought and been given permission to visit the house in Bakewell and retrieve one or two items from Beverley's possessions. In particular there was a brooch that had been given to Beverley by Wendy's mother. Richard, however, had been anxious that they only came to the house when he was present.

In the event, the Drivers and Richard Simpson had not been able to agree upon a mutually convenient time at which to visit the house, mainly because Richard was frequently away on his business trips. Some four days ago, David and Wendy had been on a shopping trip to Sheffield, and they decided on impulse to go through Bakewell on the return trip to their home in Derby. They called at the house that evening and found that Richard was not at home. After a short debate, they decided to 'seize the moment' and go in anyway. They were still in possession of a front door key, having, on a previous occasion, house-sat when Richard and Beverley had been away on a rare holiday together. After all, they were family and it was not as if they were trespassers. It was, however, not without a feeling of guilt that they began searching through drawers and cupboards in the marital bedroom.

They found the brooch soon enough, but, whilst they were looking for other items, they came across something else that they had not been expecting. It was Wendy who found the greeting cards, in a manila folder at the bottom of a drawer in one side of the double bed.

It was at this juncture that Donegani nodded towards a brown manila folder that sat in front of Bill Moore on his desk. The detective inspector handed the folder to Alan and gestured for him to examine the contents. Inside the folder were two obviously expensive greeting cards. The first one Alan picked up was a Christmas card. The printed wording inside was traditional and unremarkable. It was, however, the handwritten message that took Alan's attention:

To my Darling Richard. Can't wait for the time when we will be together. All my love, precious one. From your very own Steph.

The other card was a birthday card. It was no ordinary birthday card but, judging from the extravagantly amorous sentiments in the printed message, one that might be sent to one's husband, or, indeed, one's lover. The handwritten message left no room for doubt as to the sentiments of the writer:

Happy birthday darling Richard. Am missing you like mad. But only a few days now until we shall be together in Bakewell. Can't wait for the 14th. Lots and lots of love. From your very own Steph (who else!).

Alan's first reaction from reading the cards was 'so Richard Simpson has been having an affair – you can hardly blame him, given the activities of his wife!'

But then he realised that this was more than a casual 'fling', certainly on the part of 'Steph'. There was real passion here and an apparent commitment on the part of both parties to have a life together. Then it suddenly dawned on Alan that there was something much more significant concealed in the message from the woman in the birthday card. Somewhere in the material relating to the Simpson case, whether it be the sudden death report or in Richard's witness statement, he had seen the latter's date of birth. The 7th January 1942. Richard Simpson had had a birthday five days before his wife's death. The 14th was two days after this. He and 'Steph' were planning to be together, the plan having been hatched whilst Beverley was still alive, but due to come to fruition immediately after her unfortunate death!

Alan looked at Bill Moore. He said nothing but the expression on his face clearly said 'this is dynamite, boss!' No words were necessary. Bill simply nodded.

Donegani filled in the gaps. The Drivers, he said, also realised the significance of the cards and their contents. They had debated whether the cards should be left in their place of concealment, but had quickly understood that this was not an option. Should they go with the cards directly to the police? In the event they had decided that a better course was to pass them on to Jim Donegani, who they knew and who they knew would know how to handle them. The private investigator was aware that there was a case in west Derbyshire relating to the death of Beverley Simpson and that a man had been charged with her murder. He had not known at that time that the case against that man was about to be dropped, but he realised that the greeting cards constituted evidence that might well undermine the case against him. He therefore had no hesitation in contacting his old police colleague, Bill Moore, and bringing the cards to his attention.

He went on to tell the two officers that the Drivers had no idea of the identity of 'Steph' and he volunteered his own services in trying to locate her. Bill Moore shook his head:

'Thanks, but no thanks, Jim,' was his response to this suggestion. 'We'll take it from here. But I owe you one.'

Donegani nodded, and rose from his seat, picking up his shabby briefcase as he did so. He had known very well that his offer of assistance was not going to be accepted. The police did not work like that. But it was worth a shot! And even if Bill Moore did now 'owe him one', the debt was unlikely to be repaid. Bidding the officers 'Good luck' he left the office.

After Donegani had left the office, the two police officers sat in thoughtful silence for the best part of a minute. It was Bill Moore who then spoke first:

'I think this takes us in a completely different direction, Alan. I think you can tell your guys to put their current inquiries on hold, wouldn't you agree?'

Alan nodded.

'Yes,' he said. 'I think Simpson's our man, but it's not going to be easy proving it. We certainly haven't got enough to bring him in at the moment.'

'Agreed. So what's the way forward?'

'Well, first of all the Drivers need to go back and see Richard Simpson asap and admit that they've entered the house in his absence and recovered the brooch and whatever else they've picked up. Not the cards of course. Hopefully that will allay any suspicions he might have about what they were up to and stop him looking around for any other missing articles. The chances are that he might not miss the cards, as they appear to have been lying at the bottom of a drawer, but even if he does, at some point, realise they've gone he probably won't suspect the Drivers of taking them if they cough to taking the brooch. He may just think he's mislaid them. I know it's a bit of a gamble but we can hardly put the cards back. They're going to be important evidence in any trial.'

'What do we think about the woman, the mysterious Steph?'

Alan thought for a few moments before replying:

'Several possibilities,' he said eventually. 'She could be an accomplice to the murder. Richard Simpson has told her that he's married, and they've plotted to bump Beverley off. One thing is certain: if the two of them were planning to be together in Bakewell on the 14th January, then Beverley has to be off the scene by then. But then this doesn't stack up. If Steph knew

Beverley was to be murdered, there is surely no way she could contemplate being in Bakewell on the 14th, openly living with Simpson, at what would be only days after his wife's disappearance?'

He paused before going on:

'No, for my money Steph either didn't know about Beverley at all, or else she believed she wasn't in the picture. Simpson had spun her a yarn that he was single or divorced, or even that he was widowed.'

Bill Moore nodded.

'Yes, I agree. But what's happened about them shacking up on the 14th – that obviously hasn't happened. And is it possible that this woman has seen news coverage of the death of Beverley Simpson and of someone being charged with her murder, and maybe put two and two together?'

'Well, I think Simpson knew all along that the 14th wasn't going to happen. He could hardly have Steph in his home when he was in the process of burying his wife and the town was alive with gossip. She would have to be a complete eejit if she didn't smell a rat! He's had to find an excuse to put her off, or else he's blown her out altogether. As for press coverage, you have to remember that all the national and local papers were full of the Hughes case, and I can't remember seeing more than a few lines in the local rags about Beverley Simpson. Even if Steph is a local, and I doubt that she is, and even if Simpson has given her his correct name, I somehow doubt that she will have picked the news up and made the connection. If she had, we might well have heard from her by now!'

'Yeah, that sounds right to me too,' said Bill. 'So if we're going to make progress, we'll have to find this woman, and find her quickly.'

'Yes,' replied Alan, 'but we need to be very careful and discreet. If Simpson gets an inkling that we're looking for her, or that we suspect him, then she's potentially in danger. If he's killed one woman, he's probably not going to shrink from killing another. Mind you, it's not going to be easy to find her without giving the game away. I'll get my team together in the morning, boss, and we'll try and come up with a plan.'

'Okay. This has to be a priority inquiry now, so I'll get you any additional resources you need. Money or men, or anything else.'

CHAPTER TWELVE

February 24th

Exactly ten days after the meeting with Donegani and Bill Moore, Alan Woodman found himself driving down the A595 from Carlisle on the way to Cockermouth. Cockermouth, the West Cumbrian birthplace of William Wordsworth, the gateway to the northern Lake District. A good deal of water had flowed under the bridge in that short period.

The morning after the meeting Alan had contacted Wendy Driver by phone and asked her to go back to Bakewell, as soon as possible, and when Richard Simpson was at home, and admit to him that she and her husband had entered the house in his absence and recovered the brooch and one or two other items belonging to Beverley. She reported later that day that this mission had been accomplished that afternoon and that Simpson had seemed unconcerned either by the 'trespass' or the taking of the property. She was quite confident that he had not discovered that the greetings cards were missing, since he gave no hint of being worried or flustered and appeared 'serene and composed'.

That same morning Alan had summoned DCs Murdoch and Forrester to his office and updated them on the recent developments. They were in turn astonished and elated. They shared their sergeant's view, however, that there was not enough evidence to contemplate even arresting Richard Simpson at this stage and that there were going to be difficulties in moving the investigation forward.

The three detectives spent a good hour in discussing how they were going to trace 'Steph' and, moreover, do so without alerting Simpson to what was happening. The instinct of all three of them was that 'Steph' was someone Simpson had met in the course of his travels round the north of England in his employment as a sales and marketing representative for a Derby-based electronics firm. Beverley might have had all her casual affairs in the local area, but this was not her husband's way of operating. They might have had an 'open' marriage but Richard had no reputation for 'putting it about' locally. His wife lacked any sort of discretion; he was the soul of discretion. What they didn't know, however, was where in particular Simpson's travels took him and, more to the point, where he stayed when his work commitments demanded that he spent time away from home.

One way of tracking his movements of course was to go to his head office in Derby and request details of his recent business trips, and copies of his expenses claims, which would no doubt reveal the identity of the places where he regularly overnighted whilst away from home. The consensus was, however, that this was a recipe for disaster. There was every chance that the fact the police were making such enquiries at his place of work would reach his ears – either by deliberate leaking of those activities by office staff or simply by someone being indiscreet. It was too much of a risk.

A better course, it was decided, was to go to the 'horse's mouth' itself. Alan had a decent rapport with Richard Simpson. He had kept him up to date with the progress of the police inquiry into his wife's death. Another visit by Alan now would not arouse suspicion. The pretext would be to inform Richard that the case was not closed but the investigation was continuing, and to inquire after his welfare. This would present an opportunity to ask if he had settled back into a work routine. Was he getting out and about? Where did his travels take him? An experienced detective could use this meeting as a way of getting Simpson to talk freely about his work activities, and without arousing any suspicion.

Alan found Richard Simpson at home that same evening. Having told him that the police were still pursuing various lines of enquiry, but that there were no positive developments as yet, Alan discovered that Simpson was only too keen to talk about his work, which he said was a welcome distraction from his grief. He had thrown himself back into things, he said, volunteering to take on business trips to Belfast and Cardiff, on top of his usual commitments in the north of England. His next trip, the following day, was to Newcastle, and he would be travelling to Leeds and Manchester in the days following that. Asked by Alan how long he was generally away for at a time, he revealed that it would routinely be a couple of nights. Spent in 'grotty B and Bs no doubt' suggested Alan. 'No way!', he replied. His expenses were generous and he tended to frequent 'fairly up-market hotels'.

'You must have found a few decent spots over the years?' said Alan.

'Yes, I go back time and time again to the same places. They know me there and I get looked after.'

He reeled off a number of hotels in Newcastle, Carlisle, Manchester and Leeds. Alan made a mental note of as many as he could, and later that night he wrote down as many as he could recall.

It had been a productive meeting and Alan left the house, having warmly congratulated Simpson on getting his 'life back on track' and promising to keep him posted on any developments in the police investigation.

★★★★★★★★★★★★★★★★★★★★★★★★★★

Alan shared the information gleaned from Richard Simpson with his team the following morning. They discussed the strategy they would need to follow to make the best use of this information.

The plan they came up with was, in effect, a three-pronged one. It was going to involve a significant amount of expense, but then Bill Moore had given Alan approval to use such resources 'as were necessary' in order to locate 'Steph' and progress what was becoming an urgent inquiry into a still-unsolved murder.

The first 'prong' of the operation was to deploy plain-clothes police officers to conduct surveillance on Richard Simpson. From the moment he returned from Newcastle he was to be kept under observation, followed to his next destination in Leeds, and there watched throughout his stay. This operation would necessitate the use of officers from another part of the county as local officers, including DCs Forrester and Murdoch, were likely to be known to the target of the surveillance.

In the meantime, whilst Simpson was in Newcastle, DCs Forrester and Murdoch were to travel to Manchester and Liverpool respectively. There they would visit the hotels on Alan Woodman's list and make inquiries of hotel staff as to whether they knew of Richard Simpson, whether he was a regular resident, and, if so, whether they could say anything of his activities at the hotel, and, in particular, whether he was seen to have more than occasional female company. It was agreed that subterfuge would have to be abandoned: if the officers were to acquire any worthwhile information they would need to present themselves as police officers, and police officers pursuing an investigation into a very serious criminal offence. Whilst there was a risk involved in this approach, it was felt that impressing on hotel staff that it was vital the officers' inquiries remained confidential would be more than sufficient to guarantee the co-operative silence of those staff.

If those enquiries by the two DCs drew a blank, then they would go to the local office of Simpson's firm and make inquiries there. The device to be used here would be that they were old school or university friends of the subject and would like to track him down at his hotel in the evening, as and when he was next working in that area. Could the office staff give them an idea of his usual places of overnight stay? If any such information revealed hotels not on the original list, then there was further scope for inquiry. The silence of the office staff would be 'bought' by a plea to keep their inquiries quiet as they wished to surprise him.

In parallel with these inquiries, Alan would set in motion a plan of his own. He had a longstanding friend who was now a detective sergeant in the Cumbria police, based in Carlisle. This was a friend who owed Alan a favour. Alan would prevail on his friend to cause inquiries to be made at Simpson's Carlisle office, those inquiries to be along the same lines as those which DCs Murdoch and Forrester might have cause to make in Liverpool and Manchester.

★★★★★★★★★★★★★★★★★★★★★★★★★★

By the afternoon of the following Tuesday it was beginning to look as though the operation was doomed to failure. Nothing had been heard from Carlisle, and visits to a number of hotels in Liverpool and Manchester had not turned up any evidence of evening trysts by Simpson with any female company. Two plain-clothes officers had diligently followed him from Bakewell to Leeds on the Sunday and had spent long hours in the evenings in the foyer, the bar and the restaurant of the Queens Hotel in the city centre, keeping observations on Simpson while he read newspapers, drank and ate. On neither night of his stay did he venture out of the hotel and his only exchange with a female was when he spoke to one of the waitresses in the restaurant.

Although there was still the Newcastle end to explore, it was beginning to look as if more surveillance was going to be required, and, possibly, as if this might have to be extended to Simpson's activities outside work.

Not for the first time in the inquiry into Beverley Simpson's death, however, there was a sudden development which was destined to re-energise the investigation. It was late on the Tuesday afternoon when Alan Woodman, at the time in the canteen at Matlock police station, was given a message to ring Detective Sergeant Bill Minting at Carlisle.

Alan and Bill Minting had been at school together in Derby, had done their basic police training at the same time, and their careers had followed very similar lines, except that Bill had opted to join the Carlisle City force and live close to the Lake District, where he could pursue his love of walking the high fells, an interest which was shared by his wife. Alan had kept in touch with him over the years, and, when he was still married himself, he and his wife had joined Bill and his wife on the occasional summer holiday. More recently Alan had assisted his friend by carrying out some inquiries in Derbyshire into the activities there of a Carlisle-based fraudster, a man who had subsequently received a substantial prison sentence for offences committed across several counties in the midlands and north of England. This was the favour which Alan had called in when he had asked his Carlisle colleague to make some discreet inquiries at Richard Simpson's branch office in that city.

After the customary 'insults' and banter, Bill Minting now gave Alan some promising news. He told Alan that he had conducted the inquiry himself, had visited Simpson's Carlisle office, and, posing as an old school friend of Simpson, and using his 'legendary charm', had managed to ingratiate himself with the 'girls' in the office. It appeared that they had fallen over themselves to give information. Yes, they all knew where Richard Simpson stayed most of the time when he was in that area, and, what's more, they were all convinced that he was regularly meeting a woman there. It transpired that they didn't know Simpson had been married and they certainly didn't know that he was recently widowed. His chosen place of overnight accommodation was the Armathwaite Hall hotel near Bassenthwaite in the Lake District, quite expensive and a fair way out of Carlisle. He was always in a 'good mood' when he returned after a night there. Their female instincts told them 'there had to be a woman'. Furthermore he had been spotted on one occasion buying a necklace in a Carlisle jeweller's shop. There was no doubt in their minds that he was regularly meeting a 'lady friend' on his trips to Armathwaite. Bill had 'sworn them to silence' about his visit because he 'wanted to surprise' his old friend, although he promised to contact him first so as not to trespass on his amorous activities.

The news was music to Alan's ears. He thanked Bill profusely, and told him he would not trouble him further as he would travel up to the Lakes himself and pursue the inquiry at the Armathwaite Hall hotel.

'You don't get away with it that easily,' was Bill's retort. 'No hotel for you – you'll stop here, we'll have a few bevvies and catch up.'

★★★★★★★★★★★★★★★★★★★★★★★★★★

The following day Alan drove to the Lake District. On the instructions of Bill Minting, he left the M6 motorway at Penrith and took the A66 towards the west coast. Just after Keswick he turned off along back roads on the north side of Bassenthwaite Lake, and, eventually, and not without some difficulty, he found the Armathwaite Hall hotel. The hotel was in quite a secluded location, ringed by trees which gave it a somewhat gloomy, gothic appearance. Although the place was clearly in the first stages of refurbishment, the interior was quite dated, and hadn't moved on from its once-elegant pre-war state. Alan was, however, struck by the peaceful tranquillity of the surroundings and mused that it would appeal to an elderly couple seeking a quiet weekend stay, or indeed, to a pair of younger adults looking for a day or two of conjugal bliss.

Somewhat incongruously, given the surroundings, the girl behind the reception desk was wearing a smart beige uniform with a name-badge above her left breast. She was plumpish, dark-haired, rosy-cheeked, and disarmingly cheerful. Alan decided that the best approach was to abandon any attempt at subterfuge and adopt an uncompromising direct stance. Producing his warrant card, he introduced himself as 'Detective Sergeant Woodman'. Allowing the receptionist only a second or two to register this information, he glanced at her name-badge, and then went on:

'Kate, I'm investigating a very serious criminal offence, and I'm hoping you might be able to assist me.'

Slightly open-mouthed and wide-eyed, the girl seemed unable to speak, but nodded.

'Does the name Richard Simpson mean anything to you?' asked Alan.

Kate nodded again, but her composure was returning. 'Yes, he's one of our regulars ... He's been coming here for about six months.'

'Kate, can you tell me how often he stays here, and does he come alone or is he accompanied?'

The girl was now warming to the task and her habitual cheerfulness was back. 'Oh, he comes every three or four weeks and stays for a couple of nights. I think he's a rep of some sort. He always turns up on his own, but for the last few months he's been meeting up with a lady who also stops here quite a lot. When I say they "meet up", they take dinner together and drink together in the bar.'

'Kate, you're being very helpful,' Alan went on. 'Can you tell me how long they've been so friendly, and it would be very much more helpful if you can tell me anything more about the lady.'

There was no stopping Kate now. 'She's from Cockermouth. I think her husband's dead and he's left her comfortably off. She's a real lady of leisure. She's been coming here for more than a year, and it was a few weeks after Richard started coming that they began to get together.'

'Do they have separate rooms?'

'Yes ...' Here Kate looked over her shoulder, presumably to make sure that no-one was eavesdropping. ' But ...' and she dropped her voice, 'they may book separate rooms, but they don't sleep in separate rooms.'

'You know this because ...?'

'The chambermaids can always tell whether a bed's been slept in, and if one's been slept in by more than the one person, if you follow my meaning.'

Alan nodded. 'One more question Kate. The lady's name?'

'It's Mrs. Winter.' The girl consulted the guest register. 'Er ... Stephanie Winter.'

'That's marvellous, Kate. Just one final question. Can you give me her home address?'

Kate looked doubtful. 'I'm afraid I can't. We're not allowed to give guests' addresses out.'

'Well, it is an inquiry into a very serious criminal offence,' Alan pointed out. 'It's very important.'

The girl hesitated. 'I'll have to go and check with my supervisor,' she said. She turned away from Alan and towards the office behind the reception desk. As she did so she, quite subtly, pushed the open guest register a few inches towards Alan.

It was one of the oldest tricks in the book. Alan waited until the girl had disappeared into the rear office, and then wasted no time in turning the register round so he could read the contents of the page from which Kate had extracted the Christian name of Mrs. Winter. He quickly found the entry and saw that there was an address in Cockermouth and also a telephone number. He wrote the details in his pocket book, and then restored the register to its original position. A few seconds later Kate reappeared behind the desk.

'I can't find my supervisor,' she announced. 'If you wait ten minutes or so I'm sure she'll be back.'

'No, I think I have enough information – the address will keep,' he said. 'You've been very helpful, Kate.'

The girl smiled knowingly. 'Glad I could be of assistance.'

'Just one more thing. It's very important that our conversation goes no further. Confidentiality is absolutely vital.'

Kate nodded vigorously. 'Of course. Mum's the word, sergeant.'

Alan had no doubt that she would be as good as her word.

★★★★★★★★★★★★★★★★★★★★★★★★★★

As he drove towards Cockermouth the next morning, Alan wished that he had been more abstinent the night before. His head was heavy and he felt slightly nauseous. He had anticipated two or three pints with Bill Minting in the pub, but to his great surprise he had discovered that his old friend had become a wine buff. He had insisted on producing several bottles of claret to drink with the very good but very rich Coq au Vin cooked by Mrs. Minting, and then a dessert wine, and then a bottle of Armagnac to go with the post-prandial cigars. Alan was not used to drinking wine or spirits, but he wasn't about to abuse Bill's hospitality by not enthusiastically participating in the conviviality. But now he was paying the price. It also occurred to him that he was probably still well over the limit for driving with alcohol in his system, even at eleven o'clock, and he kept a weather eye open for roving police patrol cars.

Bill hadn't known the whereabouts of the street that Alan was looking for but he had known where the police station in Cockermouth could be found and had given Alan some precise directions. Shortly after midday, Alan found a parking place in the town's main street, which left him a hundred-yard walk to the police station. It was a long way from being the tourist season, but the town was reasonably busy and the many cafes and tea-shops seemed to have plenty of customers. Alan noted that there was an exceptionally large number of pubs – he counted seven or eight on the other side of the street, and all within a stone's throw of his parking spot. To warrant that many, and also for there to be so many places to drink coffee and tea, the town must be a thriving place in spring and summer.

The police station was a quaint old building, and the interior, Alan decided, was in need of some modernisation. The officer behind the counter was also quite venerable, very overweight, and clearly his operational days were well behind him. He was, however, well-informed as to the whereabouts of streets in the town and he gave very clear directions to the road near Harris Park which was Alan's destination and he even knew the exact location of the house and its description.

Less than ten minutes later Alan was parked outside the double-fronted detached house in a leafy road, probably only a five-minute walk from the town-centre. He guessed the dwelling was 1950s and probably four-bedroomed. Behind the laurel hedge, there was quite a substantial front garden, with a well-manicured lawn and well-stocked flower beds. There was also a tarmac drive leading to a garage. Parked on the drive was a newish MGB soft-top roadster.

Alan had decided that he would not telephone in advance to announce that he was coming. He was therefore taking a chance that the lady would be at home, but on balance he had felt that it was better just to turn up on the doorstep. This way, if she was an accomplice to Beverley Simpson's murder, she wouldn't have the opportunity to prepare a defence, or indeed to make herself scarce. A phone call, on the other hand, if she was guilty, would almost certainly alert her to the purpose of Alan's visit, and she could react accordingly. The presence of a car on the drive seemed to suggest that Alan was in luck.

He rang the front doorbell once. Half a minute went by and he was thinking of ringing the bell again when the door opened. The woman who stood in front of him was blond, probably about five foot nine and wearing a white polka dot dress. It was the dress which first claimed Alan's attention. It was longer than 'mini' length, but noticeably tight-fitting, emphasising all the curves on her body. The phrase that came to Alan's mind was 'full-bodied', just like the Burgundy he had been drinking the previous night. She could have passed for thirty-five, although, from one or two small tell-tale signs around the eyes, Alan guessed she was probably five or six years older than this. Unless she was wearing a very good foundation garment, however, there was no hint of middle-age spread around her waist. She was carefully, even expertly, made-up. Dressed to kill, Alan thought, although he suspected she routinely presented like this. There was, however, nothing 'sluttish' about her. Indeed she gave out an air of unflustered elegance.

To his embarrassment, Alan realised that he had been looking when he should have been speaking. From her rather coquettish smile, however, it seemed apparent that the lady knew she was being appraised, and, moreover, that she was far from offended. As it was, she opened the conversation:

'How can I help you?' she asked.

'Mrs. Winter, Mrs. Stephanie Winter?' he inquired.

She nodded.

Alan had quickly made up his mind that he was going to be direct and open with her, and treat her as a material witness and not as a potential suspect. His detective's instincts told him that she was most unlikely to be an accomplice to murder. It was a hasty judgment but he was confident of its correctness.

He produced his warrant card. 'Detective Sergeant Woodman, Derbyshire Police. I'm investigating a serious offence committed in the Peak District.'

She looked at him quizzically. 'I'm not sure what this

would have to do with me?'

A critical point was about to be reached. 'I believe you know a man called Richard Simpson, from Bakewell in Derbyshire?'

There was just a hint of a frown on her lightly tanned forehead.

'Yes, I know him.'

'Then you may be able to assist with my enquiry. I hasten to add that you are not under suspicion, but you may well be a material witness.' There, he had committed himself! He was breaking all the rules of investigative procedure, but he was backing his instinct.

By now Stephanie was beginning to look faintly shocked, but her reply was given in a firm voice: 'Well, I think we had better continue inside.'

She stood aside to allow Alan to enter the hallway, and then ushered him into the lounge. This room was as elegant as the lady herself, Alan noted. It was tastefully furnished with an expensive, modern three-piece suite, a highly polished coffee table, and a top-of-the-range colour television mounted on the wall. The Axminster carpet and the wallpaper were immaculate. There was not a hint of dust and there was a smell of furniture polish and carpet shampoo. Alan could not imagine Stephanie Winter, dressed and made-up as she was, involving herself in the kind of housework required to maintain such a high standard of tidiness and elegance. The answer to that conundrum, however, soon became apparent. A shout of 'Mrs. Forbes' from Stephanie brought the lady in question into the room. There was no doubt about her role in the house: she was dressed in a housecoat and headscarf. The quintessential English charlady, Alan thought to himself. A real-life 'Hilda Ogden'.

'Could we have some coffee please, Mrs. Forbes,' she instructed. Then to Alan: 'I'm sure you could use a coffee?'

Alan certainly could 'use' a coffee. He hadn't drunk anything since breakfast time and he was feeling more than a little dehydrated, largely due to the excesses of the night before. Mrs. Forbes re-appeared in no time at all with the coffee. Alan was slightly disappointed to see that this was not in mugs but in very dainty china cups, very much in keeping with the ambience, he thought.

Mrs. Forbes also thoughtfully put an equally elegant ashtray on the coffee table. She then left the room, closing the door behind her. Alan was then offered a cigarette by his hostess, which he took. A good tactic, he mused, as accepting coffee and cigarettes from Stephanie was sure to signal to her that this was not going to be a hostile interview.

Alan found himself perched on the settee, whilst Stephanie had sat back in the matching armchair opposite him. She had crossed her legs as she sat down, and her dress had ridden up a little, exposing more of her shapely legs and some of her thighs. She made no attempt to adjust her dress. Alan resolved that he was going to have to concentrate on keeping eye-contact with her, or appearing to consult his notebook which he had taken out of his pocket. The notebook in fact contained nothing that was going to assist with the interview.

Stephanie drew on her cigarette. If she had been disconcerted by any of Alan's earlier revelations, she appeared to have regained her composure now. The coquette had returned!

'Well, I'm all yours, sergeant,' she announced.

Alan decided to ignore the obvious innuendo. With some of the matters he was about to disclose, he needed to keep the conversation on as professional a footing as possible. He resolved to maintain the same open and direct approach that he had used before he had entered the house. He would hold nothing back. This might be a risky strategy, but it seemed to him to be the right one if he was going to get her to open up. He dived straight in:

'The serious offence I am investigating is in fact a murder. The victim is a woman called Beverley Simpson. She was the wife of the man you know as Richard Simpson. She was found dead at the foot of a cliff in the Peak District on the 12 January this year. We have good reason to believe that this was no accident and that she was pushed. Our prime suspect is the same Richard Simpson.'

If Alan was expecting a reaction from Stephanie, he certainly got it. Well before he had finished speaking, her composure had completely fallen away and she sat staring at him open-mouthed.

'But ... his wife died of cancer ... three years ago,' she stammered. 'It can't be her.'

'I'm afraid there's no doubt about it. Simpson identified her body himself.'

'Just a minute,' she went on, 'wasn't there some escaped criminal killing people in your neck of the woods at this time?'

'Yes, but all his victims were in the one house, and he couldn't possibly have been at the place where Beverley was killed at the time of her death. We're quite satisfied that there's no connection between the two sets of killings.'

Stephanie paused to absorb this information. She then slowly shook her head.

'The bastard. The duplicitous bastard.' She said this quietly but with real and unmistakable venom.

She got up from her chair and walked slowly away to the other side of the room. She then returned, sat down again and lit another cigarette. For the moment at least, the flirting was gone. There was now a stern and intense look on her face. She leaned forward and when she spoke again, there was a grim determination about her:

'Sergeant, I'll tell you everything you want to know.'

Alan was now feeling much more at ease. His 'risky strategy' looked as though it was going to pay off.

'Suppose you tell me how you and Simpson met, and then how matters developed from there.'

She needed no encouragement or prompting. She told Alan that her husband had been killed in a car accident two years ago. There were no children of the marriage and her family lived far away. She had friends locally but they were all married or with partners, and she found that, although they had rallied round immediately after her husband's death, after a while the dinner invitations dried up and she began to feel increasingly lonely. What she really yearned for, she said, was male company, and she got no fulfilment from women-only organisations such as the Women's Institute, a body which she had joined and of which she had been briefly a member. She had tried to meet suitable men by submitting her details and requirements to a computer dating company, but the results had been risible. As something of a last resort, she had started visiting pubs in the evening, but this had made her feel uncomfortable as she sensed that there was still a stigma about women going to pubs unaccompanied and that she was seen as a prostitute looking for custom. Then, five or six months ago, she had begun to spend whole weekends at the Armathwaite Hotel. She found that she liked the olde worlde charm of the place and enjoyed the unashamed luxury of its surroundings and cuisine. It was expensive but then she had been left very well-off as a result of her husband's demise.

Initially, she said, there seemed little prospect of meeting eligible men, as most of the regular weekend residents at the hotel were elderly couples. Then, however, one Sunday evening, about five weeks after her first visit, she went into the hotel bar and noticed a man sitting and reading a newspaper in a corner of the room. She saw that he was in his thirties, good-looking, and she felt attracted to him. Before she had even spoken to him, she admitted, she was hatching plans to seduce him.

Alan was becoming more and more astonished by the utter brazenness of this woman. Although she had shown the occasional sign of shock and anger, it seemed that soon reverted to coquettishness and a quite unashamed and uninhibited honesty about her true character.

'I make no bones about it,' she told Alan, 'I'm an over-sexed female predator. I meant to have this man as soon as I clapped eyes on him.'

She had approached the man, the only other occupant of the bar, and had spoken to him. She hadn't actually said 'Do you come here often', but it was something equally unsubtle and banal. The man had put down his newspaper and had smiled, rather self-consciously she thought. He hadn't spoken in turn, but she took his silence as at least half an invitation to sit down at the same table. She had offered to buy him a drink, but he stood up, rather awkwardly, and insisted on buying her one. She didn't demur and he went to the bar, returning shortly with two gin and tonics.

Conversation was now called for, and Stephanie said that she made most of the running, introducing herself, revealing where she was from and how often she visited the Armathwaite hotel. At first reticent, he slowly warmed to the task, and told her he was Richard Simpson from Bakewell in Derbyshire, a sales representative with an electronics firm based in Derby, and that it was his first visit to that hotel. She drew from him the information that he came up to Carlisle at least once every three weeks. The firm had a branch office there and quite a lot of customers in that area who needed regular visits from him. He had previously stopped in hotels in Carlisle but found them rather soulless and he had hankered after somewhere with more character to stay on his trips north. One of the women in the Carlisle office had told him about the Armathwaite.

She had readily disclosed that she was a widow and a lady of leisure, and she then enquired after his marital status and domestic situation. He hesitated only briefly, before telling her that his wife had died of cancer nearly three years previously, that he had not remarried, and that he lived with his mother. His mother, he said, had early-onset dementia, and his sister, who lived in Derby, would look after her on his frequent absences.

Alan interjected at this point and pointed out that the only person Simpson had shared his home with, until recently anyway, was his wife, and that his mother lived elsewhere in the county with her husband and was, to his knowledge, in good health. Stephanie nodded knowingly: 'Thinking about it now,' she said, 'he had made up his mind at this stage that he wanted and saw the potential of a relationship with me, and he was putting himself forward as a single man. The bit about the mother was designed, I believe, to discourage me from ever coming to his home, as, of course, had I done so, I would have learnt the awful truth.'

She went on to say that, by now, they were talking quite freely to each other, and it was a natural development to agree to have dinner together in the restaurant. Dinner, she said, was a leisurely affair and they lingered over post-prandial brandies, becoming more and more comfortable, she felt, in each other's company. Eventually Simpson made to get up, insisting that he had an early start in the morning. She didn't want to rush things on their first meeting, professed tiredness herself, and accompanied him to the first floor, where they both had rooms. She was, however, already plotting the next stage in the development of their relationship. As they parted at his bedroom door, she enquired as to when he would be in the area next, adding that it 'would be nice to meet up again'. He didn't need any encouragement. He had a customer to see in Kendal the following Monday and planned to stop at the Armathwaite on the Sunday night. By a happy coincidence, she told him, she was going to be here too that weekend. Perhaps they could have dinner together again? He nodded enthusiastically.

They didn't see each other in the morning, as he had to leave very early to return to Carlisle, and she was not one for early breakfasts. She knew, however, that she could 'move things on' the following Sunday.

By now Alan was becoming quite accustomed to her directness. It had been unsettling at first, but now he was seeing it as a mark of her honesty, and he was quite confident that his initial judgement about her character and his assessment that she was not an accomplice in the murder of Beverley Simpson was correct.

Lighting another cigarette, Stephanie continued with her story. On the following Sunday evening, she and Simpson met in the hotel bar and then had dinner in the restaurant. Both had consumed a fair amount of alcohol, more, in fact, than they had at the previous meeting, and they were still in the bar when the barman made it known that he was anxious to close and go to bed. At this juncture, Stephanie pointed out that she had a 'decent bottle of malt' in her room, and asked 'shall we have a nightcap?' She didn't, in fact, have any alcohol in her room, but as far as she was concerned the 'nightcap' was just a euphemism for something more intimate and she was quite certain that Simpson was on the same wavelength. In any event, he readily agreed to come to her room. Just to reinforce the signal she hoped she was giving out, she told him to 'give me ten minutes' before he knocked on her door.

During the evening Stephanie had eventually managed to steer their conversation round to more personal and intimate topics. She had drawn from Simpson that his marriage had not been a happy one, that his wife had had numerous affairs which she had made little attempt to conceal, and that he too had had 'liaisons' with other women, although on nothing like the same scale. She had volunteered the information that she had enjoyed very few affairs with men since her husband's death, and that she longed for a return to a firm and stable relationship. Having manoeuvred the conversation on to that level, she had asked Simpson if he too was looking for a proper relationship, or was he content with his life as it was. Without hesitation, he stated that he also yearned for the same thing. By the time they had temporarily parted at her bedroom door, Stephanie was certain that they had reached a situation of cosy intimacy, and that it was but a short step to raise their relationship on to a physical level.

Alone in her room, she had removed all her clothing except for her bra and knickers, put on a short light dressing gown, and awaited his knock. This came at almost exactly ten minutes after they had parted.

Her account of what followed was explicit and uninhibited even by her standards. Alan had been involved in cases of rape and sexual assault and invariably struggled to elicit intimate details from embarrassed victims, and particularly from children. He was astonished, however, at the way that this woman could describe so fully, and without a hint of embarrassment, the details of her sexual encounter with Richard Simpson. She was talking to a man that she had met only an hour before, and there was indeed no need to allude to this matter at all, let alone in a blow-by-blow account. She seemed, however, to positively revel in it. Alan could have cut her short and insisted that he didn't need to hear anything about what had happened in the bedroom, but he suspected she would have been disappointed, and he didn't want to stem the flow of the valuable evidence she was providing.

Having let Simpson into the bedroom, she gave him no chance to speak, but immediately pulled him close and kissed him full on the lips. He tensed at first, but then relaxed and responded to her embrace. She started to unbutton his shirt, at the same time allowing her dressing gown to fall open.

'I could tell he was aroused, but I was having to make all the running,' she said. 'I had to loosen his belt and unfasten his trousers and remove his shirt. He seemed reluctant to make any further move, so I had to slip out of my robe and pull him towards the bed. He had removed his shoes but he would have kept his socks on if I hadn't taken them off myself. I straddled him on the bed, and as he showed no sign of doing do, I reached behind me and unfastened my bra. I guided his hands to the underside of my breasts, a very erogenous zone for me. He eventually got the message and started to caress me there. I slid down the bed and pulled down his underpants and began to fellate him.

It was clearly something he hadn't experienced before as he again tensed and tried to pull away before he actually started to enjoy it.

'I then lay back on the bed. He muttered something about "was it safe?"' I told him it wasn't a problem. I'd had an IUD fitted some months previously. He could have been a virgin, as he had no idea about a woman's body. I had to guide his hand between my legs and towards my clitoris, and then to my G-spot.

Eventually I helped him enter my vagina. I tried to encourage him to hold back but he came in a rush. Perhaps he was just out of practice, or perhaps he and his wife just didn't have any sort of real physical intimacy.'

Alan interjected at this point to tell her about Beverley's reputation as a woman who 'played the field'.

Stephanie nodded knowingly. 'So she took her pleasure elsewhere,' she said. 'I suppose that's not surprising if he wasn't doing it for her. Or perhaps they were just incompatible?'

'Anyway,' she continued, 'afterwards he dropped off to sleep almost immediately. From my point of view it hadn't been a great experience, but I was determined to persevere. I woke him up about six in the morning, and it was a bit better the second time. He was starting to get the hang of it.'

Alan had been growing increasingly uncomfortable with her frankness and he decided he had to move things on. He couldn't face another blow-by-blow account like the last one. He wondered, in fact, if she was being deliberately forthright and explicit as a means of exacting revenge, intentionally humiliating a man who had lied to her by making him look small in front of a stranger.

'How did your relationship with Simpson develop after that night?' he asked her.

She seemed to take the hint and moved on.

'Well, it got better and better, and I don't mean just the sex. I really believed we had genuine feelings for each other and that we were soul-mates. We really enjoyed each other's company. That's certainly how I felt and I'm sure he felt the same. He used to ring ne every night, from wherever he was staying. We saw each other every weekend, usually at Armathwaite or at my home. I suppose if his wife was putting it about everywhere she wasn't going to worry about him being away. He took me to Paris for a long weekend, and also to London to see a couple of shows. He showered me with presents and flowers. He also bought me that car that's on the drive. We couldn't get enough of each other.'

Alan asked her if they had ever discussed putting their relationship on a more permanent footing. Had they talked about living together, or even marriage?

'We talked about little else from about the beginning of December,' she said. 'Christmas was coming and I knew that we would have to be apart for a week or so as he would have to spend time with his family. This kind of focused our minds on needing to find a solution to the practical problems facing us.' She paused and lit another cigarette.

'The main difficulty was his mother. Or so I was led to believe at the time. When he was working away, or when he was with me, his sister looked after her, either in Bakewell or at her home in Derby. But she was getting pissed off with the arrangement and was putting more and more pressure on him to find a place for their mother in residential care. I suppose I was doing likewise, pushing him in the same direction. Then, a week before Christmas he told me that he had succeeded – he and his sister had secured a place for his mother in a residential home near Derby and it was available for her from mid-January. I was over the moon.'

On cue, Alan produced from his briefcase the two greeting cards that had been retrieved by Beverley's parents from her bedroom. He handed them to her.

'I take it you sent these to Simpson?'

She examined them. She shook her head sadly. Then she nodded and handed them back.

'Yes, it was going to be the 14th of January. That was the day I was going to move in to his house in Bakewell. Of course, I know now that it was never going to happen. He was going to have to get rid of his wife and then he'd have to organise her funeral. He could hardly have me there with that going on.'

Alan then went on to ask her about the 14th January. Presumably he had found a reason to put her off?

'Yes. On the Monday before the 14th he rang me. This was in the morning, which was unusual. He told me that the care home had just contacted him and informed him that they would have to postpone his mother's admission as the refurbishments the home was undergoing had been delayed and were now well behind schedule. He also told me that his sister had gone ski-ing and wouldn't be available to look after his mother the following weekend, or indeed the one after that. He was obviously clearing the decks so that he could dispose of his wife and have her funeral without me being there to queer his pitch. He continued to ring me every night but, thinking back, he sounded rather distracted.'

'When did you see him next?' inquired Alan.

'It would be the last weekend in January. He came to Cockermouth. He was quite subdued at first but later he became quite animated. He expected his mother to move into the home in the next month. He had put his house on the market as he wanted to get away from Bakewell, as the house there held so many bad memories. I could empathise with that because I had always made it clear to him that, for the same reason, I wanted to move away from Cockermouth at some point.'

Alan made a mental note to check whether the house in Bakewell was in fact on the market.

'Where was he thinking of moving to?' he asked.

'Nottingham or Leicester, I think. Close enough to his office in Derby and to the home where his mother would be. Of course, knowing what we know now, he would have to be well away from Bakewell to minimize the chances of my running into someone who knew about his wife, not to mention his mother.'

There was a pause, and she lit yet another cigarette.

'So, is he going to get arrested?' she asked.

Alan nodded. 'No doubt about it, and soon. Can I take it that you're prepared to give evidence in court if necessary about what you've told me today?'

She nodded vigorously. 'Too bloody right I am. He needs locking up and the key throwing away. I suppose in one sense I should be flattered that he was prepared to kill his wife so he could be with me, but I shudder when I think I could have been living with a murderer.'

Alan decided a note of caution was appropriate. 'Well, assuming we do charge him, there's no guarantee that he will be convicted. You can never be sure how juries will react.'

'But it's obvious!' she exclaimed. 'What other explanation can there be for his wife's death? He's as guilty as sin.'

Alan smiled and inclined his head slightly. She was right but he sensed that it was going to be a difficult case to prove, all the same.

'If he's charged,' he went on, 'it's just possible that at some stage, if not immediately, he might get bail. He's going to know that you will be a material witness. Now, if he is released the court will attach stringent conditions to his bail, such as not making any attempt to contact you, but, if he's desperate, there's no saying that he won't come and look for you. Is there some place you can go to, should it be necessary, where he's unlikely to be able to find you?'

She looked alarmed. 'Surely he's not going to get bail if he's charged with murder!' she cried.

'Stranger things have happened.'

She thought for a moment, and then said 'I have a friend in Taunton. He doesn't know about her and she would put me up for as long as I want.'

'Fine,' replied Alan. 'I'll keep you posted about every development as soon as it happens. That way, you'll have time to make the necessary arrangements.'

She seemed reassured and the coquettish smile reappeared. 'Now, won't you stay for a late lunch? And it's a long way back to Derbyshire. There's a bed here for you and you could set off back in the morning.'

Alan knew only too well where this was going. He was momentarily tempted. But then common sense took over. Getting involved with a witness, particularly one as important as this, was a very bad idea. He knew of one police officer who had lost his career as a result of allowing himself to be sucked into a relationship with a witness.

'Thanks, but no thanks. I need to get back. We need to move quickly. But someone will be in touch to take a statement from you shortly.'

Will it be you?' she asked hopefully.

'Maybe, but more likely it will be another officer.'

Alan made another mental note to ensure that he was unavailable for the trip to take the statement. He then thanked Stephanie for her 'enormous help', made his excuses, and left.

★★★★★★★★★★★★★★★★★★★★★★★★★★

Alan had plenty to think about on the long drive home. Most of his thoughts surrounded the interview he had just conducted with Stephanie Winter. He was quite intrigued by the woman. She was a paradox. An enigma. She could move from flirtation to alarm to indignation and back again. She appeared to be a strong and robust personality, but Alan suspected that she was also a vulnerable and needy person. He could see why Richard Simpson had been attracted to her. But at the same time he strongly believed that she needed him as much as he needed her.

In any event, the case that appeared to have sunk without trace was back afloat ...

CHAPTER THIRTEEN

February 25th

Before he left Cockermouth Alan had gleaned from Stephanie Winter that she was due to receive a visit from Richard Simpson that very weekend, and he promised her that he would do his best to ensure that this did not take place. This meant that he would have to arrange for him to be arrested early the next day, Friday the 25th of February. He had managed to ascertain that Simpson would be at home that morning, after returning from a business trip to Manchester on the Thursday.

It was well into the evening when Alan got back to Matlock, and he was very weary after a long drive and a challenging time earlier that day. He knew, however, that there was no time to lose if the arrest was to be put in place early the next morning and if his subordinates were to be briefed and a strategy devised for the interviewing of the suspect in the hours following his arrest. With this in mind, he wasted no time, on arriving back at Matlock police station, in contacting Detective Constables Forrester and Murdoch, and convening a hastily arranged conference for later that evening. Both officers were off-duty and at home when he rang them, but neither raised the slightest objection to giving up a night by the fireside and turning out on a bitterly cold night to meet up with their sergeant. Alan also had no hesitation in contacting Detective Inspector Bill Moore at home to bring him up to date on the events of the day and the proposed course of action for the Friday. DI Moore was equally untroubled about having his evening disturbed, and, indeed, received Alan's news with undisguised glee. He too put on his coat and climbed into his car to join the meeting at Matlock police station.

It was past midnight before the meeting of the four officers broke up. But by then they had mapped out a plan for the morning, involving not only the arrest but a search for further evidence from Simpson's home and his place of work in Derby. The strategy for the interviews of the suspect was also discussed and agreed.

★★★★★★★★★★★★★★★★★★★★★★★★★★★

It was just before 8.00 am when Richard Simpson opened his front door, to find DCs Forrester and Murdoch on the step. He was surprised at the earliness of their visit but assumed that they were there to update him on the latest progress of the investigation. He quickly realised, however, from their facial expressions that they were not bringing him the sort of news he wished to hear.

'Richard, you're being arrested on suspicion of the murder of your wife, Beverley Simpson,' he was informed by DC Forrester.

He probably never heard the words of the caution that followed this statement, because he was too busy exclaiming and shouting obscenities.

'You have to be fucking joking! You bastards! Why the fuck would I want to murder my wife?'

The officers were quite taken aback by the vehemence of Simpson's reaction. They were very much accustomed to speaking to a man of a quiet and mild-mannered demeanour. They had expected a show of surprise, and even some objection, but this was right out of character. They braced themselves for a possible show of physical violence, but it seemed that Simpson's aggression evaporated as quickly as it had appeared and he submitted tamely to being handcuffed and led to the waiting police vehicle.

Accompanying the detectives was a team of uniformed police officers, who entered the house as their plain clothes colleagues departed and began to carry out a thorough search of the premises. They had been briefed earlier by Alan Woodman as to the sort of material they should be looking for.

At about the same time, two other uniformed officers set off from Matlock to travel to Derby. They had been tasked with visiting Simpson's office there and recovering his claims for expenses over the previous few months. It was hoped that these would show not only his movements across the north of England during this period but also provide some sort of timeline of his specific movements on the morning of the 12th January.

At much the same time Alan Woodman was speaking to Martin Tory on the phone. He had managed to catch Martin at home before he left for work and was relieved to find that the lawyer had no court commitments that day and was able to meet Alan a little later at the CPS offices at South Darley. There was no obligation on the police to consult with the CPS at this stage in the investigation, or indeed at any stage before any charges had been preferred, but Alan always felt that, in a serious case of this nature, it was good practice to keep the prosecutors in the picture at all times, as far as possible.

Forty minutes later, Alan was outlining to Martin all the developments in the case that had occurred over the last ten days or so. He told Martin about the discovery of the greeting cards and about their content, about the search for Stephanie Winter, and about her disclosures in relation to Richard Simpson. He went on to tell Martin that Simpson was to be arrested and interviewed that day. He also made the point that, even if there were no admissions of guilt in the interviews, all the officers involved in the investigation felt that there was enough evidence to charge Richard Simpson with the murder of his wife.

Martin had listened carefully and paused before responding. He then stood up and went across to the window, looking down on the rain-swept car park. Alan waited patiently, for a moment, at least, sensing that the CPS lawyer might be 'against him'. He needn't have worried. Martin turned back, and sat down, smiling broadly.

He began with a rhetorical question. 'It's got to be him, hasn't it? It all stacks up. He's painted himself into a corner. He's got to the point where his two worlds are on a collision course. Something has got to give, and it has to be Beverley. She has to go!'

He paused again, before going on: 'Mind you, it's circumstantial evidence with a big "C". Nothing wrong with that, if it's compelling circumstantial evidence, and I think this is. Obviously, however, if you can find anything else to support the case, then so much the better. I get the feeling that you don't think he's going to "cough" in interview?'

Alan nodded. 'That's my gut feeling', he said. 'But I've got a search team in his house, and you never know what he might have left behind. He certainly wasn't expecting to get arrested and he might have been careless.'

Alan left the building shortly after, promising to keep Martin up to date with the outcome of the search and the interviews. Martin's parting shot was, 'You'd better get them to play it by the book this time, Alan – make sure he has a solicitor, and keep PC Trousdale well out of the way!'

★★★★★★★★★★★★★★★★★★★★★★★★★★

They were taking no chances at Matlock police station. As soon as he was booked in, Richard Simpson was asked if needed the services of a solicitor, and if so, which one. It was pointed out to him that it would be very much in his interests to have legal advice and legal representation in the interviews. Simpson needed no encouragement. He was no Rex Maitland and clearly realised that he needed to see a solicitor as soon as possible and have one present in interviews. He only knew one firm of solicitors locally, and that was the company that had employed his late wife. DC Forrester telephoned Hassop's offices and was put through to Kevin Malcolm. The officer started to outline to Kevin the reason for his call, but Kevin cut him off very quickly:

'Sadly I can't act for Richard Simpson,' he told the officer. 'There's a complete conflict of interest here. It's not possible for this firm to represent someone accused of murdering one of their employees.'

Kevin did, however, suggest that a suitable alternative might be Paul Hargreaves in Chesterfield. As well as being an experienced criminal solicitor, there was also the advantage that Hargreaves was familiar with much of the evidence by virtue of his earlier representation of Rex Maitland.

DC Forrester relayed this information back to Simpson, who was quite happy to have the services of Paul Hargreaves. A phone call was quickly made to the latter's firm in Chesterfield. The solicitor was just preparing to leave for the local magistrates' court where he had a number of clients appearing that morning. He had no hesitation, however, in agreeing to come immediately to Matlock police station. His clients' files were handed over to one of his partners. The clients would be disappointed not to be represented by Hargreaves that morning, but that was too bad – it was not every day that one picked up a murder case!

★★★★★★★★★★★★★★★★★★★★★★★★★★

Paul Hargreaves arrived at Matlock police station at 9.45 am, to be met by Alan Woodman. Alan had thought very carefully about how much he should disclose of the evidence that had been gathered. He was under no obligation to tell Simpson or his solicitor anything, and the nature of the case could be sprung on them in the course of the interviews that would follow. Alan, however, was not in favour of this approach. In the first place he had always believed that it was intrinsically unfair to keep a prisoner and his solicitor in the dark and then 'ambush' them in the interviews with the evidence. Secondly, it was likely to be counter-productive, as any solicitor worth his salt would almost certainly, in these circumstances, advise his client to exercise his right of silence and decline to answer any questions. Far better, in his view, to throw the defence a 'few morsels' and disclose at least part of the evidence before the interviews commenced. In his experience, defendants were more likely to be forthcoming in interview when they had some idea of the nature of the case against them, even if they then clammed up later on when other evidence emerged. There was a balance to be struck – you gave away so much, but kept some 'up your sleeve'.

With this in mind, Alan informed Paul Hargreaves that the police knew about Simpson's girlfriend, Stephanie Winter, and that they had located her and that she would be a material witness against him. He did not, however, tell the solicitor about the discovery of the greetings cards. Hargreaves shook his head and laughed:

'So he's got a girlfriend!' he exclaimed. 'It's hardly surprising, given that the deceased was running around with every man in Bakewell. Hardly makes him a killer. If that's all you've got we're going to have another short-lived case.'

Alan decided to exercise his own right of silence at this point, and did not respond to Hargreaves' jibe. He knew, however, that the lawyer was too astute an operator not to realise that there was more to the police case than he was being told about. He gave Alan a knowing look and then allowed himself to be led away to confer with his client.

The first interview with Simpson began about twenty minutes later. Rain lashed against the single window of the room set aside for this purpose. In stark contrast to the circumstances in which Rex Maitland had been questioned a few weeks earlier, however, the room was warm and well-lit, and the prisoner had recently been provided with refreshments. He also, of course, was accompanied by a solicitor with a good deal of experience in criminal law.

The interviewing officers were once again Detective Constables Forrester and Murdoch. They took pains to enquire after Simpson's comfort and welfare and to ensure that he understood the caution that he was read before questioning started.

Paul Hargreaves interjected at this point:

'My client has nothing to hide and he will be answering your questions. However, if I think there is a need at any stage I will ask for the interview to be stopped and I will want to have the opportunity to confer with the defendant and give him appropriate advice.'

The officers both nodded. They had expected this. Hargreaves was clearly anticipating a few surprises down the line and he didn't want his client blundering into 'uncharted territory' before he had had the chance to confer with him and advise him whether he should be continuing to answer questions.

The interview began in uncontroversial areas. This was the officers' strategy for the first interview: to ask non-hostile, open questions about uncontentious matters, questions which were designed to put the accused at ease, and which he would have no difficulty in answering. Thus Simpson was asked about his employment, his marriage and his domestic situation. He told the officers that he was a sales and marketing executive for an electronics firm based in Derby, but which had branches elsewhere in the north of England and the Midlands, and customers throughout the country and in Northern Ireland and southern Scotland. His particular job entailed him travelling extensively across the northern area of the country, visiting the branch offices, and both existing and potential customers. Recently his travels had also extended to Northern Ireland and South Wales. He was away from home a lot and spent much time 'living out of a suitcase'.

Asked about his marriage, he said that he had been married for six years and there were no children from the relationship. Because of the nature of his job and also because of his wife's leisure interests, they had not often been at home at the same time. He described their relationship as 'ships that passed in the night'. He went on to volunteer the information that he and Beverley had not married out of 'love', but rather from peer pressure, as their mutual friends had all been getting married at that time and it seemed to be 'the thing to do'. They had been 'good friends' and 'still were', but it became apparent very soon after the wedding that it was not 'a marriage made in heaven' and that, essentially, it had been a mistake. There was 'no spark' and it quickly became obvious that she did not want any physical relationship with him. She had no interest, he said, in 'being with one man'. She got her 'kicks' from 'playing the field' and she made no secret of the fact that she was having one fling after another.

Anticipating the next question, Simpson told the officers that he hadn't sought a divorce or separated from his wife because it suited them to stay together. Early on they agreed that their marriage should be an 'open' one, which left each of them free to pursue their own love interests. He had had 'girlfriends' over the last five years, but not many and he was certainly not in the same league as his promiscuous and free-spirited wife. The other reason they stayed together was that they had, perhaps perversely, always enjoyed each other's company, and on the few occasions when they were both at home simultaneously, they would go out for a drink or to a restaurant and take pleasure in it.

Asked about Beverley's 'leisure interests' (other than men, that is), Simpson stated that his wife had been an enthusiastic rock-climber. She had seemed to need 'an edge' to her life, 'a buzz', whether it came from pursuing one man after another or from pushing herself to do more and more difficult climbs. He himself had never had any interest in the sport, although on odd occasions, when she not had a climbing partner, he had accompanied her to 'belay' her. By this he meant to stand at the bottom of the crag and hold the rope, with a view to holding her in the event of a fall. More recently, however, if there had been no-one to climb with, she had taken to 'soloing', climbing without a partner. Of course, he pointed out, the problem with this was that she would have no 'margin of error', and if she fell, it would probably result in serious injury or even death. But this was very much in character – 'living on the edge'.

Simpson didn't know the identity of many of her climbing partners. He was aware that Rex Maitland had been a recent partner, but he believed that she had climbed with men, and women, from local mountaineering clubs – in Sheffield, Buxton and Chesterfield. She had often gone away for weekends to climb in North Wales or the Lake District, although most of her time had been spent on the Derbyshire crags. She would climb regularly in the Peak District, mainly on the gritstone edges, but also at places like Matlock and Cromford. He didn't know who her partner was on the day that she lost her life, or if she had one, and was not aware that she was going to Curbar Edge. She didn't brag about her sexual 'conquests', but he believed that some of her climbing friends had been 'more than just climbing partners'.

So far Simpson had answered questions freely and he continued to do so in a second interview, when he was asked if he could expand on his own 'extra-marital' affairs. His 'liaisons', he said, had been, until very recently, casual and short-term. They had tended to be with women he already knew, staff in the branch offices, or once a receptionist in a hotel where he had regularly stayed. He had no social activities outside work, other than with Beverley, so he hadn't had that many opportunities for meeting the opposite sex. Then he had met Stephanie Winter. This was about five or six months ago. They had been fellow guests at the Armathwaite Hotel at Bassenthwaite in the Lake District and she had initiated a conversation in the hotel bar. At first he had been almost overawed by her. She was smart, very attractive and sophisticated, and he felt that he was 'not in her league'. But she soon managed to put him at ease. She was a good listener and she showed interest in his work and where he was from. He became quite captivated with her and after they parted company that night he had gone so far as to invent a fictitious trip to Cumbria the following weekend so that he could see her again. He found that he was thinking of her constantly during the week that they were apart.

On their second meeting, again at the Armathwaite, they had dined together and later they had slept together, after she had invited him back to her room for a 'nightcap'. Their relationship had then 'taken off'. They had spent almost every weekend together, usually at her home in Cockermouth, but there had also been a trip to Paris and one to London.

He was asked if she had visited him in Bakewell.

'No,' he replied. 'You see I had told her that my wife had died of cancer three years previously. She had already told me that her husband had been killed in a road accident, and I thought she might be put off if she knew that I was a married man. So I lied. Once I had done that I realised that I had to construct a further lie in order to rule out any possibility of her coming to my home. By this stage I was quite desperate to build a relationship with her. So I told her my widowed mother was living with me, and that she had severe dementia. So, no, she has never been to my house.'

'So you were in fact telling her that you were your mother's carer?'

'Yes, and that when I wasn't at home my sister had to come up from Derby to look after her.'

The detectives, as part of their interview strategy, decided not to ask further questions about Simpson's relationship with Stephanie at this stage, and moved on to ask the defendant about his movements on the day of Beverley's death. In answer to their inquiry he gave a detailed account of his travels from leaving home that morning. It was about 8.00 am when he came out of his house, he said. His wife was preparing for a climbing trip, but they had had no conversation about where she was going or how she was getting there. They were a one-car family and he assumed that she was going to be picked up by her prospective climbing partner. He then drove to Newcastle, joining the M1 motorway near Chesterfield and then taking the M18 and the A1 to the north-east, arriving at his destination at about 12.30 pm. He had stopped only once on the journey. This was around 10.00 at a service station near Wetherby. He was there for about twenty minutes for coffee and a smoke.

He went on to say that on arrival he had visited the firm's office in the city, and in the afternoon he had met with a customer. He had spent that night and the following one at a hotel in Chester-le-Street. He had seen further customers on the Thursday, and again on the Friday morning, before setting off back to Derbyshire on the Friday afternoon. It was 8.00 pm or thereabouts that evening when he got home. Although he had not spoken to his wife while he was away, he expected her to be at home when he got back. It was apparent, however, as he had told the sergeant at Bakewell police station later that night, that she had not been in the house since the Wednesday, as there were two days' newspapers on the mat and two days' milk on the doorstep. It was also plain that the bed had not been slept in. The next time he saw Beverley was on a mortuary slab.

Simpson had been quite matter-of-fact in his replies to the officers and up to this point had been very composed. Now, however, he put his head in his hands and appeared to be sobbing uncontrollably. Whilst neither of the interviewers were impressed by this last performance, they thought it appropriate to call a halt to the interview.

★★★★★★★★★★★★★★★★★★★★★★★★★★★

Whilst the second interview with the prisoner was in progress, the investigation had received three significant pieces of evidence from different sources. The first two had been discovered by the police team that had that morning been searching Simpson's home. In a bureau in the living room, while rifling through a pile of papers, an alert officer had come across a life insurance policy and had noticed that, not only was the insured person one Beverley Simpson, but that the policy had been issued as recently as the 15th December 1976. A quick perusal of the policy revealed that the sole beneficiary in the event of the insured's death was Richard Simpson, and that the amount of benefit was £50,000. In a drawer in a unit in the kitchen, another officer had found a sheaf of bank statements relating to the Simpsons' accounts at the Midland Bank. Further examination of these later was to prove instructive.

Not long after this discovery, another officer had arrived at the police station bearing documents he had recovered from the defendant's head office in Derby. These were forms detailing his claims for expenses over several months, together with receipts from hotels, petrol stations and restaurants to support those claims. Taking possession of these documents, Alan Woodman had turned quickly to those relating to the 12th January 1977. His interest was particularly aroused by a till receipt issued at the Wetherby Service Area on the A1. The receipt recorded the sale of coffee and a doughnut. It also bore the time of its issue: 12.10 pm.

★★★★★★★★★★★★★★★★★★★★★★★★★★★

The third interview with Richard Simpson began at just after 2pm. At this point the questions were still open and unchallenging and the defendant was still ready to give full replies. He was asked about how he had dealt with meeting, or not meeting, as the case may be, with Stephanie at Christmas and in the aftermath of his wife's death. He told the officers that Stephanie knew they would have to spend Christmas apart because he would be 'obliged to be with his mother and his sister and her family'. He volunteered the information that just before Christmas he was coming under increasing pressure to put his relationship with his girlfriend on a more 'permanent' footing. By this he meant living together.

This pressure was coming from her on the one hand, but he was also desperate to set up home with her. He had thought about divorcing Beverley, but this would have been 'financially ruinous' for him and he would also, he felt, have risked exposing the lies and deceit that he had constructed in order to sustain his affair with Stephanie. He was in 'too deep'. Instead he 'dug himself in even further'. Just before Christmas he had told her that he and his sister had found a place in a residential care home for his mother and she could take this up in mid-January. He had also told her that he didn't want to live in Bakewell thereafter, as it 'held too many bad memories'. He knew that Steph felt the same about Cockermouth, so he said he would put the house on the market and look to move to another location, close enough to his place of work in Derby and also to the home where his mother would be living.

Stephanie, he said, had been delighted with this news. He knew, however, that he was just buying time and he had no idea how he was going to resolve the problem that he faced. He had spent Christmas and

New Year at home and had then seen Steph on the first weekend in 1977 at Armathwaite. She was full of plans about where they would live and whether she should sell her own house or let it. His plans, however, were about how he was going to stall her. On the Monday following that weekend, with the deadline for his mother's 'departure' looming, he told Stephanie that there had been a 'delay', as the residential home was still undergoing refurbishment and it would be probably another month before his mother could 'move in'. Steph was disappointed but, as far as he knew, she believed his tale.

Beverley's death, he went on, came as a tragic coincidence. Having to deal with that and then the funeral arrangements meant he couldn't see Steph for a couple of weeks. He rang her every night, and added the further lie that his sister had gone ski-ing and so was not available to look after his mother. He felt sure that he must have sounded unconvincing on the phone, but Stephanie never at any time challenged his story. He saw her again at the end of the month and told her that his mother's 'departure' was now only a couple of weeks away, and that he had put the house on the market. The last part of that statement was actually true, as he had instructed an estate agent to sell the Bakewell house. Sadly and perversely, he said, Beverley's death had made things easier for him and given him some freedom to manoeuvre. He was now able to fulfil the promise he had made to his girlfriend that he would find a home for them to share, although he had to make sure it was far enough away from Bakewell to prevent his lies and deceit from catching up with him.

At this point the officers said that they would stop the interview so that Simpson and his solicitor could be shown some documents that they had recovered.

★★★★★★★★★★★★★★★★★★★★★★★★★★★

Paul Hargreaves had been presented with the greeting cards, and copies of the other documents that the police had discovered that morning – the insurance policy, the receipt from Wetherby Services and the bank statements felt to be relevant. He had then disappeared to consult with his client.

The fourth interview commenced twenty minutes later. Paul Hargreaves was now looking more thoughtful than he had previously, but he indicated that Simpson intended to continue answering the officers' questions as he 'had explanations' for any issues that might arise from the content of the disclosed documents. In accordance with their planned strategy the detectives' approach now became more probing. The questions were now 'closed' and challenging.

Simpson was asked to look at the two greeting cards. At this point his solicitor demanded to know how the police had come by them. Were they found by the police team that morning, or, as he suspected, had they been retrieved in an 'unlawful' search on an earlier occasion by either police officers or other persons being in the house without the defendant's permission? He was told that they were found by Beverley's parents, who had always had her consent to enter the premises, and who were looking to retrieve some personal items belonging to their daughter. Hargreaves nodded and said that he would not take the matter further at this time but that there may well be 'a challenge to the admissibility of that evidence at any trial'.

Undaunted the officers pressed on. Did Simpson accept that the cards had been received by him and were addressed to him? Did he agree that one was a Christmas card and the other a birthday card? The defendant did agree, and also that his birthday was on the 7th January.

DC Forrester then put this to him:

'It's quite clear from those cards that Steph was intending to come to Bakewell on the 14th January, and that the two of you were going to be living together in your home from that date.'

'It might look like that,' retorted Simpson, 'but it obviously couldn't be, as I was already living with someone else. She's got hold of the wrong end of the stick. All I told her was that my mother would be moving out then. I never told her she could come to Bakewell. Why would I? It would be madness.'

'But Steph's clearly of that opinion,' said DC Murdoch. 'The point is of course that she could come to Bakewell on that date, because you had already decided to dispose of your wife before the 14th January, and your mother was never there anyway.'

Simpson shook his head.

'Why would I do that?' was his response to the accusation. 'I had nothing to gain from it and a lot to lose. Anyway, the arrangement as it stood was perfectly satisfactory. I had the best of both worlds – an easy-going domestic situation and an exciting relationship away from home. I was having my cake and eating it.'

'Can I remind you of what you said to us in an earlier interview,' DC Forrester pointed out. 'You were "thinking of her constantly" and you were "desperate" for a relationship. This was not just a casual fling. You wanted to live with this woman. And it's quite clear from the cards that Stephanie certainly wanted this. You had built a network of lies and fiction so that you could perpetuate your relationship. You were setting it up so that you could share your lives – as man and wife, not just "playing away from home".'

Simpson shook his head again.

'It was never going to happen.'

'So what was going to happen, if your wife hadn't so conveniently died?' asked DC Murdoch. 'How were you going to resolve things? Matters were coming to a head. As far as Steph was concerned your wife was long dead and your mother was out of the way in a home. You were a free man. You could sell up and buy a house elsewhere. How were you going to explain your lack of action?'

'I was in a bit of a spot, I admit. But at the end of the

day I would have had to either end the relationship, or come clean to Beverley and ask her to let me go.'

'You were seriously going to end your relationship, just like that?' said DC Murdoch. 'Your grand passion. With a woman you had showered with gifts, taken to Paris, provided with a new car. And as far as Beverley is concerned, she wasn't going to just let you go, just like that either. She would take you to the cleaners financially. You've already told us that divorce, or separation, would be ruinous.'

At this point, Simpson's attention was drawn to the selection of the bank statements that had been retrieved from his home. He agreed that they related to him. He said that he had a current account and a deposit account at the Midland Bank. The accounts were in his name. Beverley had had her own account. There were no joint accounts.

He confirmed that the latest statements showed that the deposit account had a balance of £2, and that his current account was heavily overdrawn.

'What those statements show,' said DC Forrester, 'is that from having a credit balance on your current account six months ago, you have progressively gone into the red month after month. What has been coming in every month has been consistently exceeded by what is going out. Basically you have been living beyond your means. Would you agree with that?'

Simpson nodded.

'Yes. I've had a lot of outgoings recently. As well as my normal household costs, mortgage et cetera, I've had HP payments on the car I bought Steph, and then the costs of trips to France and London, hotels and that sort of thing.'

'So you've added to the expenses you had before the additional cost of entertaining a high-maintenance girlfriend, with all that that involves – buying her cars and presents, weekends away, expensive hotels and so on. Clearly that was a lifestyle you couldn't afford. What was the attitude of your bank to all this?'

'I've had the bank manager on my back. He's given me some latitude because I've been a good customer, but I've had to tell him that I would be trimming my expenditure and also putting the house on the market with a view to moving to a smaller, cheaper property.'

'But how realistic was that?' asked DC Murdoch. 'Obviously, as you didn't have a joint account, your wife wouldn't have known about your additional expenses. If you suddenly told her you were planning to sell the house and downsize', she's going to be asking questions? And I can't see that there was much scope for reducing your expenses if you were going to keep Steph in the lifestyle to which she had become accustomed?'

'Yes, well something was going to have to give. Either end the relationship, or divorce or separation from Beverley.'

'Yes!' was the response from DC Forrester, 'and it was

Beverley that had to "give", wasn't it? Because you had already decided before the end of the year that divorce or separation wasn't going to come into it. You were going to dispose of her for good.'

Simpson made no reply, but sadly shook his head.

'You said earlier that you had nothing to gain from her death,' said DC Forrester. 'But that's not true is it?'

The life insurance policy recovered from his home that morning was placed in front of him. Simpson agreed that he had been provided with a copy earlier, that he had been responsible for arranging the policy in December 1976, and that he was the sole beneficiary in the event of his wife's death.

'It's right, isn't it, Mr. Simpson, that you stand to gain £50,000 from your wife's death? Or you would if you'd had no hand in it.'

Simpson nodded assent.

'Have you claimed under the policy?' he was asked by DC Forrester.

'Yes, but the insurance company have told me that they won't consider paying out until the police investigation is complete, and any court proceedings arising from that are finalised.'

'Why did you suddenly decide to take out insurance on your wife's life?'

'It was a joint decision. Beverley felt that her climbing activities were becoming more adventurous and consequently more hazardous, particularly with her doing a lot more solo climbing. She knew that she was taking a lot more risks. She said that she wanted me to be able to pay off the mortgage if she had a fatal accident.'

'I find that a little hard to believe,' said DC Murdoch. 'You're almost suggesting that she had some sort of death wish.'

'Well, that's how she was with her climbing. She was always pushing herself a bit further, but she knew the risks.'

'I'm sure you would agree that it's an astonishing coincidence that she died only a month after the policy was issued.'

'Well, that's all it is, a coincidence,' was the reply.

DC Forrester then told Simpson that before finishing the interview they wanted to ask him some questions about what he'd said earlier about his journey to the north-east on the morning of the 12th January. He was asked to look at the copy of the till receipt that had been issued at the Wetherby service area.

'Would you agree that this receipt was issued at 12.10 pm?' he was asked.

Simpson examined the receipt closely.

'Yes,' he replied.

'Well, you told us earlier that you left home at about 8.00 am and that you didn't stop until Wetherby

Services, which you reached about ten o'clock. Now, that's clearly wrong, but it wouldn't take you four hours to drive from Bakewell to Wetherby, would it? What we're saying is that, if you are telling the truth, you must have left home a lot later than 8.00 am?'

Simpson shrugged.

'Well, I've obviously got my departure time wrong. I've had a lot on my mind lately and it's clearly affected my memory. It must have been closer to 10.00 am when I left home.'

'Alright,' said DC Murdoch, 'but if that's the case then you must have been at home when your wife left the house, bearing in mind that her body was found just before 10.00 am. So you should be able to tell us who picked her up?'

'Well I can't. Thinking about it now, she must have left the house before I was out of bed.'

'But you told us earlier that, and I use your words, "she was preparing for a climbing trip". Are you now telling us that you are mistaken about having seen her that morning?'

'Yes. I'm sorry about that.'

'This is just not credible, Mr. Simpson,' DC Forrester now interjected. 'Your wife has died in a "tragic accident" that same morning, and you have no precise recollection of the time or the circumstances in which you last saw her. Surely you would be very focused about what would have been the last hours of her life and how and when you last saw her?'

Simpson shook his head apologetically. 'I know what you're saying but the fact remains that events have affected my memory.'

'Isn't the truth of the matter this ...' said DC Murdoch. 'You have a very clear recollection of events that morning because you were her driver, you took her to Curbar Edge, as you had planned all along. There was no third party involved?'

'No, no, you've got it all wrong,' was the reply.

'You told her you would belay her while she climbed,' the officer went on. 'You walked along the top of the crag with her while she decided which climb she was going to do and then waited with her while she changed into her climbing shoes. Am I right?'

'No, you're way off the mark. Anyway she would plan her climb from below the crag, not on the top of the edge.'

'As soon as she was changed, it would be very easy for you to push her over the edge. She had no reason to suspect you of anything, she wouldn't have seen that coming, and it would have the appearance of a tragic accident?'

Simpson sadly shook his head again. 'Look, I know you've got to make that allegation, but you're so wrong. She was forever pushing herself to do harder and harder climbs, and often without a partner. She was going to come to grief one day.'

'If she was on her own,' put in DC Forrester, 'can you explain why she was so scantily dressed on a very cold morning? No warm clothes, no rucksack, nothing.'

'No, I can't. Maybe there was another person present, and maybe there was foul play, and maybe he's removed her gear after he's pushed her. But it wasn't me.'

'So you are agreeing it may not have been an accident, but the culprit was some person who had it in for her?'

'Possibly. She will have pissed a few men off in her time. You found one of them – Maitland.'

'We're about done,' DC Forrester then told Simpson, 'but what we're saying is this. We're quite satisfied that your wife's death was no accident, and that she was murdered. Your two lives, your life with Beverley and your secret life with Stephanie were on a collision course, and, to use your own words "something had to give". You couldn't give up your grand passion and divorce was not an option. You couldn't run the risk anyway of your girlfriend finding out that your wife was still alive and exposing your lies. The only way out for you was to dispose of Beverley. That solved most of your problems. You could sell the house, move away from Bakewell and set up with Stephanie. And as long as you made her death look like an accident you had the bonus of an insurance pay-out which would solve your immediate financial difficulties, and give you a nice sum to start your new life. Very neat.'

'Is there meant to be a question in there somewhere?'

asked Paul Hargreaves. 'It sounds more like the prosecution address to the jury.'

The officers didn't reply to this, but simply announced that the interview was over, and that there would be no more. Simpson was returned to his cell.

Thirty minutes later, following a discussion between the two detectives and Alan Woodman, and after a telephone call made by the latter to Detective Inspector Moore, Richard Simpson was charged with the murder of Beverley Simpson on the 12th January 1977.

CHAPTER FOURTEEN

May 13th

Richard Simpson made his first appearance in court at Bakewell on the morning of Saturday the 26th February. He was remanded in custody after Paul Hargreaves told the single magistrate sitting that there would be no application for bail that day, although there would be a full bail application at the next hearing.

Over the next few days, the investigators began the process of gathering the formal witness statements that were required to make the case against the defendant. This included a long statement from Stephanie Winter that was obtained by DC Forrester after a trip to Cockermouth. She had already been spoken to by Alan Woodman on the phone on the Saturday of the court appearance and informed that Simpson had been charged, that he was in custody, but may be granted bail in a week's time. She was advised to make the necessary arrangements to move to Taunton, should the need arise.

On the Monday, Martin Tory had been informed of developments since he had spoken to Alan Woodman on the previous Friday. He was made aware of the evidence that had been retrieved from Simpson's home and his workplace, his response to questioning in the interviews, and now that he had been charged. Martin, in turn, had relayed this information to his boss, Robin Caulfield.

'It's not going to be an easy one to prove,' Caulfield had opined. 'You had better make sure we get a prosecuting counsel with some balls. Fascinating case though!'

Later that afternoon the case was the talk of the CPS tearoom. After Martin had provided his colleagues with a snapshot of the evidence, he found that opinions were sharply divided. Some thought the case had little prospect of success; others saw the evidence as overwhelming. The most vocal protagonist of the latter view was, not altogether surprisingly, Ronnie Fox. With the case against Richard Simpson up and running, the investigation was over and he no doubt thought he was free from any prospect of being caught up in any further police probing into the deceased's murky past.

Martin also took time to sit down with George Noble, the chief clerk in the CPS Crown Court section, a man who had many years' experience of dealing with barristers and their clerks. Martin knew that George would have a very good idea of who might be currently suitable to take on the job of prosecuting the Simpson case in the higher court, and, almost inevitably, to trial. George listened to Martin's description of the case and the evidence, and then thought for a few moments before replying:

'I would strongly suggest Brian Cattermole,' he eventually said.

Martin knew him well. He had prosecuted many serious cases for Derbyshire CPS in the past as a senior junior counsel, and with a good deal of success. He made no secret of the fact that he much preferred prosecuting to defending criminals. Martin, however, had just one reservation:

'He's only just become Queens Counsel, hasn't he? This would be his first murder.'

'Yes,' said George. 'That's quite right. But I would see that as a plus. He's going to want to push hard and make an impression. You don't want anyone too laid back, and I can see some of the more experienced silks being a bit lukewarm about this case.'

Martin nodded his agreement. 'How about a junior?'

'Brian will probably want Tom Edwards,' said George. 'They'll work well together.'

Martin grimaced. Tom Edwards was as prolific and as successful a prosecutor as Brian Cattermole had been, but he was someone whom Martin actively disliked. He regarded Edwards as arrogant and condescending.

Police officers tended to be irked by his tendency to talk down to them, and this view was shared by most of the CPS lawyers that came into contact with him. There was no doubting, however, that he was very good as a prosecuting counsel, and that he would be more than able to take over the conduct of the case should his 'leader' become indisposed. Martin reluctantly nodded his assent.

★★★★★★★★★★★★★★★★★★★★★★★★★★★

Richard Simpson succeeded in securing bail on his second appearance at court, on the 4th March. Although Martin resisted the application for bail made on Simpson's behalf by Paul Hargreaves, he wasn't entirely surprised that the magistrates, after a long deliberation, agreed to release him. Hargreaves played the 'they got it wrong last time' card for all it was worth, and he was able to remind the bench that Simpson was a man of unblemished character, with a good job and a fixed local address. Moreover, he said to the court, even if he had killed his wife, the prosecution could hardly suggest that he was going to offend again as there was no evidence that he harboured any murderous feelings against any other person. In any event, he was not guilty and the case against him was 'weak, speculative and circumstantial.'

There were conditions attached to the defendant's bail. He was required to surrender his passport, report to Bakewell police station every Saturday, and to make no attempt to contact or communicate with Stephanie Winter. The conditions were not particularly onerous, but then the court was anxious not to restrict his ability to do his job. Martin suspected that the one condition that would cause him a problem was the last one. Alan Woodman thought the same, and he hastened from court at the first opportunity to ring Stephanie. She was clearly waiting for the call, and although she expressed disappointment and concern over the result of the hearing, she indicated that she was ready to set off to her friend's house in Taunton that same day.

★★★★★★★★★★★★★★★★★★★★★★★★★★★

On the day that Richard Simpson made his first appearance in the dock at Nottingham Crown Court, well-groomed and smartly dressed in a charcoal grey suit, winter had given way to spring. May 13th was a warm, sunlit morning in Nottingham and on the crags and moors of the Derbyshire Peak District there was no trace of the heavy snow that had lain into early April.

The weeks between Simpson's appearances in Bakewell Magistrates' Court and May 13th had been largely uneventful. The machinery of the criminal justice system had ground its inexorable way through the customary routines of preparation for a criminal trial: the prosecution evidence had been bundled together into an acceptable form, served upon the defence and the courts, and presented to Brian Cattermole and his junior counsel. During this period the case went quiet. The press had nothing to report as there was nothing to report, and it would have nothing to report until the trial took place. Richard

Simpson, apart from a couple of conferences with his solicitor and his own barrister, went about his normal business, albeit without any visits to Armathwaite Hall. Alan Woodman and his detective colleagues busied themselves with investigating more mundane cases. Martin Tory went to court and worked on the rest of his caseload.

There had been one short-lived incident that had briefly threatened to disturb this peaceful hiatus. In early April Alan Woodman had been contacted by the private investigator, Jim Donegani. Donegani had received a phone call from an individual who had identified himself as 'Richard Simpson'. The caller had wanted to recruit Donegani to locate a woman for him, a woman who he had lost touch with but for whom he had news 'which might be to her significant advantage'. The woman was called Stephanie Winter. If it was Simpson who was the caller, he had, of course, chosen the wrong private detective to ring. Donegani knew enough about Simpson's case from the newspapers and from his own previous involvement with it, to be immediately suspicious. He told 'Simpson' that he would have to meet him personally to take instructions, he would need a photograph of the woman, and he would need paying 'up front'. The caller quickly made excuses and rang off.

Alan discussed the phone call with Martin Tory and they agreed that it could be construed as an attempt to contact the witness, and hence a breach of Simpson's bail conditions. That is, of course, if it was Simpson.

Alan strongly suspected that if Simpson was arrested for the breach and was confronted with that evidence, he would almost certainly deny that he was the caller. On the other hand, if there was no follow-up, he might believe he had got away with it and try his luck with another private investigator in another area, someone who might not have been conversant with the finer detail of the case. Simpson was therefore arrested. As Alan suspected, he did deny being the caller in question, and suggested that some 'hostile' third party was intent on making trouble for him. The decision was taken to release Simpson and not to bring him back before the court, but Alan was confident that the arrest had served its purpose. If Simpson had indeed been the caller, he would now, in all likelihood, be deterred from making any further such attempt to locate Stephanie, knowing that the police clearly had the means to discover his actions and knowing that the consequences of discovery would probably be a remand in custody until the trial.

★★★★★★★★★★★★★★★★★★★★★★★★★★★

The clerk of the court rose to his feet in order to read the indictment to Richard Simpson. Jeremy Ramsbottom had a strong resonant voice and a commanding presence. He had, before the creation of the Crown Court in 1972, been the Clerk of Assize, but now bore the somewhat grander title of Chief Clerk of the Crown Court. He was a pompous and self-important man. One of his subordinates could just have easily have acted as clerk of the court on this occasion, but the judge was a High Court judge and it was a high-profile case, so no-one else but Jeremy Ramsbottom would do! He was in fact just a middle-grade civil servant, but, in his wig, and sitting in front of the red-robed judge, he gave the impression of being much more important than he was. To his staff and legal practitioners he was a figure of fun. He would have been mortified if he had been aware that he was widely known as 'Shepherd's Delight'.

'The particulars of the indictment are that on the 12th day of January 1977 you murdered Beverley Simpson,' the clerk intoned. 'Do you plead Guilty or Not Guilty?'

'Not Guilty,' was Simpson's clear and defiant response.

Both prosecution and defence counsel then provided the court with information about the number of witnesses that were to give evidence in the trial, when they were available and how long it was estimated the trial would last. The judge consulted briefly with the clerk and then made his pronouncement about the date of trial.

'The trial in this matter will begin on the 25th July, 1977.'

★★★★★★★★★★★★★★★★★★★★★★★★★★

It was only a short walk to Brian Cattermole's chambers on High Pavement. Here, Martin Tory, Alan Woodman, DC Forrester and the CPS law clerk allocated to the case, David Cragg, were ushered into a large and splendid conference room, where they were joined by Brian and Tom Edwards. A female clerk arrived almost immediately with a large coffee pot and an expensive-looking tea service.

'Would you mind being mother, Tom?' said Brian to his junior counsel.

Although he obliged, Tom Edwards was clearly not suited to being treated as a lackey. His body language gave his feelings away. Martin could barely suppress his amusement.

Seated round the table, all waited for Brian to speak. There was no need for introductions, as both barristers had been involved in cases with each of the others on more than one occasion in the past. Brian pulled his file of papers towards him, but did not open it. He was very familiar with the contents by now. He sat back slightly in his chair and put his hands behind his head.

'A fascinating and most unusual case,' he began. 'I've not come across anything like it before, and I know Tom hasn't either. It's not a stone-waller.' By this he meant that conviction was by no means a certainty. 'But I'm sure a sensible jury would be convinced of his guilt, because it's the only logical conclusion you can come to.'

'This is how we present the case to the jury,' he went on. 'The defendant's two worlds were about to collide. He could not allow this because the result for him would have been catastrophic. On one side we have Stephanie Winter. The exotic 'femme fatale' with whom he was obsessed. On whom he had showered gifts and who had led him into a lifestyle he clearly had no intention of giving up. Such was his obsession, that he had spun a web of lies and deceit in order to keep that relationship going. He had told her that his wife was dead, and that he was living with his mother who was stricken with dementia. Both terrible and calumnious falsehoods. Were Stephanie to discover the truth, it seems inevitable that this would spell the end of the relationship with Simpson. "Hell hath no fury" et cetera. And now she was putting increasing pressure on him to make their relationship a more permanent one, to create a home for them to share.

'Then, on the other side, we have the equally larger-than-life figure of the free-spirited, independent Beverley Simpson. Cheated-upon and cheating, but not in equal measure. But despite her feckless lifestyle, the evidence tends to suggest she had no intention of giving up on her marriage. She and her husband appear to maintain an amicable relationship. They continue to socialise together. He supports her climbing activities. She would no doubt indulge his "flings", his casual affairs. She is scarcely in a position to do otherwise. But this is very different. He is wanting to discard her in order to pursue a separate life with another woman. Unbeknown to Beverley he has driven himself deep into debt through the extravagance of his secret lifestyle. She does not know that he has "killed her off" in order to sustain his other relationship. He does not want to end his marriage, because he is certain that, having discovered the horrible truth, Beverley will "take him to the cleaners". Already deep in debt, he is not going to be able to make a new home for himself and his girlfriend and keep up the lifestyle to which he and she have become accustomed. That is even if he is able to maintain the pretence that his wife has died some time previously, and of course prevent Stephanie learning the truth about his mother.

'He is in a dire situation. How is he going to square the circle before it is too late?

'The answer of course is to do what he did. By disposing of his wife, informing Stephanie that he has found a place in a home for his mother, and arranging to move as far away as possible from Bakewell, he can, hopefully, pursue his preferred course without his new partner discovering the truth. And as the cream on the cake he has a tasty pay-out from an insurance policy that he has recently and conveniently taken out. He can clear off his debts and set himself up for his new life.'

The QC paused at this point and looked around the table, as if inviting comments. No-one spoke. Everyone present had already come to the same conclusions in his own mind. The silence indicated assent.

Cattermole went on: 'Of course the defence will say this was a very high-risk strategy and one that no sane person would think about embarking on. There was always a chance that Stephanie would discover that Simpson's wife had died recently and not some years ago, or that his mother was not in a home. What if the police didn't buy the scenario that Beverley's death was an accident, and there was an investigation with publicity that might reach as far as Cumbria. And he was always going to have to keep Stephanie away from Bakewell, away from his friends and relations, away from his work colleagues. He was always going to be looking over his shoulder. Our answer to that has to be that he was a desperate man and desperate measures were required. An intelligent man, and he would surely have realised that he wasn't about to commit the perfect murder, but there was a certain grim logic about it all, and no doubt he would have thought that, with a fair wind, he had a good chance of getting away with it.'

Brian paused again, before continuing. 'The spectre at the feast of course is Rex Maitland. The defence will milk that for all it's worth. "Members of the jury, the police got it very wrong there. How can you be sure they didn't get it wrong again. They needed a quick fix. They casted around for another patsy and they alighted upon Mr. Simpson". We'll just have to roll with the punches on that one and just hope the jury don't get too distracted by that argument.'

Tom Edwards clearly decided that he wasn't going to be overlooked, as he took the opportunity to get his own small contribution in, piping up with, 'It also helps our cause that he has lied about his movements that morning.'

He was rewarded with a few nods around the table, although his leader didn't join in.

'OK,' said the QC, 'we're probably about done here. There's no great work needs doing on the case. I'll draft an opening statement for the judge and I'll draw up a batting order for calling witnesses. There should be some scope for agreeing quite a bit of the evidence too. Are we happy that Miss Winter isn't going to go flaky on us?' He looked at Alan Woodman at this point.

'No, she'll be fine,' said Alan. 'She's really fired up and ready to go.'

★★★★★★★★★★★★★★★★★★★★★★★★★★

CHAPTER FIFTEEN

July 25th

The last Monday in July was to be the hottest day of the year so far, and not only in the south of England. By 10.30 am it was already uncomfortably humid in the streets of Nottingham, and unbearably hot in the Crown Court building. In court number one, however, the trial judge in the case of Regina versus Richard Simpson, was in no mood to allow any departure from the normal dress code. Mr. Justice Sweeney was attired in his customary heavy robes, the Queens Counsel in their buttoned-up jackets and gowns, and their juniors in three-piece suits and gowns. All wore wigs. Nor were any exceptions made for those who sat behind the barristers. The solicitors, clerks and police officers were expected to be dressed in their usual work attire – suits and ties, or uniforms, as the case may be. Members of the public could dress as they liked, within reason. Only the defendant, Richard Simpson, and the Clerk of the Court, Jeremy Ramsbottom, were formally dressed by choice. The former because he needed to make an impression; the latter because he saw it as a mark of his status and importance to be wearing a wig, not because he was required to do so.

Once it had been confirmed that Simpson was maintaining his plea of Not Guilty, the judge asked the jury bailiff to bring the jury panel into court. Once assembled, the panel were provided with the name of the defendant, the terms of the indictment, and the details of the witnesses that were to be called in the trial. This was to give the potential jurors the opportunity to disclose if they knew anyone who might feature or be named during the hearing. One man announced that he had known the deceased 'quite well', and was discharged from the panel. Whether 'quite well' was a euphemism for 'intimately' was not revealed, although many of those present on the court benches suspected it might have been.

The twelve members of the actual trial jury were then selected by drawing names out of a box that Jeremy Ramsbottom had in front of him. He made an unnecessary meal of the process, producing each slip of paper with an elaborate flourish and then enunciating each name slowly and with great emphasis on the surname. Needless to say, no-one was impressed, particularly the judge, who made a rather obvious point of looking at his watch. Jeremy, of course, would not have seen this, as he had his back to him.

At last the selected jurors were seated in the jury box, and the judge thanked them for their attendance at court and gave them what he referred to as 'the ground rules'. They were to talk to no-one other than each other about the evidence they were to hear, including their family members when they went home. They should forget anything they might have read about the case in the newspapers, heard on the radio or seen on television. They were sworn to reach a verdict in the case purely on the evidence that they would hear in the trial.

Martin Tory was pleased with the appearance of the jury. It was an exact mix of men and women, and most were smartly dressed. There was a marked absence of jeans and T-shirts. They looked attentive. You could never tell, but they seemed to be the sort of jurors who would listen to and have regard to the evidence, and not be swayed by such irrelevancies as 'liking' or 'disliking' one of the barristers, or believing that the defendant must be guilty 'because the police wouldn't have brought the case if he wasn't'.

Having established that neither counsel wanted to raise any preliminary legal issues, that would have had to be dealt with in the absence of the jury, the judge then invited Brian Cattermole to make his opening address.

★★★★★★★★★★★★★★★★★★★★★★★★★★★

For the prosecution, the opening address to the jury was one of the most important ingredients of the trial process. Prosecution counsel would tell the jury what evidence they were going to hear, and set out in clear and unambiguous terms how that evidence established the guilt of the man in the dock. The first two or three days of the trial would belong to the prosecution. The jury would only hear from prosecution witnesses. Brian Cattermole knew that at the end of the prosecution case, if the accused was to be convicted, the jury must have been left with a strong sense of his guilt. So strong indeed that the defence case which followed would not dent or undermine that sense. Brian knew that he would have to reinforce that feeling in the jury's mind from the outset. His opening address would have to be robust and unequivocal, so that the prosecution had claimed the 'high ground' right from the start.

By the same token, the QC had also decided that he would need to deal in his opening address with what he saw as the 'red herrings' in the case: the points he knew the defence would make to 'muddy the waters'. By this he meant the initial police view that the death was an 'accident', and, more particularly, the 'Rex Maitland dimension'. If the defence was allowed to 'spring' these points or this evidence on the jury in the course of its case, then there was a danger that the jury might become so distracted by these issues that the strong case that the Crown had set out might be undermined. So, Brian decided, he would seek to disarm these weapons in advance, so that the jury would not be later taken by surprise, and hopefully would treat these factors with the insignificance they deserved, indeed as no more than the red herrings they were.

Having risen to his feet and smiled benignly at the jury, Brian introduced himself and his junior counsel as the prosecution team, and he also told the jury that the defendant was represented by Ms. Alison Lancaster QC and Ms. Jacqueline Lamont. He then began his speech, as he always did, by informing the jury that this was a criminal trial, that the prosecution brought the case and it was the prosecution which had to prove it, and that they, the jury should only convict the accused if 'they were sure of his guilt'. Martin Tory had heard this all before and he knew that it was a deliberate ploy on Brian's part to make this point at the outset. The intention was to get the jury to see that he was a fair prosecutor, not a persecutor, someone worthy of careful attention and consideration. Martin had no doubt that most juries were impressed by this approach.

But this was the first and last concession that Brian would make to the defence in his address. He then launched into his outline of the prosecution case and followed it up with a powerful statement as to how that case pointed overwhelmingly to the prisoner's guilt. He began thus:

'Members of the jury, what is this case about? It is about the murder, the callous execution, by the defendant of his wife on the 12th of January 1977, by pushing her off a clifftop to be dashed to death on the rocks many feet below. The prosecution say that the defendant's action was pre-planned and was designed to allow him to freely pursue a relationship with another woman with whom he had become infatuated. It was also designed to allow him to enjoy the proceeds of an insurance policy he had recently taken out on the life of his wife, proceeds which would have freed him from debts he had accumulated as a result of his illicit relationship.'

Brian then began to methodically outline the evidence that the Crown intended to call as part of its case. He described how a woman's body had been found at the foot of Curbar Edge in the Derbyshire Peak District, that she appeared to have been a rock-climber, climbing alone, and that the assumption at this stage was that she had fallen to her death from near the top of the crag. A tragic accident, but an accident nevertheless. He then told the jury about the identification of the body as his wife by Richard Simpson, more than forty-eight hours later. Simpson he said had attended Bakewell police station on returning home after a business trip and finding that his wife had not been at home for two days. He had last seen her, he said, on the morning of 12th January just before he left home himself. She was a climber and was preparing for a climbing trip. Since he had got home he had become aware that a woman, believed to be a climber, had been found dead below Curbar Edge. He suspected that this was his wife Beverley. His 'suspicions' were confirmed when he was taken by a police officer to the mortuary in Chesterfield and was shown the body of a young woman, which he was able to identify as that of his wife.

'And that might have been that,' Brian went on. 'A climber on her own. No partner. No ropes. Poorly clad. A bitterly cold morning. Cold hands. Slips and falls to her death. For all the world nothing more than an accident. It's fair to say that at this time no-one had any reason or inclination to regard what had happened as anything other than an accident, whether this was the mountain rescue team, the medical authorities, or, indeed, the police. The police in particular saw no need to mount an investigation into the death. In any event, the police in North Derbyshire at this time were engaged in a massive manhunt for a violent and very dangerous escaped prisoner. You may have heard, members of the jury, of the case of William Thomas Hughes, and if you haven't, you will have done by the end of this trial. This was a man who had stabbed his prison escort on his way to court in Chesterfield, stolen the car in which he was being carried, and made off across the moors. He was eventually shot dead by a police officer, but not before he had murdered four of the inhabitants of a cottage in which he had sought shelter. This was probably one of the most notorious crimes ever perpetrated in this country, and certainly in Derbyshire. The manhunt, which began on the same day as Beverley Simpson's body was recovered, involved a very large number of police officers. You may think, ladies and gentlemen, that in the circumstances, it was hardly surprising that the constabulary spent so little time and energy in looking into a death that did not appear in any way suspicious. They had much bigger fish to fry.'

But then, Brian continued, there had been a 'fortunate' turn of events. 'Not fortunate for the defendant, indeed, but fortunate for the interests of justice.' He then outlined how 'an alert and experienced' detective sergeant, reading a report of Beverley's death a few days later, had realised there might have been more to her death than had at first appeared. The name of the deceased was known to him, and, at first out of curiosity and then 'with growing suspicion', he began to examine in detail the circumstances of the supposed 'accident'.

Brian paused here and checked to make sure that he had the attention of the jury. There was no doubt about this. Their body language made it clear that they were hanging on his every word. He went on:

'The conclusions that were reached by Detective Sergeant Woodman, ladies and gentlemen, form part of the prosecution's case. Our case is that Beverley Simpson's death was no accident. How so? Because, in the first place, as an experienced rock-climber, even climbing alone, she would not have been so skimpily dressed on a freezing cold morning– jeans and a thin shirt, and no helmet. And she had no rucksack with her. A rucksack that should have contained warmer clothes to put on after her climb, and a change of footwear so that she could slip out of her climbing shoes and walk back to the car park in comfort. But then there was apparently nothing for her back at the car park, no car and no-one waiting for her when she got there to give her a lift. The crag was a long way from her home. How was she going to get home, and, indeed, how had she got there in the first place? Public transport in these parts is almost non-existent, and, anyway, she was found to have no money in her possession. Beverley had nothing but the clothes she stood up in, the clothes she was wearing when her body was recovered. The inescapable conclusion, members of the jury, is that there had to have been a third party involved. Someone who took her to Curbar Edge, who removed her extra clothing, and then left her there to die. The only and irresistible inference is that that someone was responsible for her death. Beverley Simpson did not fall, she was pushed.'

The jury were then told that, following DS Woodman's conclusions, the police treated Beverley's death as suspicious and embarked on a murder investigation. Beverley Simpson had a reputation in and around Bakewell of being a woman who had had casual sexual relationships with a number of different men, and the initial police inquiries were directed at identifying these persons, and, in particular, those who might have borne a grudge against her, either as 'rejected suitors' or whose relationship with her had ended in acrimony.

Again Brian paused at this point, before going on:

'Members of the jury, I have to tell you that the police investigation initially went down the wrong road. A suspect who fitted the bill was identified, a young man called Rex Maitland, who had been a climbing partner of the deceased. He had aspired, however, to be more than just a climbing companion. He wanted to be her lover. She, however, did not want that sort of relationship and made it plain that she did not. Unfortunately he could not accept this position, and continued to press his suit, showering her with gifts and other tokens of affection. All in vain. She remained totally unmoved, and at one point publicly humiliated him in front of a bar-room full of people.

'It seemed to the investigators, therefore, that here was a man worthy of their attention: rejected, desperate, scorned and ridiculed, and possibly, as a result, with a motive for doing her harm. Their suspicions were fortified when they went to his place of work and recovered Beverley's rucksack from the rear of his van, a vehicle which matched the description of a van seen by a witness in the car park at Curbar Edge early on the morning of her death. The young man also had no credible alibi for that morning, a morning when he was not at work.

'To cut a long story short, ladies and gentlemen, Mr. Maitland was arrested on suspicion of Beverley Simpson's murder and later charged with the offence after he had made what appeared to be a full confession to that crime. It is fair to say, however, that the confession was made in unusual circumstances, and, indeed, in circumstances which would have rendered that "confession" unreliable. The irony was, however, that he could not have committed the murder because at the material time he was committing another serious offence some twenty or thirty miles away. Further investigation revealed that on the morning in question, Maitland was responsible for sexually assaulting a female student in countryside near Sheffield. He has since pleaded guilty to that offence and is serving a custodial sentence for it. He had a perfect alibi as far as the death of Beverley Simpson was concerned, even if it was not the sort of alibi he would have desired.

'So that was an end of the case against Maitland as far as the murder of Beverley Simpson was concerned, and the police investigation was back to square one. It is certain, members of the jury, that the defence will make much of this failed case. They are fully entitled to do so. They will say to you: "The police got it completely wrong once. How can you be sure that they haven't got it wrong again?" But you mustn't be distracted by this. It really has no relevance to the case against Richard Simpson. There were good reasons why Maitland was arrested and charged with the murder. He was a genuine suspect and there was evidence against him. A mistake was made but I would suggest it was a very understandable one. You should put it out of your mind and concentrate instead on the case before you.'

Brian then described how the police investigation, although 'back to square one' and looking very much as though the 'trail had gone cold', was suddenly boosted a month later by information from an unexpected quarter. He told the jury of the news brought by the private investigator Jim Donegani as to the visit to Simpson's house by Beverley's parents after her death, whilst Simpson himself was absent, and their discovery in a drawer in the marital bed of two greeting cards. He brandished the cards aloft (the defence had decided not to challenge the lawfulness of their seizure):

'Ladies and gentleman, you have photocopies of these two cards in front of you. They were clearly intended for Richard Simpson. One is a Christmas card. The other is a birthday card. Simpson's birthday was on the 7th January. You will hear evidence that these cards were sent to him before last Christmas, and in time for his birthday last January. You will note the content of the handwritten messages inside the cards. The prosecution say that these cards were sent to Simpson by someone, 'Steph', who clearly regarded herself as involved in a passionate love affair with the defendant, and, moreover, expected to be living with him as 'man and wife', by the 14th January 1977. You will note that this is two days after Beverley Simpson's death. We say that this was not just wishful thinking on Steph's part, but was part of a joint plan by the defendant and Steph to be together, a plan that was obviously hatched before Christmas, and was due to come to fruition a week after Simpson's birthday. The obstacle to the success of the plan was Beverley. She would have to go. She would have to be removed.'

The prosecutor then described the inquiries made by the police to uncover the identity of the mysterious 'Steph', and how she was revealed to be a woman from Cockermouth in Cumbria, who had met Simpson in a hotel in the Lake District, while he was in that area on one of his business trips. The jury was told how the pair had fallen into a passionate relationship, spending weekends together, often at her home and also on occasions in Paris and London. He showered her with gifts and rang her every night. They discussed how they might contrive to be together permanently.

'What is plain, however,' Brian told the jury, 'is that Steph was not a party to any plot to kill Beverley Simpson. You will hear evidence from the lady, Stephanie Winter. She will tell you that her relationship with Simpson was based on her belief that Simpson was a single man. He had told her that his wife had died of cancer some three years previously. She was told that he lived with his mother, who suffered from dementia, and that his sister in Derby looked after her during his frequent absences from home. Simpson was now building one lie upon another. When Stephanie pressed him to make their relationship and their cohabitation permanent, he told her that he and his sister had found their mother a place in a residential home, and that she would be able to take up the place on the 14th January. Hence the reference to that date in the birthday card.

'But Simpson was painting himself into a corner. He was running out of options and his lies were about to catch up with him. Beverley, of course, was still very much alive. His lover was on the brink of coming to Bakewell to share his life. His mother was not living with him and was not suffering from dementia. His two worlds were about to collide. The easiest course for him would have been to break up with Stephanie. It is plain, however, that this was never an option. He was infatuated with her. It was his grand passion. He could tell her the truth about Beverley and tell Beverley that he was leaving her. But this was not an option either. The truth would probably fatally jeopardise his relationship with his lover, and, as you will hear, he could not afford a scorned wife "taking him to the cleaners" in a divorce settlement. He had, members of the jury, in reality, only one course open to him: remove his wife altogether, and then remove himself far enough away to a place where no-one would know of his life in Bakewell. It was a risky and desperate strategy, but he was a desperate man. So that was his plan.

'What Simpson knew, of course, but Stephanie did not, was that there was never any prospect of them coming together on the 14th January or, indeed, for some little time thereafter. He would be too busy arranging his wife's funeral and dealing with her affairs, and then arranging the sale of his house. You will hear that he fobbed Stephanie off with the excuse that the place for his mother in the residential home was not yet ready for her, so Stephanie could not yet move in with him.'

'There was another reason, too, that Simpson needed his wife to die. You will hear evidence that when his home was searched following his arrest, the police seized a quantity of bank statements. These showed that he was in ever-increasing debt. He was leading a double life and living a lifestyle that he could not sustain on his income. The police also recovered from the house an insurance policy. It was a life insurance policy. The subject of the policy was Beverley. The sole beneficiary in the event of her death was the defendant. The insured sum was £50,000. This would have solved all Richard Simpson's financial problems. He stood therefore to gain in more ways than one by his wife's early death. You will hear that Simpson claimed under the policy, within little more than a month after his wife's death. Sadly for him, the insurance company stated that there would be no pay-out whist there was a police investigation into the death and before these proceedings were concluded.'

Brian paused again. The jury were listening intently. But it was time to draw his address to a close:

'Members of the jury, it is very likely that the defendant will give sworn evidence himself, once the prosecution has concluded its case. He will deny murdering his wife. He will no doubt tell you that he had never given Stephanie the impression that she would be able to join him in Bakewell on the 14th January. He may well agree that he was deeply involved with this woman and that matters were coming to a head, but that, nonetheless, she was dispensable, he could break off the relationship. Alternatively he could divorce his wife. As easy as that! He will provide you with an alibi for the morning of his wife's death. It is, however, one that is full of holes. He will also tell you that the insurance policy was as much Beverley's idea as his own

– she was conscious that her climbing activities were becoming ever more hazardous and she was anxious to leave him financially comfortable in the event of her untimely death. She was dead within less than a month of the policy being taken out. Astonishing coincidence, or was it part of the evil plan?'

What the prosecution say, members of the jury, is that there are just too many coincidences in this case for them to be just coincidences: to regard the events that unfolded, in the manner and sequence that they unfolded, as coincidence would be an affront to common sense. They were part of a wicked plan by Simpson to free himself of an encumbrance and of his debts. He must have thought he had got away with it, and he may well have done, had it not been for chance and his own carelessness.'

After another brief pause, Brian nodded at the jury, and sat down.

The judge peered at the clock on the wall at the back of the court.

'It's not late in the day,' he said, 'but I think that's a convenient place to finish. We'll resume at 10.30 in the morning.'

CHAPTER SIXTEEN

July 26th

Martin Tory was unable to stay for the second day of the trial. His routine court and casework commitments meant he could not afford the luxury of being away from the office and court for two successive days. He had noticed that Ronnie Fox had been sitting at the back of court and he would, no doubt, be there for the rest of the trial. His rank enabled him to dictate his movements at work and Martin was aware that he had 'booked' himself out of court for the week and delegated some of his more urgent casework to other lawyers. Martin wondered what the senior staff at the County Council would have thought of this, had they known of it. After all, even though he might have a 'personal' interest in the Simpson case, he would be hard put to justify a week-long attendance observing a case in which he had no professional involvement.

Martin had been quietly confident about the prospects for the case after listening to Brian Cattermole's opening address to the jury. Like Brian he had been impressed by their attentiveness, and he had noticed also that some of the individual jurors had looked knowingly at their neighbours on occasions when Brian made a particularly telling point. He had asked the CPS law clerk, who would be in court throughout the trial as part of her duties, to give him a call each day to update him on progress, and he had planned to get back to court himself when the defendant was due to give evidence. Once Alan Woodman and the other police officers had been in the witness box, he would also be able to get their impressions on the way things were going. Alan Woodman himself would be at court until the jury delivered its verdict.

★★★★★★★★★★★★★★★★★★★★★★★★★★★

The second morning of the trial was given over to evidence about the events of 12th January 1977. Almost all of it was uncontroversial, and most of it indeed in the form of written statements which were read to the court by junior prosecuting counsel.

The jury heard evidence from the two climbers from Sheffield who had discovered the body, and from the Mountain Rescue and police officers who had attended the scene. One of the police officers described the scanty clothing that the deceased was wearing, and also the weather conditions. He also stated that he had checked in vain for a motor vehicle in the car parks which might have brought her to Curbar, and he was able, from his local knowledge, to tell the court that there was no bus service that could have delivered her to the scene at that time of day.

A statement from a senior police officer who had been involved in the search for William Hughes detailed the time of his escape from the custody of the prison officers and also, in brief terms, the tragic events at Pottery Cottage and the shooting of Hughes himself. This evidence served the dual purpose of providing the jury with a picture of the massive operation the police were engaged in that day, but also of making it clear that Hughes could not have been responsible for the death of Beverley Simpson.

In the afternoon, solicitor Bob Hassop went into the witness box to tell the jury that on the morning of 12th January, his secretary Beverley Simpson had not turned up for work. This he said was not entirely out of character, as she had done so on occasions in the past, and without giving notice, as on this day.

For the first time in the trial, the defence QC got to her feet. She began to cross-examine Mr. Hassop. Martin Tory arrived at the back of court to witness this. He had taken advantage of his own cases finishing early at Ilkeston Magistrates' Court to make the short journey to Nottingham, and he now had his first glimpse of leading counsel for the defence. The woman came across as impatient, waspish and haughty, characteristics that were unlikely to endear her to a provincial jury. Martin wondered why Simpson's solicitors had chosen this barrister from a set of chambers in London, when there were some very good QCs in Nottingham, Sheffield or Leeds who would have jumped at the opportunity to take on the case. It didn't appear to be a particularly inspired choice, or certainly not at first glance anyway. But as well as being unimpressed, Martin was at the same time quite delighted. Whilst an intelligent jury might not be distracted from their consideration of the evidence by the unattractive attitude of defence counsel, there might always be some jurors who could be tipped towards 'the other side' in a finely balanced case by an instinctive dislike of the defence barrister.

'Not the most reliable employee, Beverley Simpson, was she?' Ms. Alison Lancaster QC snapped at Bob Hassop. Bob had to agree.

'It's right, isn't it, that she also had a reputation for having many casual sexual partners?'

Bob was by now feeling uncomfortable. 'Well, I believe she had a few men friends,' was the best he could do.

Counsel noticeably rolled her eyebrows. 'A few men friends! Not to put too fine a point on it, she was a slut!'

The judge looked as though he was about to intervene, but before he could do so, Ms. Lancaster had swiftly moved on. 'You would have come across the Simpsons together on several occasions, office parties and the like?'

Bob agreed that he would have done.

'And it would be fair to say, wouldn't it, that they always seemed to be happy in each other's company?'

Bob again agreed.

'Despite being married to a libertine and a philanderer, he acted like a good and caring husband?'

'Yes, it appeared like that.' Before Bob had completed his reply, defence counsel had sat down and was looking at her papers.

Bob's articled clerk, Michael Donald, was next in the witness box. He described how he had gone to Beverley's house on the 13th January, after she had again failed to appear at work, and had found that there was no-one at home.

Michael wasn't to escape the attentions of Ms. Lancaster either, however, and was treated with no more respect than his principal had been:

'With her reputation, I don't suppose that you were surprised when you didn't find her at home?'

Michael hesitated, not sure of the right reply.

'Well, let me help you, Mr. Donald. She was what's commonly known as a "tart", and I'm not referring to the local Bakewell delicacy. That's right, isn't it?'

Michael felt himself reddening, with a mixture of anger and embarrassment. 'She was a lovely woman, friendly and easy-going,' was the best he could muster.

'Yes, I'm sure she was,' responded Ms. Lancaster, with a pointed look at the jury.

★★★★★★★★★★★★★★★★★★★★★★★★★★

The evidence of the post-mortem was not challenged, and consisted of a written statement from the pathologist who had conducted it, read to the jury by Tom Edwards. It told of the cause of death being multiple injuries consistent with a fall of eighty to a hundred feet onto bare rocks. There was no evidence of sexual trauma. There was no means of establishing the identity of the deceased at that time, and the massive injuries to the face meant that there could be no meaningful comparison with dental records.

The evidence of identification of the body followed in the person of Inspector Tyzack. He told the jury of Richard Simpson's visit to Bakewell police station on the evening of the 14th January, his account of coming home after a business trip that day, finding that his wife had not been home for two days, and his fears after reading in a local newspaper of the discovery of a woman's body below Curbar Edge. The inspector said that he had been 'a little surprised' that Simpson had not asked more questions about the discovery of the body, even though it was quite apparent that he believed it to be his wife. Inspector Tyzack also told of taking the defendant through to Chesterfield to identify the body and of Simpson's 'low-key' reaction on identifying the woman on the mortuary slab. What was more surprising, however, he said, was the defendant's decision to drive home after the inspector returned him to Bakewell Police Station.

There was no way that the inspector's testimony was going to be left unmolested by Alison Lancaster. She laid into him like 'a terrier snapping at one's heels', Martin Tory thought:

'Isn't it right that next-of-kin and bereaved persons react in different ways when identifying a body in such circumstances, or indeed when they believed that they were going to be asked look at a body which may well turn out to be someone close to them?' she asked.

The inspector agreed.

'So there was really nothing suspicious or sinister about Mr. Simpson's demeanour, either at the police station, or at the mortuary, or afterwards?'

The inspector said he would have to agree with that.

★★★★★★★★★★★★★★★★★★★★★★★★★★★

The day concluded with the evidence of Rex Maitland's conviction at Sheffield Crown Court for an offence of attempted rape, committed on 12th January 1977. There was also a short statement from his victim, Annette Collins, to confirm that the offence was actually committed on the morning of that date in High Bradfield, near Sheffield, and that Maitland had been in her company all that morning. The purpose of this evidence was, of course, to demonstrate that Maitland could not possibly have been responsible for the murder of Beverley Simpson.

CHAPTER SEVENTEEN

July 27th

Martin Tory had contrived to get to court for the third day of the trial, mainly by taking work home the previous day and 'burning the midnight oil'. He had been determined to see that day's evidence because he knew that this was to be the day that Stephanie Winter was due to testify and that her evidence was critical to the success of the prosecution case. Should she fail to turn up, or if she fell apart in the witness box, then the case was likely to founder.

In the advocates' room in the court building, before proceedings for the day started, the prosecution team mulled over the progress of the trial thus far. Brian Cattermole felt the case had gone largely to plan, even though he conceded that the defence had 'scored' one or two points on day two. They had succeeded in blackening Beverley Simpson's character, whilst portraying her husband as a long-suffering martyr. Brian felt that this was always to be expected at this stage in the trial. It was, however, in his view very much a 'two-edged sword'. The jury may loathe the deceased and have a lot of sympathy for Richard Simpson, but all that was going to do was engender a feeling of 'no wonder he killed her'. They may think he is a 'saint', asserted Brian, but she 'would test the patience of a saint'. He also didn't think defence counsel's abrasive approach to cross-examination was helping her client's cause overmuch.

★★★★★★★★★★★★★★★★★★★★★★★★★★

Day three opened with evidence from Beverley's mother, Wendy Driver. She told of the visit to her daughter's home in Bakewell, some days after the funeral. Simpson had not been there but she and her husband were able to enter because they had long been in possession of a key to the front door. They were looking for a brooch belonging to Beverley that had been something of a family heirloom. Simpson had previously agreed that they could have it. They found the brooch, but also came across the greetings cards in a drawer under the double bed in the marital bedroom. They realised the significance of the cards immediately, and had decided that they must be passed to the police. They arranged this through the private investigator, Jim Donegani, whom they knew, and he had advised that this was the correct course.

Mrs. Driver, whilst in the witness box, was shown the two greetings cards, and identified them as the cards she and her husband had found in the matrimonial home. At this point the witness dissolved into tears.

She had kept her composure up to then, but it was plain, even months after the event, that she had not at all come to terms with her daughter's tragic death. Whatever sympathy the jury may have felt for the defendant hitherto, and whatever distaste they might have felt for the lifestyle of the deceased, it was clear from the body language and facial expressions of the jurors that they had been moved by this outpouring of grief on the part of Mrs. Driver.

Defence counsel, probably wisely on this occasion, did not cross-examine the witness.

There then followed a short statement from Jim Donegani relating to passing the greetings cards to Detective Inspector Moore. He knew of the police investigation into Beverley's death and that 'foul play' was suspected, and he therefore realised that the cards may well have been 'of enormous significance'.

★★★★★★★★★★★★★★★★★★★★★★★★★★★

Brian Cattermole informed the judge that the next witness for the Crown was Stephanie Winter. The court usher disappeared into the corridor to call her. In the short interval that ensued, an almost deathly hush had fallen on the courtroom. But Martin sensed there was an atmosphere of anticipation, an atmosphere you could cut with a knife, almost as if heralding the arrival of a celebrity or a royal personage. Then the door opened and the witness entered, followed by the usher, who guided her to the witness box.

This was the first time that Martin had seen Stephanie

Winter, and he could see why Richard Simpson might have been so infatuated with her. She was dressed in a beige trouser suit that was as immaculate as the white silk blouse that she was also wearing. The clothing might have seemed unremarkable on many women, but on Stephanie, when set off by a mane of well-groomed blonde hair, they served to create a picture of supreme elegance. Looking at the jury, it was apparent to Martin that the male members, and indeed some of the females, were in awe of her. She had won over the jury before she had even opened her mouth!

She took the oath and answered Brian's initial few questions in a clear and confident voice. Her facial expression remained neutral. There was no hint of the coquettish smile that she had sported through much of the interview with Alan Woodman.

Stephanie described her first meetings with Richard Simpson at the Armathwaite Hotel, how a relationship had developed and grown into a passionate affair. She told the jury how they spent weekends together, how he rang her every night when they were apart, showered her with expensive gifts, and treated her to short breaks in Paris and London. Before Christmas 1976 they were planning a life together. As far as she was concerned, the only obstacle to this was Richard's mother, who lived with him and suffered from dementia. He had told her very early on that his wife had died from cancer some three years previously. She was asked by prosecuting counsel how they were going to move to a situation where they could live together. Her response was that before that Christmas Simpson had told her that he and his sister had made arrangements for his mother to live in a residential care home, and that the place for her would become available on January 14th 1977. Was she certain that he had spoken of these plans, and was she sure of the date?

'Yes, I am very certain,' she replied. 'I even referred to the date in the birthday card I sent him. It's imprinted on my mind because it was exactly a week after his birthday. I had cancelled the milk and newspapers from that date and was planning to travel to Derbyshire on that day. As far as I was concerned that was to be the first day of our life together.'

Stephanie was then shown the two greetings cards that had already been exhibited in the trial. She identified them as cards she had written and sent to Simpson.

'Did you travel to Bakewell on the 14th January?' she was asked.

She shook her head. 'No. Richard rang me earlier in the week to say that the place for his mother in the home wasn't yet free, and there would be a delay before I could join him.'

'Did you believe him?'

'Yes, I had no reason not to. And I carried on believing him until Sergeant Woodman came to see me in Cockermouth at the end of February.'

'What happened in the weeks between the 14th

January and the end of February?'

'We continued to see each other, in Cockermouth mostly. Not in Bakewell of course. He told me that there was an on-going delay with the room for his mother becoming available, because the refurbishment of the home was taking longer than expected to complete.'

Brian paused for a few seconds, looking down at his papers. Then he looked up at the witness:

'How do you feel about Richard Simpson, now that you know the truth – now you know that there was no dead wife, no mother with dementia, and no place in a residential home?'

Stephanie also paused before replying. She wistfully shook her head.

'At first when I found out I was very angry. I had been deceived, and lied to from the very beginning of our relationship. But after a while the anger disappeared. I realised that he had probably loved me and genuinely wanted us to be together. He was trapped in his own lies. He had dug himself into a deep hole and did not know how to dig himself out without resorting to extreme measures. In truth I now feel sorry for him.'

Brian nodded slowly, looked at the jury, and then sat down.

Defence counsel rose to her feet and pulled her gown back over her shoulders. She stared intently at the witness. Perhaps she paused too long before asking the first question in cross-examination, because the judge took the opportunity to intervene:

'I think that's enough for today. We'll resume at 10.30 tomorrow morning.'

CHAPTER EIGHTEEN

July 28th

Martin Tory had decided he couldn't justify any more time away from his other duties, but, in order to allow him to continue watching the trial, he had taken a couple of days leave. He hadn't told his wife that he had done this, as she would not have been too pleased that he had sacrificed two days of his annual holiday for this purpose. He was confident, however, that she would not find out.

He encountered Alison Lancaster QC striding along the concourse inside the court building. She was clearly particularly bad-tempered that morning, complaining loudly to her entourage of junior counsel and solicitor's clerk about the way that the judge had undermined the impact of her cross-examination by cutting her off just as she was going to ask her first question of the witness. 'The effect will be lost,' she was saying. 'She'll have had time to gather herself.'

In the advocate's room, the conversation amongst the

prosecution team was that Stephanie Winters, thus far anyway, had been an exemplary witness.

Alan Woodman and the two detective constables, as witnesses still to give evidence, were not present at this meeting, but Martin knew they would be anxious to know how she had presented in the witness box. Martin found them drinking coffee in the room set aside for police officers. He was aware that he shouldn't be talking to them about what had gone on so far in the trial, but when Alan Woodman looked at him quizzically, Martin smiled broadly and nodded his head. The silent message was received and understood.

★★★★★★★★★★★★★★★★★★★★★★★★★★

Day four of the trial. Alison Lancaster stood up, a little apologetically it seemed, as if she was afraid that the judge might once again step in and deprive her of the chance to ask a 'devastating' opening question in cross-examination. She soon regathered her normal demeanour, however, and set about trying to unsettle the witness.

'Before you met Richard Simpson, you were a lonely middle-aged spinster, were you not?' was her opening gambit to Stephanie Winter.

If she expected the witness to crumple in the face of this question, then she was disappointed in the result. Stephanie met her head-on:

'Middle-aged, yes. A spinster, no. I believe a spinster is

a woman who has never been married. I am a widow. My husband died after a road accident some years ago. Lonely, never. I have friends, male and female.'

Counsel tried again. 'But lonely enough to hang around in bars, looking for men to pick up?'

'I think you are describing a prostitute. I have met men in bars, even slept with some of them, but I have never been paid for it.'

'Then how would you describe the nature of your regular unaccompanied visits to places like the Armathwaite Hotel?'

'I was single and comfortably off,' replied Stephanie. 'Quite simply I enjoyed the luxury of occasional weekends spent in a country house hotel.'

Counsel wouldn't let go. 'But the real purpose of these visits was to find a man, wasn't it?'

'I wouldn't deny that I am fond of male company and that I hadn't had a satisfactory relationship since my husband had been killed. But if you are suggesting that I was some kind of sexual predator, then you are wrong. If I met a man I liked, and he liked me, and something developed, so be it. But it would have to be a mutual thing. I would never pressurise any man to go to bed with me.'

Sitting at the back of court, Martin recalled that Alan Woodman had told him that Stephanie Winter had indeed described herself to him in those words – a 'sexual predator', had said in terms that she was hungry for male company, and that she had set out to 'seduce' Richard Simpson. When she had dictated her witness statement, however, she had drawn back from such extreme claims. Defence counsel may have been not too far from the truth in her challenging assertions, but clearly the witness was not about to give her the satisfaction of portraying her as a 'scarlet woman'.

Undaunted, defence counsel pressed on. 'It's right, isn't it, that when you saw Mr. Simpson in the residents' bar of the Armathwaite Hotel, you approached him and offered to buy him a drink, rather than the other way round?'

'Yes, that's right. I saw him and admit I was attracted to him from the off and I spoke to him and, yes, I offered to buy him a drink. But I am a confident and, some would say, a direct person, and I have never believed that it is wrong for a woman to make overtures to a man, rather than sitting there and waiting for him to do it.'

'Your "directness" went to the extent of seducing him on the next occasion you met him.'

'No, I didn't seduce him,' Stephanie replied. 'I admit I may have made most of the running, but he didn't seem to have much of an idea how to progress things. I invited him to my room for a "nightcap" and he came. He didn't need any encouragement. Remember that he had already lied about his marital status. Both of us knew that he wasn't coming to my room for a glass of whisky. To put it crudely, he was definitely up for it.'

Several of the male members of the jury smirked at this remark, although it seemed likely that the witness hadn't intended it to be taken that way. Or had she? thought Martin. It would certainly accord with Alan Woodman's description of the brazen way in which the woman had talked in his interview with her.

Perhaps anticipating the next question from defence counsel, the witness went on:

'I also accept that I took the lead in our lovemaking. He came across as a novice. I assumed it was because he was out of practice since the "death" of his wife. He told me that she was ill for a couple of years before her death and had lost any interest in the physical side of their marriage. Anyway, he soon picked things up again and we never looked back after that.'

'Yes, and that was all your relationship was about as far as he was concerned – just sex?'

'Not at all,' retorted Stephanie. 'From early on he made it plain that he wanted us to have a life together. He'd already invented a dead wife and a sick mother, and then he rang me every night when we weren't together, showered me with gifts, flowers, holidays. He even bought me a car. I have no doubt that he was in love with me. It was he who started the discussion about how we could live together. He was going to get his mother into residential care. And he was going to sell his house and move away, as the home in Bakewell had too many sad memories for him and he wanted us to have a new life elsewhere.'

'This is just fantasy on your part, isn't it?' counsel suggested. 'You were lonely, desperate for a lasting relationship, and you were badgering him to make arrangements for you to be together?'

'No. He even gave me that date when I could move to his home in Bakewell. That's why I put the "14th" in his birthday card. This was to be the start of our life together. I got that date from him. I didn't pluck it out of the air.'

'Well, that's exactly what I am suggesting you did do. You see, he will tell the court that he never told you that you could come to Bakewell then, but simply that his mother would be moving out on or about that date. It was wishful thinking on your part?'

'No, we agreed that I could move in then. I had even made arrangements to let my house.'

'But, we know now that there was no way you could move to Bakewell then. It would have been madness on his part to invite you when he had a wife living there.'

'I agree,' said the witness. 'It would have been madness. But then I think he had already planned to dispose of his wife.'

'Even if that was the case, the 14th would have been a non-starter for you to be there, as he would have had to arrange a funeral, and surely there would have been a lot of people locally who would have put you wise about his wife and her very recent death?'

'Yes, I realise that. But I think he had told so many lies that he had ceased to think things through. He would have had to put me off travelling down to Bakewell, and, when it came to it, that's exactly what he did.'

Listening to the cross-examination, Martin Tory could see what defence counsel was trying to achieve. She was attempting to show the jury that Stephanie Winter was a domineering temptress, who had seduced a weak man, an 'innocent abroad', and, desperate herself for a permanent relationship, was trying to bully him into arranging his affairs so they could live together as man and wife. It was a risky strategy in some ways, for if she succeeded, the jury could possibly conclude that Simpson had indeed succumbed completely to her persuasive 'charms' and was prepared to resort to a desperate course of action to be with his lover. So, at the same time, counsel was seeking to demonstrate that Simpson was obsessed with the witness only in a physical sense, and had no real intention of committing to a life together. He was, in other words, only in it for the sex! But it was surely difficult for the jury to appreciate the distinction that counsel was seeking to draw?

Stephanie Winter, of course, was having none of that. She had conceded in her evidence that she might have 'led from the front' to begin with, but she had made it fairly plain that Simpson had quickly bought into the relationship, literally in fact, and that their feelings for each other, and their desire to share their lives, was entirely mutual. Martin recalled how Alan Woodman had told him that his impression of Winter was that, underneath the hard, composed exterior, there was a vulnerability, a 'neediness'. Perhaps, therefore, one could find credence in the line being pursued by Alison Lancaster?

But how would the jury view the situation? Would they accept Stephanie Winter's version of events? Martin had observed them carefully during the course of her evidence. It was difficult to tell, but his impression was the men on the jury were totally smitten. No doubt some of them were fantasising about being seduced by this elegant and sensual woman, and she had them 'eating out of her hand'. By the same token there was no obvious indication that the female members were outraged or appalled by her directness and transparency about the way she had initiated the conversation and then the bedroom encounter with the defendant. But then there was something quite disarming and refreshing about her candour and composure in the witness box. Martin would not have been surprised to hear that the jury had found her evidence completely compelling.

★★★★★★★★★★★★★★★★★★★★★★★★★★★

Alan Woodman's evidence began after lunch on the fourth day of the trial. In reply to questions from Brian Cattermole, Alan gave an overview of the police investigation up to the point of the charging of Richard Simpson. He included in his outline the abortive prosecution of Rex Maitland.

When he had finished, Alison Lancaster was on her feet with alacrity.

'So,' she began, 'when you first clapped eyes on the sudden death report into Beverley Simpson's death, you were quite happy to regard her death as an accident?'

'Yes, that's how it appeared at first glance. But it was only a glance at this stage, as I was pre-occupied with my own involvement in the William Hughes case. You could say we had bigger fish to fry at this point.'

'Maybe,' counsel went on, 'but then everyone else who had anything to do with the finding of the body also were satisfied that this was an accident – the police officers at the scene of the death, the mountain rescue, the paramedics, the pathologist?'

'Yes,' said Alan, 'that's how it appeared to them all – at that point.'

'But then, five days after the discovery of the body, you suddenly leap from seeing it as an accident to launching a murder inquiry! Why was that?'

Alan explained that it was learning the identity of the deceased that made him think that he ought to have a closer look at the evidence surrounding the death. He knew of the deceased's reputation locally as a woman who had had many affairs with men, and his intelligence was that some of her former 'suitors' had parted company with her in acrimonious circumstances. His 'policeman's instinct' told him that there might be more to the death than meets the eye. He had looked closely at the evidence relating to the finding of the body, and also what the defendant had told Inspector Tyzack about his wife's movements that morning, and he had become convinced that 'this was no accident'.

'It didn't stack up. She was dressed completely inappropriately for the weather conditions, she had no warm clothing to change into, she had no money in her possession, no vehicle, and no means of getting to or from the scene without the involvement of a third party. And given what Mr. Simpson had said, there was clearly someone else with her at the beginning, someone who should have been taking her home, someone who had left the scene. It was plain to me that there had been foul play.'

'But it's right, isn't it, Detective Sergeant, that no-one has seen any third party with the deceased at the scene or prior to her death that morning?'

Alan agreed that was the case.

'So your conclusion that there was someone else present is compete speculation, is it not?'

'No, its logical deduction. I think it's the only conclusion that can be drawn from the evidence.'

Alan was now being pressed hard by defence counsel. 'But nonetheless you cannot possibly completely rule out that the deceased was alone immediately before her death, and, indeed, that her death was an accident.

Something that everyone seems to have regarded it as, until you decided otherwise?'

Alan shook his head. 'I believe it's highly unlikely to have been an accident.'

Alison Lancaster was now warming to her task, perhaps sensing that she had found a loophole in the prosecution case.

'Well, let's just assume for the moment, Sergeant Woodman, that your "logical deduction" is correct and that there was someone with Beverley Simpson at the material time. Even in that situation you can't rule out an accident.'

Alan shook his head again. 'I don't follow your argument,' he said.

'Well, let me put this scenario to you. The deceased was climbing solo, without a partner or a rope. She slipped or lost her grip on a hold, and fell from a height to the rocks below. The third party, observing this, panicked, or simply didn't want to get involved, decided she was beyond help, and left the scene, taking her rucksack and other clothing with him, or her. Not very Christian, inhuman in fact. But you can't rule that out, can you?'

Alan thought for a moment. 'No, I suppose you can't, but I would find that scenario too improbable to be accepted.'

'Improbable but not impossible!' This was clearly meant to be a rhetorical statement, and counsel moved on, not waiting for any response from the witness. There was also a sideways glance at the jury, with just a hint of triumphalism about it.

'Well, let's go a stage further and take the prosecution's allegation that, not only was Beverley murdered, but she was murdered by Richard Simpson. It's right, isn't it, Sergeant, that there is not a scrap of evidence from any witness that the defendant was with the deceased on Curbar Edge that day or, indeed, anywhere near the place?'

'No witness evidence, no,' Alan agreed.

'Nor is there any such evidence that his car was in any car park near the crag?'

'No.'

'So I wonder why we are here, Detective Sergeant Woodman. There is no cogent evidence that a) this was not an accident, or b) if it was murder, that Richard Simpson was responsible.'

'The case is based on circumstantial evidence,' Alan pointed out. 'And we say strong circumstantial evidence.'

'You might say that, officer, but whether it is or not is a matter for the jury,' insisted counsel.

'Yes, I would agree with that.' Alan pointedly looked in the direction of the jury.

★★★★★★★★★★★★★★★★★★★★★★★★★★

Martin Tory had sat through the cross-examination of

Alan Woodman, and despite the officer's last retort to counsel, which at least had the merit of reminding the jury that the outcome of the case was their decision and not that of anyone else, he felt quite despondent when it was over and the jury were dismissed for the day. The defence had scored a good few points that afternoon, and Martin was beginning to wonder if the prosecution case was fatally wounded.

To his surprise, however, Brian Cattermole did not share his pessimism. When he met with prosecution counsel in the advocates' room at the end of the day, and after defence counsel had departed, he found that Brian was quite sanguine about the way that the case had gone in court.

'With a circumstantial case you've got to expect that sort of questioning. The defence are bound to milk the situation that there are no eye-witnesses to the event, and that the possibility of accident or murder by another cannot be ruled out. Alan is back in the witness box tomorrow and he's going to get more of the same. But that's going to be the high point of the defence case. I'm quite confident that when we get Simpson in the box, and he's going to have to give evidence, then the jury are going to see just how strong and compelling the circumstantial evidence is.'

CHAPTER NINETEEN
July 29th

The cross-examination of Alan Woodman continued on the morning of the fifth day of the trial. Defence counsel was now probing him about the police investigation that led to the arrest of Rex Maitland.

'As I understand it, Sergeant,' she commenced, 'the investigation was targeted at those known to be former boyfriends of the deceased, and then specifically at those who might have been rejected by her or who had parted company from her in acrimonious circumstances?'

'Yes, that was the line of enquiry we were pursuing'.

'And that line of enquiry eventually threw up Rex Maitland?'

'Yes.'

'And Richard Simpson was never considered as a suspect at this stage?'

'No.'

'You and your colleagues were convinced of Maitland's guilt?'

'Yes. We found Beverley's rucksack in his van, he had no coherent alibi for that morning, and ultimately of course he made a confession.'

'Ah yes, a "confession" that was obtained in oppressive circumstances and after the bizarre intervention of an officer who was not connected to the investigation. Not a very clever or professional state of affairs, Sergeant, was it?'

'I would have to agree with that,' was Alan's response.

'And as it turned out you had got it completely wrong.'

'Yes, Rex Maitland in fact had a cast-iron alibi.'

Alison Lancaster looked at the jury, and then back to the witness. 'Not to put too fine a point on it, Sergeant, this was a quite inept investigation.'

'Mistakes were made, but we felt we had a strong case against him at the time. He never actually came forward with his alibi, of course, and we only learnt of it by chance.'

'Isn't it right, Sergeant, that there were many other men in the locality, or, indeed, elsewhere, that you could and should have interviewed, men who had had an affair with the deceased?'

'It's quite possible that there were others,' said Alan,' but we only spoke to those where we had at least some information or evidence that they had been involved with her.'

'Indeed, one or two senior police officers, and also a senior lawyer in the County Prosecuting Officer's office?'

'I know nothing of that,' was Alan's reply. 'There were always rumours, but if we interviewed everyone who was rumoured to have had any sort of relationship with Beverley Simpson, then we would still be at it now.'

Martin noticed that Ronnie Fox was not in his customary position at the back of court that morning. Had he had an inkling of what was to come out?

Defence counsel paused and was sifting through the papers in front of her on the lectern. She then looked at Alan again:

'Does the name David Syrett mean anything to you?' she asked.

Alan hesitated. He hadn't expected this name to crop up. He wondered where the questioning was going.

'Yes,' he said eventually. 'He was a local man who was convicted some years ago of the manslaughter of a woman on the moors between Baslow and Chesterfield, not far in fact from Pottery Cottage, where William Hughes committed four murders in January this year. I think he was sentenced to eight years imprisonment.'

'Were you aware that he had been released from prison

recently?'

'No, I wasn't.'

'Were you also aware that he had had a brief relationship with the deceased not long before this offence, and that during that time he had been violent towards her?'

Alan again admitted that he was not.

'Then you will also have been unaware that on the 11th January this year, the same David Syrett was staying at the Chequers Inn at Froggatt, less than a mile, as the crow flies, from where the deceased's body was found?'

At this point Brian Cattermole leaned over towards his opponent. 'Is there going to be any evidence of this?' he asked, *sotto voce*.

His opponent simply nodded, and pressed on.

'I take it, Sergeant, that the answer to the last question is "Yes"?'

'It is.'

'Clearly, if you had been aware of this information, then you would have been investigating Syrett as a potential suspect?'

'Yes, of course.'

At this point defence counsel sat down. Cross-examination of Alan Woodman was over.

Martin Tory had initially regarded Alison Lancaster

QC as unimpressive, full of noise and bluster but with no great substance to her performance, and her cross-examination of Stephanie Winter had not changed his view at all. But now she had gone up in his estimation. She had exploited the obvious weaknesses in the prosecution case, but more than this, by stopping her cross-examination of Alan Woodman where she had, she had shown that she was very tactically aware. Having scored a number of points for the defence, she had not gone on to quiz Alan about the actual investigation as it related to Richard Simpson. The prosecution were on much stronger ground here and it would have given Alan the opportunity to emphasise the strength of the circumstantial evidence against Simpson, highlighting the greetings cards, the insurance policy and so on. This would have detracted from the high ground counsel had managed to reach in the cross-examination. Her exit strategy, Martin thought, was timed to perfection.

★★★★★★★★★★★★★★★★★★★★★★★★★★

The rest of the day was taken up with evidence that was agreed or not tested by cross-examination. Statements were read from officers who had recovered the documents from the defendant's house and from his head office in Derby, and also from persons who could show the provenance of those documents – bank officials, insurance company staff, and people from Simpson's office who dealt with his travelling expense claims. DC Forrester gave evidence of what the defendant had said in his interviews with the police. These were not challenged: not surprisingly as he had made no startling admissions.

The prosecution case was brought to a conclusion shortly before 3 pm. Although it was still early, there was no way that the judge was going to allow the defence to begin its case at that point. The weekend beckoned, and the judge indicated that it was a convenient and logical place to call a halt. The jury were released until Monday morning, the judge warning them again about not discussing the case with family or friends over the weekend.

As soon as the judge had left the courtroom, Brian Cattermole called Martin over, and also DS Woodman and DC Forrester who were at the back of the court.

'I know the sun's not over the yardarm yet,' he announced, 'but let's go back to chambers for a beer and a chinwag.'

★★★★★★★★★★★★★★★★★★★★★★★★★★★

Fifteen minutes later, Brian, Martin and the two officers were sat round a conference table in the QC's chambers, Tom Edwards, a reluctant 'go-for' if ever there was one, having been despatched to fetch bottles of beer from the fridge in the kitchen.

Once Tom had returned and drinks had been poured, Brian handed round copies of a document he had been given by defence counsel at the end of that day's proceedings. It was a witness statement by one Norman Smith, landlord of the Chequers Inn,

Froggatt, a village just down the road from Curbar.

Brian explained that what Mr. Smith was saying in his statement was that he had known David Syrett for twenty years, and knew that he had recently served a prison sentence for manslaughter of a woman at Holymoorside. He went on to state that Syrett had stopped at the inn on the nights of the 10th and 11th January 1977 and had left about 8 am on the 12th January, having paid for his stay in cash. He had told Smith that the car he was driving belonged to his mother, and that he was in the area 'looking up old friends', persons he had not seen for more than eight years.

Brian said that the defence were proposing to call Mr. Smith to give evidence, no doubt with a view 'to muddying the waters further' and showing that there was someone else at large at the material time who possibly had a motive and an opportunity, and even a propensity, to cause harm to Beverley Simpson.

'No doubt another red herring,' Brian continued, 'but one we need to kill off, if we can.'

He looked towards Alan Woodman and DC Forrester, who, in turn, looked at each other. The junior officer anticipated the next question:

'I wasn't doing anything else this weekend, I'll see if I can track down Syrett. Hopefully he'll have an alibi for the morning of the 12th!'

Brian looked relieved. 'Good man,' he said. 'We'll all

be in your debt if you can get a result with that.'

Putting the witness statement aside, Brian paused, put his hands behind his head, and then went on:

'I think we've come through this week okay, and as I said yesterday I have no qualms with the points scored by the defence in cross-examination. I'm confident that Simpson will probably be, in fact, the best witness we've got, better even that Stephanie Winter, as excellent as she was.'

Martin asked if Brian was confident that the defence were going to allow Simpson to actually go into the witness box. There was no obligation for him to do so, and it might be the case that Alison Lancaster believed she would be in a stronger position not to call Simpson to testify and subject him to some difficult cross-examination.

'I think he's got to give evidence,' replied Brian. 'He's got a lot of explaining to do, and the jury inevitably are going to think he's got something to hide if he doesn't. The clincher is, in any event, that Alison Lancaster wouldn't have served Smith's statement on us and been talking about calling him to give evidence if there was no intention of putting Simpson in the witness box. By the way, before you ask, the fact that she has served this statement tells me that she will not be inviting the judge to throw the case out at this stage on the basis that the defendant has no case to answer. It would be a loser anyway, given the circumstantial evidence.'

The conference then broke up. There was a noticeable whiff of optimism in the air as the team bade each other 'have a good weekend'. For DC Forrester and Brian Cattermole, however, it was not going to be a restful one.

CHAPTER TWENTY

August 1st

The hot, even oppressive, weather that had characterised the last week of July 1977, continued into August. Martin Tory, who had managed to negotiate another day away from his normal duties, found Brian Cattermole in the advocates' room at just after 9.30 am, still in open-necked court shirt, delaying as long as possible the moment when he would have to put on his wing-collar and tabs.

'Any sign of DC Forrester?' he enquired earnestly.

Martin agreed to go and seek him out and also find a conference room where the team could meet before court started. He found Alan Woodman and the DC in the police room, and the expressions on their faces when they greeted him were clear indications that they were the bearers of good tidings.

A little later, in a conference room in the court building, DC Forrester handed round copies of two witness statements he had obtained over the weekend.

One was from the Reverend George Inskip, the other from David Syrett.

The officer explained that on Saturday he had contacted the prison in which Syrett had recently been held, and had managed to acquire the address of his next-of-kin, his mother. The mother lived in Burton-on-Trent, and the officer had hastened there, found the address, and then Mrs. Syrett when she had returned from Saturday morning shopping. The mother told DC Forrester that her son had lived there 'on and off' since his release from prison in early January 1977, but while he was in prison 'he had found God' and was spending more and more time in a religious retreat in Derbyshire. The pastor at the retreat had visited her son regularly in prison, and she recalled that in early January he had borrowed her car, and some money, and had set off to the retreat, but intending to look up some old acquaintances on the way. She said that he had more or less taken permanent possession of the car, and had not repaid the debt. She did have the address of the retreat and was able to give the details to the officer.

The retreat was in Carsington, about 30 miles south of Bakewell, and it was to there that DC Forrester drove after leaving Burton-on-Trent. He found it, not without some difficulty. It consisted of a rambling, rather decaying Edwardian mansion surrounded by several acres of farmland and market gardens. The building itself had been crudely converted into a number of flats and meeting rooms. The officer found the pastor, the Reverend George Inskip, in an office on the ground floor. He wore no clerical garb, but was dressed in jeans and a T-shirt. He explained to DC Forrester that the organisation he ran, known as Bedford Farm, was a religious retreat. It was available only to practising Christians, and provided an existence removed from the stresses of normal life. Those who were accepted into its bosom were provided with food and accommodation in return for working on the farm and the market gardens which formed part of the estate. They were also expected to attend the twice-daily religious services run by Inskip and to surrender any income or capital they might accrue from any source. It was in effect a monastery without the monastic garments.

The pastor said that he had 'recruited' Syrett when he was a serving prisoner, and now he had been a member of the sect since the previous January. Inskip kept a diary, to which he now referred, and he was able to tell DC Forrester that Syrett's first day at Bedford Farm was 12th January, and that he had arrived there in time for the first devotions of the day at 9.30 am. The pastor agreed to make a witness statement recording these details.

A little later DC Forrester tracked down Syrett himself, who was working in the gardens. Syrett confirmed that he had set off from the Chequers Inn at just after 8.00 am on the 12th January and had driven directly to Carsington. He had paid for his stay at the pub with the cash he had borrowed from his mother. He had been in the area, 'looking up old friends', people he had not seen since he had been imprisoned, and who he probably would not see again once he had joined the retreat. When asked by the officer about Beverley Simpson, he stated that he had known her and had had a relationship with her six or seven years ago, but he had not seen her since, and as they had parted on 'bad terms' he had had no intention of seeking her out. He agreed that on one occasion he had been violent towards her, but 'all that' was 'behind him now'. He was 'a very different man' since his conversion to Christianity whilst he was in prison.

DC Forrester was of the opinion that Syrett was being truthful. In any event, if the times given in the statements of Norman Smith and the pastor were anything like accurate, it would have been quite impossible for Syrett to have gone to Bakewell after leaving the Chequers Inn, picked up Beverley, driven her to Curbar, killed her, and then driven down to Carsington, a distance of about 40 miles, much of it on minor roads.

Brian Cattermole nodded vigorously. 'Yes, I think that's another red herring we can lay to rest,' he asserted.

★★★★★★★★★★★★★★★★★★★★★★★★★★

Brian provided copies of the statements of Syrett and Inskip to Alison Lancaster before the court hearing resumed that morning. She read them thoughtfully. 'Are these men available to give evidence?' she asked.

'Yes, given notice,' Brian replied. He wasn't in fact sure how much notice they would need to attend court, but he wasn't about to let his opponent think that they might be unwilling to attend.

When the hearing began, Alison asked the judge for a short adjournment, so that she could 'discuss something that had just arisen with the defendant'. The judge was more than happy to acquiesce.

Ten minutes later, she re-appeared and informed Brian that the two witnesses were not required. Nor would she be calling Norman Smith to testify.

'All right,' said Brian, 'let's scotch all three witnesses, but the jury will need to be told somehow that they should ignore the references to David Syrett that had been made in the cross-examination of Detective Sergeant Woodman. In fact I think you should draft a form of words to the effect that Syrett couldn't have been at Curbar Edge that morning, I'll sign it and it can go before the jury as a formal admission of facts.'

'Agreed,' was the response.

★★★★★★★★★★★★★★★★★★★★★★★★★★

Fifteen minutes after that conversation between counsel, Richard Simpson was being sworn as a witness. Brian Cattermole had been right when he had predicted that a) defence counsel would not be asking the judge to dismiss the case at that stage, and b) Simpson would be giving evidence on his own behalf.

Prompted by his barrister, Simpson told the jury about his work and his marriage. He was a sales and marketing executive for an electronics firm based in Derby, but which had branches throughout the north of England and customers all over the country, and in Northern Ireland and southern Scotland. The nature of his employment meant that he had to travel widely, visiting branch offices and actual and potential customers. Mainly his travelling had been in the north of England, although this had extended, after his wife's death, to Scotland and Northern Ireland. He would often have been away for 'days at a time', and when he was at home, his wife was not always there, as her own leisure pursuits often kept her away from the house as well.

He described how he had met Beverley about eight years ago in a pub in Bakewell. They had married about eighteen months later. They had got on well before this, but he realised that they had little in common and their characters were very different. He was quiet and reserved and had only a few friends, all male; she was lively, extremely gregarious, and had numerous friends of both sexes. He had proposed to her because he was aware that all his friends were getting married, one by one, and he didn't want to be left 'alone and high and dry'. Although he was fond of her, and they enjoyed each other's company, he knew it was no 'love match', and they both quickly realised after the wedding that as a marriage, it was not going to succeed. There was 'no spark'. The physical side of their marriage had 'never really got off the ground' and Beverley had made it plain fairly early on that she derived no satisfaction or pleasure from being with just one man. She 'got her kicks' from 'playing the field', and didn't regard her marriage vows as in any way binding. Albeit reluctantly at first, Simpson said he had agreed that their relationship should be 'an open one' and that each should be 'free to pursue their own love interests'.

In time he said that he found that the arrangement suited him. He derived much satisfaction from his work and he could be away from home for several nights without feeling guilty, and could seek 'liaisons' of his own without his conscience being troubled and without 'fear of discovery'. Over the last five years he had had occasional affairs with women from work or who he had met in hotel bars. Her emphasised that these were far from numerous. He was not 'in the same league' as his wife. He was very aware from one source or another that she had had 'countless' affairs with many men, ranging from 'one-night stands' to short-term relationships of no more than a few days. She had set out to 'play the field' and was succeeding.

Asked if he knew who these men were, Simpson stated that he had heard that they were mainly local persons, from Bakewell and the surrounding area, men she had met in pubs or at parties. He also knew that she had had affairs with some of her climbing partners. He had also heard rumours that she had been with one or two professional people, including a senior prosecutor, and high-ranking police officers.

Counsel asked him why he hadn't sought a divorce from his wife. His reply to this was that he had become accustomed to the arrangement. He was unhappy about his wife's promiscuity, but, at the same time, their lack of 'togetherness' suited him. Moreover, despite the situation, they had always got on well, and remained 'good friends'. When the opportunity presented itself, they would go out together for meals or for a drink. Although he had no interest in rock climbing, he would also occasionally accompany her on local climbing trips if she had no climbing partner, and would 'belay' her from the bottom of the climb. She was an obsessive climber, and was constantly pushing herself to do harder and harder 'routes'.

He was asked how she dressed when rock-climbing. She had proper climbing shoes, he said, but would otherwise wear just jeans and a T-shirt in summer, and the same in winter plus a jumper or a light cagoule. She would also take a small cylindrical rucksack which would contain spare or warm clothing, and food and drink. He had never seen her without a helmet when she was climbing. However, more recently she had started climbing alone, without a partner or someone to hold the end of the rope. It may well have been that in these circumstances she would not bother with a helmet, as a helmet would probably not have made much difference if she had fallen from any height.

Simpson then described his first meetings with Stephanie Winter, and how their relationship developed. He had met her in the residents' bar of the Armathwaite Hall Hotel near Bassenthwaite in the Lake District. This was a place he stopped at occasionally when his work travels took him to Carlisle or the north-west, but not always as it was rather expensive. He had noticed her sitting in the bar, reading a newspaper, but he had decided that she was 'out of his league' and it had therefore never occurred to him to initiate any conversation with her. She was expensively dressed, very elegant, and extremely attractive. She was not likely to be interested in a 'glorified sales rep' he decided. Much to his surprise, however, she came over, sat down and initiated a conversation. She offered to buy him a drink. He was quite overawed by her, but managed to compose himself sufficiently to decline her offer and issue the same invitation to her. She graciously accepted and he bought her a gin and tonic. She was a great conversationalist and a 'very good listener'. Soon he felt very much at ease with her, and by the end of the evening he was 'enraptured'. They parted company, but, learning that she would be at the Armathwaite the following weekend, he invented a fictitious business trip that, by chance, would bring him into the area again then. They agreed to resume their acquaintanceship then.

The following weekend, he said, their relationship went up a level. At the end of the Sunday evening, she invited him to her room 'for a nightcap'. He knew that this was a euphemism, and this was confirmed when she opened the door to him, wearing a thin dressing-gown and, clearly, nothing much underneath. He was nervous. The lack of intimacy with his wife, and the unsatisfactory nature of his occasional extramarital affairs, had left him quite inexperienced in sexual matters. Basically, he said, she carried on from where she had started in their short acquaintanceship, leading from the front. She 'made all the running, I just followed her instructions'. She was clearly very experienced and accomplished in the sexual arts. He was astonished at how little he knew and how much he learnt then, and again in the morning, after he had spent the night in her bed.

They went their separate ways after breakfast, but he knew they had become an 'item'. He had become infatuated with this elegant, glamorous woman. So desirous was he of continuing their relationship, that he had 'obliterated' his marriage, telling her that his wife had died three years ago. Furthermore, to safeguard the lie and to prevent her discovering the truth by visiting his home, he had also told her that he was the carer for his elderly mother who suffered from dementia.

From that point their 'affair' blossomed. He went to her home in Cockermouth at weekends. He showered her with gifts, including a sports car on which he was making the hire purchase payments, and treated her to a weekend in Paris and another in London. He rang her every night that they were apart. He knew that he was living beyond his means, but he didn't care.

Counsel inquired as to whether he thought Stephanie had the same intensity of feeling about him as he had for her. He believed that she did, but there was one important difference. He felt that, underneath the calm sophistication, she was quite 'needy'. By this he meant that she needed a relationship, and a permanent relationship, with a man. She made it plain fairly early on that she wanted them to live together, as man and wife. Although he very much wanted the same outcome, he knew that it couldn't happen. He couldn't risk her finding out the truth about his domestic situation; nor could he 'ditch' Beverley, as, perversely, he knew she wouldn't tolerate him being involved in a permanent relationship with another woman, any more than she, herself, would ever form such a relationship with another. She would divorce him and 'take him to the cleaners'. He would be financially ruined, and wouldn't be able any more to lead the lifestyle to which he had become accustomed with Stephanie.

By December 1976, Simpson said, he was coming under ever-increasing pressure from Stephanie to make arrangements for them to live together. He was in a very difficult situation and he had no idea how he was going to resolve it. To 'buy himself time', however, he told her that he and his sister had found their mother a place in a residential home, a place which would become available in mid- January. He may have mentioned the 14th January as the actual date. He was adamant, however, that he had never led

Stephanie to believe that she could come to Bakewell at that time. She had jumped to the wrong conclusion in that respect. It would have been madness to allow her to come to his home at that time, a time when his wife was very much alive, even though his mother would not have been there.

How then, his counsel inquired, did he deal with the situation as the 14th January approached? Simpson's response was that he had contacted Stephanie at the beginning of that week and informed her that the care home was being refurbished and that the place for his mother would not become available for another month. She was clearly disappointed but appeared to be convinced by this latest lie. And then, within two days of this phone call, his wife was dead. He was 'devastated' by this, but had to pull himself together to organise the funeral. He was still ringing Stephanie every night but he had to find another excuse for not being able to see her for a week or so. He once again was forced to lie to her, telling her that his sister had gone ski-ing and that he had to stay at home to look after his mother. Stephanie again appeared to accept the falsehood, as she never challenged it.

How did things develop after that? he was asked. His response was that he carried on going to Stephanie's home from the end of the January, or meeting her at Armathwaite. He also continued to prevaricate about the place in the care home, pushing its availability further into the future. The difference now, however, was that he was under less pressure. He was able to tell his lover that he had put the house on the market and was intending to find a home for them in another area. This was in fact true, as he had decided that Bakewell held too many sad memories for him. Stephanie was 'over the moon' about this and stopped pressing him about when the care home place would become free. His intention now was to move well away from Bakewell and invite Stephanie to join him. He didn't need to be that close to his main office and there was much less chance of his 'getting found out' about Beverley and his mother. Then, of course, he was arrested.

Alison Lancaster then asked Simpson to explain about the insurance policy that had been taken out just before Christmas 1976. This was mainly Beverley's idea, he said. She was 'pushing the boundaries' as far as her climbing was concerned, and the risk of serious injury or death was increasing. She wanted to ensure that their mortgage would be paid off 'if the worst came to the worst'.

Counsel then asked him to recount his movements on the day of her death, 12th January. There was a pause, during which the defendant appeared to be gathering his thoughts. He accepted now, he said, that he could not have left home before 10.00 am and that Beverley had gone by this time. His recollection now was that she had still been in the house when he got up that morning and he was aware that she was preparing for a climbing trip. He must have been in the house when she was picked up by her climbing partner, but he didn't see that person. Perhaps he was in the bathroom at the material time?

'Did you go with your wife to Curbar Edge that morning?' counsel asked.

'No, I didn't.'

'Did you kill your wife?'

'No, I did not,' was the emphatic reply.

★★★★★★★★★★★★★★★★★★★★★★★★★★★

Brian Cattermole's cross-examination of Richard Simpson began immediately after the lunch adjournment. It is sometimes the way of counsel to start their questioning of a defendant with something unexpected, in an attempt to unsettle the witness at the beginning of his 'ordeal'. It was Brian's way.

'Do you believe in coincidences?' was his opening gambit.

The defendant was clearly surprised by this question, and paused to swallow before replying.

'Yes ... up to a point.'

Martin Tory thought this was masterful. It was almost a 'no-win' situation for the witness. He couldn't answer 'No' without undermining his whole case. But in replying 'Yes' he had to be careful. If he was too positive, he may come across as flippant or implausible. If he was hesitant, he was providing ammunition for the prosecution. By qualifying his answer in the manner that he had, Simpson was indeed already highlighting the weaknesses in his evidence, that his case was based on the occurrence of more than one coincidence. Right from the start of cross-examination Brian was strongly reminding the jury of how fallible Simpson's story was.

'Because if the jury are to believe your evidence, then they are going to have to accept the existence of more than one coincidence. Isn't that the case?'

'Yes, I suppose so,' was the reply from the witness.

Having made his point, Brian moved on, although he would be returning to the 'coincidence' issue later.

'Mr. Simpson, its right, is it not, that your wife was extremely promiscuous?'

'I wouldn't disagree with that.'

'One shouldn't speak ill of the dead, but, in fact, to borrow your counsel's terms, she was a "slut" and a "tart"?'

'Yes, that wouldn't be an inaccurate description.'

'It must have been a thoroughly unpleasant experience for you, with people looking at you in local pubs and in the street, and no doubt thinking "there goes poor, cuckolded Richard Simpson"?'

'It was. I tried to avoid going out in Bakewell as much as possible. I tried to grow a thick skin.'

'But with the best will in the world, there must never have been a time when you didn't feel bitter and humiliated?'

Simpson, for a moment, seemed close to tears. 'Well, yes, I suppose I got used to it all, to an extent anyway. But I was never happy in Bakewell. I made a point of keeping away as much as possible, spending days at a time away on business trips.'

'Forgive me for asking, but if you were so unhappy with your marriage and the situation, why didn't you put an end to it? You would have had ample grounds for divorce.'

'Perhaps I should have. But the irony was that, despite everything, we were and always had been very good friends. We still socialised together. We enjoyed each other's company. And I didn't want the hassle of divorce proceedings. I just put up with it.'

'So you were a martyr or a saint, or perhaps both?'

'Maybe some would say that.'

'You had affairs yourself,' Brian said, 'but I get the distinct impression that they were short-lived and unsatisfactory?'

'Yes, until I met Stephanie anyway.'

'Yes, Stephanie. Let's get on to Stephanie. It's right, isn't it, that whatever had gone before with you, this was no casual fling, this was a full-blown love affair. This was your "grand passion".'

'Yes, I was very much in love with her.'

'And she with you, judging by the sentiments in the greetings cards she sent you?'

'I believe so.'

'You showered her with presents, and you "killed off" your wife and made a dementia patient of your mother?'

'Yes.'

'You were determined to do whatever it took to preserve that relationship and prevent Stephanie from coming to your home, which of course would have jeopardised that relationship?'

'Yes, but it didn't involve killing my wife.'

Brian paused at this point. Just to let the defendant's last answer register with the jury, Martin thought. It had been Simpson who had first brought up the actual killing of Beverley, as opposed to the fictitious death he had created for Stephanie's benefit. Martin noticed that two male jurors in the front row of the box had looked at each other at this point. Significant perhaps?

'It's right, isn't it, Mr. Simpson,' Brian continued, 'that you were as keen as Stephanie for your relationship to become permanent, to be living together, as a couple?'

'I wanted that, but I couldn't see how it could happen.'

'But she was pushing you to make it happen, wasn't she?'

'Yes, this was why I had to lie again, and make up the story about the care home place for my mother. To stall her.'

'You were making a big cross for your own back,

getting deeper in the mire, with one lie after the other.'

'Yes, I was painting myself into a corner.'

'Your words, not mine,' said Brian, with a quick glance at the jury.

'So,' Brian went on, 'if your wife hadn't died, how were you going to get out of your predicament?'

The defendant paused and looked down at the lectern on the witness box. 'I was either going to come clean with Beverley and ask her to let me go, or I was going to have to end the relationship with Stephanie.'

'But you have already said that Beverley would have taken you to the cleaners, and you couldn't afford that. And you aren't going to suddenly end your "grand passion", are you?'

Simpson didn't reply, so Brian continued. 'Let's face it, Mr. Simpson, neither option was remotely acceptable to you. But then there was a third way, wasn't there, which would have spared you the agonies of having to make an impossible choice?'

Simpson shook his head. 'I know what you're suggesting, but that was never an option. I could never have harmed my wife, whatever the situation.'

'But, as you say, you'd painted yourself into a corner. You couldn't stall Stephanie for ever. And, as you told the police, you also had another problem which made doing nothing not an option either. You had the bank manager on your back?'

Simpson nodded. 'Yes, that's true. He was expecting me to put my house on the market.'

'And how was Beverley going to react to that? Selling the house, for no obvious reason, and downsizing. How were you going to sell that to her?'

'I would have thought of something.'

'But then the problem wouldn't have gone away. You would still be living beyond your means, and all the time Stephanie would be pushing you into a permanent relationship?'

Simpson again remained silent. This time the judge intervened: 'You need to answer counsel's question.'

'Yes,' came the reply.

Brian Cattermole 'twisted the knife' a little further. 'Of course, by killing your wife, providing you could make it look like an accident or that someone else was responsible, you also had a big insurance pay-out to look forward to. With that, on top of selling your house, your problems would almost have been over?'

'The insurance policy was Beverley's idea,' insisted Simpson. 'I just went along with it, and paid the premiums.'

'Well, we've only your word for that. And you were the beneficiary under the policy, weren't you?'

'Yes, I was.'

'Have you tried to claim under the policy?' asked prosecuting counsel.

'Yes, but the insurance company aren't going to pay out until these proceedings are over.'

'And not at all, if you're convicted.'

Simpson didn't reply, but this time the judge didn't intervene, presumably regarding the question as rhetorical, which it clearly was.

Brian Cattermole paused at this point, shuffled his papers, and then looked up at the defendant again.

'Let's go back to the "coincidence" issue, Mr. Simpson. It's quite a coincidence, I'm sure you'll agree, that your wife's death occurred within a month of the insurance policy being taken out?'

'Yes, but that's all it is, a coincidence.'

'It's a matter for the jury, of course,' Brian continued, pointedly looking at the jury at this point. 'But probably most people, and certainly most insurance companies, would regard that occurrence as more than a little suspicious?'

This time Alison Lancaster intervened: 'As it is a matter for the jury I hardly think the defendant can be expected or required to answer that.'

'Yes, my learned friend is quite right. Please don't answer that, Mr. Simpson.'

Despite his apparent contrition, Martin Tory, looking on, knew that the 'question' was a deliberate ruse by Brian Cattermole to score a point with the jury. An old advocate's trick. The 'question' wasn't a permissible one, but the jury had heard it and the damage was done.

Brian pressed on: 'But there is an even greater coincidence, isn't there? I refer of course to the date of your wife's death. This was two days before the 14th January, the day that Stephanie was expecting to come to your home in Bakewell?'

'I've already said that she's got hold of the wrong end of the stick there. I never told her she could come to Bakewell on that day. It was out of the question.'

'Yes, as it turned out it was out of the question – for you. But whether she's got it wrong or not, you have also said that the 14th was the date that you told her your mother would be going into residential care?'

'Yes, I agree with that.'

'Well,' said Brian, 'the point is, either way, I am sure you would agree that it's a staggering coincidence that your wife should meet her end only two days before the date that you've given out as the day on which you were going to be "free" of your mother, and, as far as your girlfriend was concerned, the removal of the only obstacle to the two of you living together?'

'Yes, I know what it looks like, I know what you're saying, but again it's just a coincidence, believe me.'

'Well, that is a matter for the jury, Mr. Simpson!' The cue for prosecuting counsel to once more look at the jury, this time with slightly raised eyebrows.

After another short pause, Brian went on: 'You

contacted Stephanie a few days before the 14th January and told her the place for your mother was not yet available?'

'Yes, I was just trying to play for time again, stall her a bit more, to give me some more breathing space.'

'Yes, and then a couple of days later you got all the breathing space you needed, when you killed your wife.'

'No, it's just another coincidence.'

'Another coincidence!' exclaimed Brian. 'But the truth of the matter, Mr. Simpson, is that this wasn't "another coincidence". It was part of your black-hearted plan to kill your wife, a plan you had conceived before Christmas, when you took out the insurance policy on her life?'

'No, no!'

'You knew you would have to put Stephanie off because you knew you would be involved in arranging a funeral by the 14th January?'

Simpson was sadly shaking his head as counsel was asking this question. 'No, it's just not true.'

Another pause, more shuffling of papers. Brian then looked up again at the defendant. 'Can I ask you about your so-called alibi?' he said. 'As I understand it, you maintain that at the time your wife met her end you were either at home or you were on the way to the north-east?'

'Yes.'

'Your account now is that she left home some time before you did?'

'Yes.'

'Although, on the day that you identified your wife's body, you told the police at Bakewell police station that she was still at home when you left the house?'

'Yes, but I wasn't thinking clearly then. I was obviously wrong about the sequence of events.'

'But this was not much more than forty-eight hours after you had last seen her. How could you be so wrong so close to the events occurring?'

'I wasn't thinking straight, as I had cause to believe that my wife had been involved in an accident.'

'But you told the same story to the police when they interviewed you weeks later. It was only when you were confronted with the evidence, the receipt from the service area at Wetherby, that you came up with a different account. One, indeed, that fitted the facts?'

'I realised then that I must have left the house much later than I had originally thought.'

'Basically, Mr. Simpson, what you told the police on the 14th January and again when you were first interviewed, was yet another lie?'

'No, it was just that I hadn't been thinking clearly.'

'Alright,' Brian went on, 'if you were at home when

your wife left the house, you must have seen who picked her up?'

'No, I didn't. I think I must have still been in bed when she left, or in the bathroom.'

'But you told the police at Bakewell police station that she was preparing for a climbing trip, and that you said goodbye to her. How could you know that and how could you say goodbye if you didn't see her?'

'I must have made an assumption that she was going climbing, and I am obviously mistaken that I had said goodbye.'

Brian gave an audible sigh. 'There's no mistake here, is there? You were the one who drove her to Curbar Edge that morning?'

'No, it wasn't me.'

'I'm sure you would agree, Mr. Simpson, that it's as plain as a pikestaff that there was someone with her at Curbar Edge, someone who has taken away her outer clothing, shoes, rucksack, and left the scene.'

'Yes, it would seem so.'

'It must have been the case that she had more than one rucksack, because the one that was recovered from Maitland's van was clearly nothing to do with what happened that day?'

'Yes, I think she had more than one rucksack.'

'And I am sure you would also agree that it is inconceivable that a bona fide climbing companion would have left her to die if she had simply fallen from the crag?'

'Yes, it seems inconceivable.'

'So, we are left only with the proposition that she was pushed by someone intent on killing her, someone who was also set on making it appear that the whole thing had been an accident? Someone indeed who bore her such ill will or who had very compelling reasons to see her dead?'

'Yes.'

'That someone was you, wasn't it, Mr. Simpson?'

Brian had sat down before Simpson could utter a reply. He began to say something, then gave up and just shook his head.

★★★★★★★★★★★★★★★★★★★★★★★★★★

Following the end of the cross-examination of Simpson, defence counsel announced that there were no other witnesses to give evidence. The judge glanced at the clock and informed those present that he would hear the closing speeches of both counsel the following day.

CHAPTER TWENTY-ONE

August 2nd

Entering the advocates' room the following morning, Martin Tory was a little surprised to find Brian Cattermole quite subdued, and not in any way expressing pleasure in the undoubted success of his cross-examination. A marked contrast, in fact, to his upbeat manner in previous days when there was perhaps less to be pleased about. But Martin soon realised that Brian was not displaying a lack of confidence, but rather was preoccupied with the issue of how to structure his final address to the jury, which he would have to deliver fairly shortly.

It was noticeable also that his opponent was no less subdued. Alison Lancaster sat in a corner with a cup of coffee and her file of papers open in front of her. She looked uncharacteristically pensive and showed no interest in engaging in conversation with her junior counsel. But then she also had a difficult speech to prepare.

★★★★★★★★★★★★★★★★★★★★★★★★★★

At shortly after 10.30 am Brian got to his feet for the last time in the trial of Richard Simpson. The jury appeared to be attentive and expectant, as they had throughout the hearing.

'Members of the jury,' he began, 'you have sat patiently throughout all the evidence that has been presented in this case, and I do not want to detain you much longer. It falls to me, however, to address you for a second time, and then you will hear from my learned friend, and finally from His Lordship, who will sum up the evidence and direct you on the law. Because His Lordship will go over the evidence, I do not propose to rehearse what has been said by the witnesses in any detail. I would be insulting your intelligence anyway as you have heard it all and, no doubt, you have already formed opinions as to where the truth lies in this case. I shall therefore be brief, or, at least as brief as I can, and I hope you will forgive me if I go on too long.

'It's a matter for you how you approach the evidence in reaching your verdict, but you might find it useful, or you might not, to start at the end of the process, and look at the awful predicament that faced the defendant, and then work backward from there.

'However you want to phrase it, Richard Simpson was in a dire situation – between a rock and a hard place, between the devil and the deep blue sea, or, to use his own words, he had "painted himself into a corner". On one side he had a girlfriend with whom, by his own admission, he was very much, hopelessly, in love. He was obsessed. He had showered her with presents, gone into significant debt, and so desperate was he to keep her that he had invented a sick mother, and he had, figuratively speaking at least, "killed off" his wife. A self-fulfilling prophecy perhaps, ladies and gentlemen?'

Brian paused at this point, perhaps to allow his last comment to register with the jurors. Martin noticed that at least two of them exchanged what could only be described as 'knowing glances'.

'On the other side was his wife of six years, a philanderer and a libertine, a woman completely devoid of any morals. A woman, nonetheless, for whom he still nurtured some affection. But more to the point, a woman who he knew would ruin him financially if she discovered that he intended to form a permanent relationship with another. His financial situation was already parlous. Divorce or separation would tip him into bankruptcy and, indeed, he would be unable to maintain his high-maintenance lover in the manner to which she was clearly accustomed.

'An appalling situation, ladies and gentlemen, but one that could only get worse. Doing nothing was not an option. He had the bank manager on his back and his lover was pushing him ever harder to make arrangements for them to live together, and, whether she was right or not, by the middle of January, she clearly expected that the moment was imminent. His two worlds were about to collide.

'Desperate times, but as the ancient physician Hippocrates once said, "desperate times require desperate measures". Something had to give, didn't it, and had to give once and for all. Could Simpson give up his grand passion – he didn't think so, did he? Or did he dispose of the woman who had consistently betrayed and humiliated him? No contest, you may think ladies and gentlemen.'

After another short pause, Brian moved on: 'Let's now have a look at the so-called "coincidences", members of the jury. First of all regarding the insurance policy. The event against which the defendant insured occurs within a month of the creation of the policy. You may think that that in itself was suspicious. But, perhaps, taken on its own, it could be passed off as mere coincidence? The deceased was engaged in an activity which could be hazardous, and, if you believe the defendant, was becoming more so as Beverley was "pushing the boundaries" of her chosen sport.

'But, of course, this is not the only coincidence. It needs to be looked at alongside the quite astonishing proximity of Beverley's death to the 14th January, the date originally announced by Simpson as the date on which his mother was to move into residential care, and the date on which Stephanie Winter believed would see the removal of the only obstacle to their living together. At the same time, of course, it won't escape your attention that as well as freeing him up to be with his lover, Simpson would also be the beneficiary of a large sum of money under an insurance policy, which would take him out of crippling debt. Always assuming of course that Beverley's death could be perceived as an accident – which it was, initially in any event. Or at least the deed of another. He would also be in a position to put his house on the market, sell up and move away from Bakewell. His problems would be over, at a stroke!

'Members of the jury, can you seriously believe that this conjunction of events can be attributed to coincidence? It's a matter for you. If you don't believe it then you will have something in common with the defendant, who, you will recall, only believed in coincidence "up to a point". Isn't the truth plain to see? These were no coincidences but stages in the development of a pre-conceived plan by the defendant to murder his wife, a plan set in motion before Christmas 1976 when he took out that insurance policy?'

Pausing again, Brian leafed quickly through his papers, before looking back at the jury. 'Of course, ladies and gentlemen, the element of coincidence does not stop there. There is what one may term the ultimate coincidence. I refer to the events on Curbar Edge that fateful morning. It's a matter for you but I think we can lay to rest the notion that what occurred was the result of an accident. Even the defendant, when he gave evidence, did not believe this. It is plain isn't it that the deceased was not on her own that morning – she needed a lift to get to Curbar, public transport was non-existent, she had no money with her and clearly expected a lift back as well. She had no warm clothing or ordinary shoes with her when she was found. In short, she started off with a companion – if that is an appropriate description? It is surely the case, is it not, that it would be inconceivable that a genuine climbing partner would have left her to die if she had fallen whilst climbing, and compounded the callousness by removing her rucksack and clothing, thus making the whole incident appear like an accident? The defendant was of the same opinion.

'So we have straightforward murder. And by a person who had some motive, some deep resentment, loathing or hatred of the deceased. Someone who was prepared to resort to a "desperate measure" to rid himself of Beverley Simpson. Consider, ladies and gentlemen, that if this was not Richard Simpson, there was someone else out there of the same desperate mindset and someone who was prepared to do the deed at the very same time as the defendant needed to do it. Coincidence again? Or the last act in a preconceived and murderous plot?

'What I am saying, and what the Crown is saying in this case, is that to accept all these occurrences as coincidences is an affront to common sense. I leave it to your common sense as to whether you agree with that proposition or not.

'Finally, ladies and gentlemen, I refer, but only briefly, to Simpson's so-called alibi for the 12th January. His initial account of his movements that day is given to the police not much more than forty-eight hours after he had last seen his wife. You may think he would have a clearer recollection of the sequence of events then than he would after a passage of time. But he changes his story when he is confronted with the evidence of the till receipt from Wetherby Services, putting his first account down to woolly thinking. Or is it yet another lie, members of the jury, by a guilty man trying to cover his back?

'He now says that he was at home when his wife left the house, but did not see who picked her up, and did not say goodbye. No discussion apparently about where she was going or who was taking her. I'm sure, members of the jury, you can determine whether this has the ring of truth or not. Or is it just another untruth by a man who, by his own admission, has told one lie after another?

'Thank you for listening.'

★★★★★★★★★★★★★★★★★★★★★★★★★★

Brian had barely sat down before Alison Lancaster had leapt to her feet. The subdued character of an hour earlier had gone; she was back to her feisty best.

'Members of the jury,' she began, 'as you deliberate, the one ball you must keep in the air is the one marked "beyond reasonable doubt". I make no apologies for returning to this theme again and again during this address because I cannot understate the importance of it. His Lordship will also remind you that you cannot convict the defendant of the charge in the indictment unless you are *sure* of his guilt.

'As the prosecution have already conceded, this case is based entirely on circumstantial evidence. There is no direct evidence that Richard Simpson has committed this offence: no eye-witnesses, no fingerprint evidence, no forensic evidence, no confession. There is indeed no such evidence that the death of Beverley Simpson was anything more than as the result of an accident. What this means for you is that if you are to convict the defendant you must do it by drawing inferences from that circumstantial evidence, inferences that can only be drawn if you are sure that they can be. It follows, ladies and gentlemen, that the evidence in question must be strong, and more than this, it must be compelling. There is a thin dividing line between "inference" and "speculation" – one is legitimate, one is not. What the defence say in this case is that the evidence only permits speculation, not inference.

'I ask you first of all to look at the circumstances in which the deceased's body was found. There is no direct evidence that there was anyone with her at the time, no evidence indeed that anyone took her to Curbar Edge. Even if you can "infer" that there was a third party present, as the detective sergeant himself conceded, you cannot rule out that she fell unassisted to her death and, however callous and inhumane, that the third party deserted her. Because there is no direct evidence that she was pushed off the crag, DS Woodman agreed, however reluctantly, that this could have been an accident. That is speculation, but then isn't the alternative of murder also speculation, members of the jury? Of course, if you are not sure that this was not an accident, then you are not sure that there was a crime. If there is no crime, then you need deliberate no further, the defendant cannot be guilty of murdering his wife.'

Listening to this argument, Martin Tory thought that if defence counsel could stop now, then she might have a reasonable chance of success. But this would be too risky a strategy. She needed to go on because the jury might not be with her on this initial issue, and she would need to deal with the other evidence in the case. It was inevitable in fact that she had to go on. Furthermore, although her opening points were interesting and, at first glance at least, quite compelling, they were submitted in isolation and failed to take into account the rest of the evidence that had been presented. She was also ignoring the fact that the defendant himself in his evidence had acknowledged that it seemed inconceivable that a) his wife was alone at the material time, and b) her death was the result of an accident. He had only been expressing an opinion of course, but the reality was that the jury would be unlikely to think otherwise when the man himself thought it was murder!

As Martin predicted, defence counsel did not stop there.

'Let us assume, members of the jury, that, as the Crown allege, the deceased was pushed to her death, was murdered. Again there is no direct evidence that Richard Simpson is the culprit. There is no evidence that he was present at the material time. There is no evidence that his car was seen in any car park close to Curbar Edge at any time. There is no evidence, indeed, that he was ever within five miles of the scene of the incident that day. So we are into the realms of "inference" again; or "speculation" I would suggest. Granted, the perpetrator must have had a motive for killing Beverley Simpson. He or she must have harboured feelings of loathing, hatred, a need for revenge. The defendant, you may say, fitted that bill. He had a motive, a need, he had been humiliated by his wife's antics over some years. But he does not seem to have entertained feelings of hatred or loathing. Otherwise, you may think, he would have done the deed before. And why him? There may well have been a number of men out there who had been ill-used or humiliated by this woman, and who may have had cause to wish her serious harm or worse. Not to mention of course a number of women whose husbands or partners had been, temporarily anyway, seduced by her dubious charms. One should not speak ill of the dead, but the truth remains that Beverley Simpson was a menace and a danger to the stability of many marital relationships. And you may think that if you play the field you are likely to make as many enemies as friends.

'The police of course identified a man who did fit the bill. Rex Maitland. They felt they had a strong case against him. They thought they had their man. How wrong they were, ladies and gentlemen. They are now just as convinced that Simpson is the "man". But if they were wrong about Maitland, why should they be right about Simpson? If they have got it wrong once, can you be sure they have got it right this time?'

It seemed to Martin Tory that defence counsel was somewhat losing her way now. She was skating over or ignoring the evidence that pointed towards Simpson. The tactic seemed to be to spread doubt and confusion by throwing into the pot a string of possibilities, possibilities for which no evidence existed.

But perhaps that was the tactic? And who was to say it may not be successful.

The rest of counsel's address seemed to reinforce the point that this was indeed the strategy.

'Members of the jury,' she went on, 'what is at the heart of the prosecution case is the claim that the defendant had been forced into a situation, largely of his own making, where he had no option but to dispose of his wife in some final manner.

'The defendant is the first to admit that he was in an appalling situation, that he had, as he says, "painted himself into a corner", and he didn't know how to deal with it. He is adamant, however, that he had no intention of harming his wife. Richard Simpson, members of the jury, would not be the first husband to find himself in such a situation, and he surely will not be the last. And the fact is of course that most men in such predicaments manage to extricate themselves without resorting to "desperate measures", however ruinous it might be emotionally or financially. And killing his wife would not necessarily solve the problem. He would have needed to move away from the area and his family; he would have been looking over his shoulder for the rest of his life in case Stephanie should learn the truth about Beverley; and how was he going to explain to her why he was not visiting his stricken mother in her care home?

'What was so terrible about the non-lethal options? Despite what Mr. Simpson may have said under cross-examination, he had told the police previously that he had considered ending his relationship with Stephanie. Whatever she may have said, is there any doubt in your minds that she seduced him, and led him into infatuation and obsession? Despite his feelings for her he makes it plain that it was she that strongly and urgently wanted their togetherness. He knew it couldn't happen. She was squeezing him emotionally and financially. At the end of the day, ladies and gentlemen, it might have been a terrible wrench to break with her, but it would have been a relief. You may think that this was an option he could have and might have pursued when push came to shove as it was about to do in January this year?

'If anything, perhaps divorcing or breaking with Beverley was a tougher option than leaving Stephanie. He could be left in a situation where he was in dire straits financially and unable to sustain his relationship with a high-maintenance girlfriend, and at the same time Beverley would still be around, presenting a residual danger that Stephanie would discover the truth about her. And there would still be the problem of concealing the truth about his mother. On the other hand, these may not be insurmountable difficulties for a determined man. Certainly plainer sailing than killing his wife and the difficulties that would arise if he were to be revealed as the culprit! The point is, ladies and gentlemen, these non-lethal options were a long way from being unachievable. If they were I would suggest that you might have a much easier task in drawing an inference that the only way was murder. Otherwise it is speculation once again, is it not?'

Defence counsel paused at this point and turned a page in her file. Then she continued: 'Of course what the prosecution say to you is that the fact that Mr. Simpson took the extreme course of killing his wife is entirely supported by the bizarre conjunction of circumstances surrounding her death – what they refer to as the "so-called coincidences" presented by the proximity of dates and events. In effect what is being said is that the only inference that can be drawn from this sequence, this scenario, is that the defendant must have killed his wife.

'What the defence say, however, is that once again this is no more than speculation. Coincidences, as we know, do occur. You can't dismiss them as being "an affront to common sense" simply because there is more than one. It's often been said, hasn't it members of the jury, that "fact is stranger than fiction".

'The deceased meets her death within a month of

the creation of an insurance policy which made the defendant the beneficiary of the policy if that event occurred, as a result of accident or the unlawful act of a third party. Highly suspicious say the Crown. But why should it be? If Beverley's death was an accident than it was one that could have occurred at any time, given that she was taking more risks in her rock-climbing, and indeed one that she seems to have anticipated to an extent by suggesting the making of such a policy. And remember no-one can dispute that it wasn't her idea. And if she was murdered, it's a big leap to maintain that it must have been down to the defendant simply because he was the sole beneficiary of her death. The prosecution would have you believe that this was part of a pre-conceived plan by Simpson – to kill his wife but make it look like an accident so that he can successfully claim under the policy, pay off his debts and live happily ever after. No-one with such a plan, ladies and gentlemen, is surely going to invite suspicion by killing his wife within a month of the start of the policy?

'The Crown lay particular store by the conjunction of the event of 12th January and the date 14th January. It is beyond coincidence, it is said, that Beverley meets her death two days before the date announced by Mr. Simpson as being that when his mother is to be removed to a care home, thus clearing the path, in the eyes of his lover at least, for she and the defendant to begin their lives together.

And Simpson has told Stephanie at the start of that

week that the 14th will not happen because he knew he would be organising a funeral on or shortly after that time. His explanation of course is that he had to provide Stephanie with a date at this time because she was pressing him to make arrangements to find his mother a placement, and the death of his wife two days before, whether by accident or otherwise, is pure coincidence. He put off the moving date for his mother because he was stalling for time, not because he knew his wife would be dead by then.

'It's certainly an unfortunate coincidence of dates, members of the jury, but why should it be any more than this? Can you be sure, as indeed you must be, that these events are all stages in the development of a master plan conceived by Richard Simpson to murder his wife? I would suggest it calls for speculation once more to reach this conclusion, and not an irresistible inference.

'What we have here is a man, members of the jury, who lacked resolution, was indecisive, put up with disloyalty and humiliation from one woman in his life, and was lured into slavish infatuation by another. "A saint and a martyr" was a description suggested by prosecuting counsel, even though it was not intended as a compliment. Not, you may think, the ingredients that make up a man who could devise a cunning and ruthless plot to murder his wife, make it look like an accident, and then claim on the insurance policy?'

So the entire strategy is revealed, Martin thought to himself. Present the defendant as a weak, ingenuous, hard-done-by, ditherer. The helpless plaything of strong, self-willed women. And then throw into the mix a few red herrings, and a layer of 'it's just speculation'. All this intended to distract the jury from considering the hard evidence. Whether or not this would prove a recipe for success remained to be seen, but it was a clever approach.

Counsel was now coming to the end of her address.

'Can I finish, members of the jury, by having a quick look at the defendant's alibi for the morning of the 12th January, which the prosecution claim is flawed and was manufactured after he was caught in another lie. You will appreciate that what the defendant has told the police at Bakewell police station initially is at a time when he says he has cause to believe that his wife has died in an accident. If that is the case then surely it is no wonder that he is not in complete command of his recollection of the sequence of events of two days before. Confronted with evidence that he is wrong, he comes clean and accepts that he must be wrong about the exact nature of his movements. And then he is preparing for a business trip, he has packing to do and he has to attend to his ablutions. His wife has her own agenda and is otherwise engaged. Why should it be strange that he does not see her depart. There are no "goodbyes" – sad perhaps, but this is the nature of their relationship.

'I have taken up enough of your time, ladies and gentlemen. For my parting shot I simply remind you of my opening one. You must be sure. Sure this was not an accident. Sure that it was the defendant who committed the murder, if there was one. Given the lack of direct evidence in this case, the possibility of other scenarios, and the character of the man before you, I would humbly suggest that you cannot be sure of his guilt.'

★★★★★★★★★★★★★★★★★★★★★★★★★★★★

Mr. Justice Sweeney began his summing-up to the jury after the lunch adjournment on the seventh day of the trial of Richard Simpson. He started by telling them that in due course he would give them directions on the law involved in the case, but that they were the sole judges of fact: they and they alone were to determine where the truth lay, and if he should, inadvertently, be perceived to be expressing any opinion or view on the evidence, they were entitled to ignore it and make up their own minds.

It was not unknown for some judges to allow their own views on witnesses and the evidence to creep into their summing-up of the facts. Mr. Justice Sweeney's address to the jury, however, was a model of rectitude – clear, balanced and entirely neutral. There would be no room for any appeal on the basis of any misdirection by the judge.

He carefully summarised the evidence that each witness had given, and then said this to the jury:

'Members of the jury, you are essentially faced with making two decisions in this case. The first decision is whether the death of Beverley Simpson was the result of an accident, or was the result of a deliberate act by a third party. As both counsel have told you this is a criminal case and you can only find the defendant guilty of the charge set out in the indictment if you are sure of his guilt. I reiterate now, members of the jury, that that indeed is the position. You must be sure. Nothing less will do. It follows, therefore, that if you are not sure that the deceased's death was not the result of an accident, then that is the end of the matter. You must find the defendant "Not Guilty".

'It is a matter for you how you consider the evidence – whether you do as prosecution counsel suggested and start at the end and work backwards, or whether you begin by examining the evidence immediately surrounding the death. At the end of the day you will have to look at all the evidence in its entirety, in the round, and not just any part of it in isolation. If you start at the beginning, as it were, then you may, or may not, make life easier. If you look at that evidence immediately surrounding the death of Beverley Simpson, then you will need to consider whether you believe she was alone or not at the time of her death. You have no direct evidence to assist you. There are no eye-witnesses, no scientific evidence, no confessions. As has already been said, the case is based entirely on "circumstantial evidence" – this means that you will need to rely solely on drawing inferences from the circumstances to establish the facts. It goes without saying, as defence counsel has pointed out repeatedly, that you must not speculate. You can only draw inferences if you are satisfied that the circumstantial evidence is sufficiently compelling to allow you to do so.

'Given those circumstances, you may infer that the deceased was not alone. That she was accompanied by someone who took her to Curbar Edge, and whom she expected to take her home. It is not in dispute that she had no money in her possession, no vehicle of her own, and that there was no evidence of any warm clothing or ordinary shoes available to her. It is, however, a matter for you whether you can draw that inference. If you are sure she was not alone, can you go on and infer from those early circumstances, as the prosecution claim you can and should, that she did not die in an accident? The prosecution say that it is inconceivable that a genuine friend or climbing partner would have abandoned her, if she had fallen, then gone on to take away her rucksack and spare clothing, and not told the emergency services. The inevitable conclusion from this would be that she was unlawfully killed and did not die in an accident. This is a harder decision for you, based on the circumstances immediately surrounding the death, but if you are sure that you can draw the inference that the Crown claim you should draw, then you have reached the stage where you are sure that this is unlawful killing and not an accident. Then you only, and I say "only", need to decide whether the defendant was responsible for the unlawful act.'

The judge paused, adjusted his spectacles, then went

on: 'At this point, members of the jury, I need to draw two points to your attention. Firstly, you have heard that the emergency services, initially in any event, were of the view that the death was the result of an accident. They were not, however, in possession of all the evidence that you possess. It is only an opinion and you should ignore it. The only opinion that counts is yours, an opinion that is formed from the evidence before you.

'Secondly it would be appropriate for me to remind you at this stage of the law that relates to an offence of murder. You must be sure that an identifiable person unlawfully killed the deceased with intent to kill her or to cause her grievous bodily harm. That is the only definition of murder that you need to concern yourselves with in this case. Suffice it to say that if you are sure that Beverley Simpson was killed by pushing her off a crag, then you will almost certainly conclude that it is murder.'

Martin Tory was pleased that the judge had told the jury that they must look at the evidence 'in the round'. This was perhaps a non-too-subtle dig at defence counsel, who had, in Martin's view, tried to 'compartmentalise' the evidence. The direction about ignoring the opinion of others also needed saying.

The judge now paused again, seemingly to gather his thoughts, before going on: 'If, members of the jury, from considering that evidence immediately surrounding the death, you cannot be sure that it was not the result of accident, you must then go on to consider all the evidence in this case in its entirety, "in the round" as I have said. If, on the other hand, you are sure that this was murder, then you will need to look at the rest of the evidence anyway to determine if the defendant is guilty of the offence.

'I have summarised that other evidence already for you and I don't need to go over it again. It is all circumstantial evidence, and the extent of its significance depends on whether you subscribe to the arguments presented by the prosecution, or to those laid out by the defence.

The prosecution case is that there was a deliberate plan by the defendant to kill his wife and that it is an affront to common sense to dismiss the sequence and conjunction of events as coincidences.

'On the other hand, the defence argue that indeed these are just coincidences, and that to find the defendant guilty on the back of these would be the result of speculation not inference. It is accepted that Mr. Simpson was in a very difficult situation, to some extent of his own making, but that there were ways out of it without resorting to murder, a course of action which would not necessarily solve his problems anyway. They say the evidence shows the defendant to be a man quite incapable of murder. Rather he is "an innocent abroad", indecisive, and manipulated by the two women in his life. He has lied but only to try and preserve his relationship with the woman who has seduced him and led him into obsession, and at a cost. His alibi is credible they say. His change of story can be explained by his mental confusion at a time when he first believed his wife to be dead.

'If, at the end of the day, you are sure that the totality of the evidence leads you to conclude that the prosecution arguments are right and that the deceased was murdered by the defendant, then you should convict. If, on the other hand, you are not sure of this, or you accept the defence position, then you must find the defendant 'Not Guilty'.

'Finally, members of the jury, I need to warn you to exercise caution in relation to two matters when you are considering your verdict. First of all, you have heard about the abortive prosecution of Rex Maitland, and the acceptance by the investigating officer Detective Sergeant Woodman that the police got the wrong man and that the investigation could be classed as inept. You should put this part of the evidence out of your minds and simply focus on the evidence in the case against Richard Simpson. That is what matters and not that the police got it wrong in an earlier investigation. It is the evidence gathered that is important not how skilful, or otherwise, are the police officers who gathered it.

'Secondly, you will recall that at one point during prosecution counsel's cross-examination of Mr. Simpson, it was put to the defendant that he wouldn't be able to give up his relationship with Stephanie Winter or leave his wife. He made no reply to that question. You may be tempted to think that his silence was tantamount to an admission of guilt, that the only option open to him was to kill his wife, as Mr. Cattermole went on to suggest was the case. You are perfectly right to look at the defendant's demeanour in the witness box when examining the evidence, and take into account his responses to questions during cross-examination, but you should be careful not to attach too much significance to that one piece of silence on his part. Given his replies to other questions, was he really saying, by implication anyway, 'Yes I had no alternative but to kill my wife'? You may think that the question was really rhetorical and that the defendant felt it didn't require a reply, he having dealt with a similar line of questioning already.

'Ladies and gentleman, it's now up to you to deliberate and consider your verdict. However, it's late in the day, so I am not going to send you out now to do that. Go home and you can start your consideration of the evidence in the morning. I remind you that it is very important that you do not discuss what you have heard with your family, friends or anyone else, other than each other.'

CHAPTER TWENTY-TWO
August 3rd

The judge sent the jury out at just after 10.30 am on August 3rd. They were instructed to elect a foreman and told that, at that stage, only a unanimous verdict would be acceptable. After the jury had trooped out, the courtroom emptied and the barristers, solicitors, solicitors' clerks, and police officers dispersed to sit and wait for the verdict, whenever that might be delivered.

Having telephoned his office, Martin Tory went into the advocates' room. Brian Cattermole and Tom Edwards were avidly watching a one-day cricket match on the television and were clearly not going to be sitting around chewing their fingernails, anxiously waiting for the jury to come back. Alison Lancaster, her junior and their instructing solicitor's clerk were sat round a table in the corner of the room, drinking coffee and smoking. They were chatting and laughing and were also showing no signs of concern or anxiety about the outcome of the trial.

Martin withdrew to another corner and settled down to read his newspaper. He was more than a little surprised when, about ten minutes later, he looked up to see Alison Lancaster offering him a cigarette. He declined but put aside the newspaper, and she sat down. Previously he had regarded her as aloof and unapproachable, ignoring his 'good mornings' spoken as they passed each other on the concourse on several days of the hearing. But now she showed a different side of her personality, warm and friendly. Perhaps, he thought, it was a sign that the trial was over, the die was cast, and the pressure was off.

'You're the CPS lawyer in the case,' she said. So she knew who he was.

'I believe there was one of your senior colleagues at the back of court earlier in the hearing?'

'Yes, that was Ronnie Fox, Deputy County Prosecuting Solicitor,' Martin told her.

'My guess is that his interest in the case was personal rather than professional?'

Martin saw no need and had no inclination to shield his superior. 'Yes, you could say that,' was his reply.

Alison nodded knowingly.

'What do you think the jury are going to do?' she asked.

Given her previous attitude, Martin was quite surprised and not a little flattered that she should be seeking his opinion. He decided, however, not to sound over-confident.

'Oh, fifty-fifty,' he ventured.

Alison smiled. 'I think you're being a little pessimistic,' she said. 'I think the guy is as guilty as hell, and my instinct is that this jury have got him weighed up. Brian is right – too many coincidences, an affront to common sense. And looking at this jury I detect a good helping of common sense there. Now if it was some of the juries from the east end of London that I often come across, we might be in with a shout. But not here I fancy. But you never know!'

'Don't you think some of the jury at least are going to have a good deal of sympathy for him?' Martin suggested.

'Yes, but it's not going to help him. Okay, they are going to say Beverley was a tart, she'd led him a hell of a life, she had it coming, and why didn't it happen before. But then it gives him a very clear and strong motive to bump her off. And when you add in the Stephanie Winter factor, I think it makes it even stronger. They'd have to be pretty perverse to say the least to cast the sympathy vote in his favour!'

Martin knew that counsel, both defence and prosecution, could often be deliberately downbeat about their chances, once the trial itself was over. To some extent it was a defence mechanism, to put them in a more relaxed frame of mind should the verdict go against them. But he somehow felt that Alison Lancaster was being genuine in her pessimism.

★★★★★★★★★★★★★★★★★★★★★★★★★★★

Lunchtime came and went. The jury had now been out more than five hours. It was Martin's turn to start to entertain depressing thoughts. Generally speaking, the longer the jury were deliberating, the more likely that there were doubts, the more likely they would come back with a 'Not Guilty' verdict. In a less serious case, the judge by now would be bringing the jury back and directing them to bring in a 'majority verdict' if they couldn't all agree one way or the other. But he wasn't likely to be doing that in a murder case just yet, and probably not before the end of the next day. A 'majority verdict' would allow the jury to convict, or acquit as the case may be, if at least ten of their number agreed on the outcome. What was also a depressing thought was the possibility, Martin mused, of a 'hung jury'. This occurred where the jury was split and unable to agree on even a majority verdict. The result would be that the judge would discharge the jury and the prosecution would have to decide whether or not to ask for a retrial. Not a pleasing prospect.

Just as everyone's thoughts, however, were turning to coming back the following day, shortly before four o'clock a court usher burst into the advocate's room to announce that the jury were 'coming back with a verdict'. The room emptied rapidly and barristers, solicitors and clerks headed for the courtroom. They were joined on the way by police officers and members of the families of the deceased and defendant who had also been alerted by court staff that a verdict was imminent.

The judge re-entered the court shortly after the parties and the onlookers. There was then an expectant hush as the jury filed back and took their seats in the jury box.

Martin watched the jury closely as they entered the courtroom. Although by no means a totally reliable guide, there was a widely held view amongst regular users of the Crown Court and observers of jurors' body language that the jury that was about to announce a 'Guilty' verdict would not look at the defendant in the dock as they came into court. Conversely, if they did look at him, they were going to find him 'Not Guilty'. It was quite noticeable that not one of this body of men and women even glanced in Richard Simpson's direction. Whilst the length of time that the jury had been out did not augur that well for a favourable verdict, Martin reasoned, he felt quite reassured by their body language.

As the jury resumed their seats, Jeremy Ramsbottom came into his own again. For more than a week he had been compelled to sit in silence while the trial went on around him. Now he was going to make the most of his moment in the limelight. He rose slowly to his feet, needlessly adjusted his wig and his gown, and asked for the jury foreman to stand. A well-dressed, middle-aged lady in spectacles, stood up from her seat in the front row.

'Madame foreman,' intoned Fred, 'has the jury reached

a verdict on the single count in the indictment, a verdict on which you are all are agreed?'

'Yes,' was the reply.

'Then in respect of that count in the indictment, does the jury find the prisoner in the dock, Richard Simpson, Guilty or Not Guilty?'

'Guilty,' came the clear response.

Jeremy looked as though he wanted to say more, but the judge never gave him the chance, intervening quickly to thank the jury for their 'patience and attentiveness' in 'an important and difficult case'. Some judges often could not resist the temptation to express their view on the jury's verdict, usually to approve it. Professional to the last, however, Mr. Justice Sweeney was not going to be drawn, although his later sentencing remarks would clearly indicate where his sympathies lay.

The reactions in court to the announcement of the verdict were markedly different. There was an audible gasp from Beverley's parents, who had sat through the whole trial. By way of contrast, Simpson's mother and father sat stony-faced. Perhaps they were not surprised by the verdict, Martin thought.

Martin had his back to Richard Simpson, but was later told that the defendant simply bowed his head when the verdict was given.

Alison Lancaster showed no surprise, rather confirming her sentiments expressed in her earlier conversation with Martin. Brian Cattermole merely allowed himself the ghost of a smile.

After the jury had filed out of court, the judge turned to prosecuting counsel to enquire if 'anything was known' about the defendant. Brian confirmed that he was a man of 'hitherto unblemished character'. This exchange was almost entirely academic, since there was only one sentence that the judge could pass. A conviction for murder meant one thing and one thing only: life imprisonment. It would be up to the Home Secretary to decide what minimum term Simpson would serve before he became eligible for parole.

The judge then asked Alison Lancaster if she had anything to say. She rose for the last time in the hearing: 'My Lord there is nothing useful I can say at this point. There is of course only one sentence Your Lordship can pass and the defendant is well aware of this. I have to inform Your Lordship that, notwithstanding the jury's verdict, he still maintains that he is innocent of the crime.'

The judge expressed no surprise at this last remark. He had heard it all before. He now spoke directly to the defendant:

'Richard Simpson, please stand. You have been found guilty by the jury of the murder of your wife, Beverley Simpson. There may be those who would have some sympathy for you and the predicament in which you found yourself. I am not one of them. I have no doubt at all that you carefully planned the manner and timing of the killing of your wife, and that it was your intention to benefit from her murder, both by allowing you to be free to make a life with your lover, and also financially. In my book there can be no sympathy for someone who conceives and callously implements a plot to dispose of his wife for his own selfish ends. As you have already heard I can only pass one sentence, and that is one of life imprisonment. Take him down,' he added to the prison escorts.

After Simpson had been taken down the steps to the cells below, the judge commended Detective Sergeant Woodman, and Detective Constables Forrester and Murdoch, for their 'zeal' in carrying out the investigation which had led to Simpson's arrest and charge. He then thanked both leading counsel for their conduct of prosecution and defence respectively, then rose to his feet, and left the court.

CHAPTER TWENTY-THREE

June 8th 2002

Martin Tory and ex-Detective Inspector Alan Woodman met for a drink in the Chequers Inn at Froggatt one warm Saturday morning in June 2002. They had met frequently over the last twenty years or so, a friendship forged from working together on dozens of criminal cases.

Alan had retired from the police service in 1992 and, much against his better judgment, had entered into partnership with Jim Donegani in the latter's private investigation business in Derby. When Donegani had retired a few years ago, Alan had carried on in the firm as the sole partner. He had never found the work particularly congenial but it was better than being a security consultant or working behind the counter in a filling station, the sort of post-retirement jobs that many of his former colleagues had taken. It was also better than sitting at home watching daytime television or pottering in his garden. He dreaded the prospect of final retirement from work, something that was only a few years off, particularly as there was no-one else at home, he having never remarried after the failure of his first relationship.

Martin still lived with his wife only a few miles from where they were sitting now. He had stayed with the office of the County Prosecuting Solicitor in Derbyshire, and, five years after the creation of the new Crown Prosecution Service in 1986, he had become the Chief Crown Prosecutor for the same area, a post he still held. Fortune, however, had not smiled on his erstwhile superiors. Robin Caulfield had 'hit the bottle' in a big way from the early eighties and had 'taken early retirement' following a motoring accident in which he had knocked over and seriously injured an elderly lady in 1991. He had somehow turned out to be not over the blood-alcohol limit at the time, which was a great surprise to everyone who knew him. Ronnie Fox had remained in post until 1986, but then had found the regime of the new Crown Prosecution Service which came into being in that year as not at all to his taste. He had departed and joined a firm of solicitors in Nottingham, but his indolent ways were soon exposed and his partners in the firm decided he had to go. His third wife had come to the same decision about him at much the same time, and he left the area and no-one had seen or heard of him since.

As they sat over their pints, it dawned on them that it was twenty-five years since the verdict in the Simpson case. There were probably few persons amongst present or past local police officers, or indeed in the local legal fraternity, or indeed in the population of the county in general, who had heard of the case, dwarfed as it had been at the time by the notorious Pottery Cottage murders. But then again, despite it being one of the most infamous murder cases in the annals of serious crime in England and Wales, there were not that many locals who could now recognise the name of William Thomas Hughes and the nature of his notoriety. Even the local press and other media appeared to have erased the case from their collective memory, and the twenty-fifth anniversary of the horrific murders had passed without any kind of public acknowledgment. It was, Alan said, as if everyone wanted to forget that those events ever happened.

The whereabouts of the tragic Gill Moran were unknown. Rumour had it that she had remarried some years later, but she had disappeared from the locality, to try and rebuild her shattered life in pastures new.

For Alan and Martin, however, the murder of Beverley Simpson had been the most memorable case of their respective careers. More memorable and significant in some ways than the Hughes affair, a case which had not given rise to any prosecution and trial. As they sat and drank, they mulled over how time and fate had dealt with the main 'players' in the case.

Richard Simpson had never ceased to maintain his innocence. His legal team had advised him that he had no grounds to appeal against his conviction, unless he was able to discover fresh material evidence.

His family had mounted a crusade on his behalf and had instructed private investigators to search for this 'new evidence'. Three years of searching had yielded nothing, and the crusade withered away. The Home Secretary had decreed that Simpson should serve a minimum of eighteen years imprisonment before he could be considered for parole. The prospect of at least another fifteen years behind bars was clearly too much for Simpson to swallow, and in 1981 he hanged himself in his cell. His supporters said 'that showed he was innocent'; others said it showed nothing of the sort.

At the end his only regular visitor was his mother, who had apparently forgiven him for the lie he had told about her. In 2001 she was admitted to a residential care home, suffering from acute dementia.

Stephanie Winter continued to live in Cockermouth and to frequent the Armathwaite Hall Hotel. In 1987 she met there and married a man fifteen years her junior. They emigrated to New Zealand shortly afterwards, and, as far as anyone knows, are there still.

The hapless Rex Maitland, having served his custodial sentence for the offence of attempted rape, was able to return to his previous job as a farm labourer, courtesy of his former employer, David Hersey. Mr. Hersey's act of kindness, however, proved to be in vain. Maitland's co-workers knew of his offending and its nature and made life unbearable for him. He was 'sent to Coventry' from the start of his re-employment, and he handed in his notice after less than three months.

He tried but completely failed to get any sort of work in the local area, and found that he was unwelcome in the pubs in Bakewell. Even his own family were unsympathetic towards him, and, in some despair, he hitch-hiked to London. Last heard of, he was living in hostels for the homeless or on the streets, working only intermittently in hotel or restaurant kitchens. There had been no news of him or his whereabouts since the mid-eighties.

The barristers involved in the trial had had contrasting fortunes. Brian Cattermole had become a High Court judge. His opposite number, Alison Lancaster QC, had failed to reach the same heights, but had, by way of some consolation, belatedly been created a circuit judge and sat in Preston Crown Court. Tom Edwards' career had stalled and he was still a senior junior barrister, practising, as he had been in 1977, in the Crown Courts in the north-west.

Both of Alan Woodman's colleagues on the investigating team had retired from the police service in the last few years. Detective Constable Forrester had found employment as head of security in a supermarket in Derby; DC Murdoch was still working for Derbyshire Constabulary as a civilian clerk in the Prosecutions Department in Chesterfield. As for the much-maligned Ernie Trousdale, a man arrested for shoplifting made a complaint that he had been assaulted by the officer. Unfortunately for Trousdale the incident had been witnessed by two members of the public and he was suspended from duty while the matter was investigated. Whether or not there were Masonic influences at work, Trousdale was not prosecuted but was allowed to resign. This meant he kept his police pension, which would not have been the case if he had been dismissed. He did not live, however, to enjoy much of that, succumbing to bowel cancer in his mid-fifties.

As for Beverley Simpson's former employers, Hassop, Brook & Co. was still in existence in Bakewell, although the eponymous senior partner, Bob Hassop, had long retired from the firm. The senior partner now was Kevin Malcolm. His wife Deborah still worked at the CPS office in South Darley. To the surprise of many she had stayed with her husband, although rumour had it that she had had numerous affairs with other men over the years. She was never going to be in the same league in this department, however, as the firm's former secretary had been. Michael Donald was the firm's litigation partner. He and Kevin were now the only members of the firm to have any real memory of the unfortunate Beverley.

As they talked about the case, both realised that neither had ever seen the site of Beverley Simpson's death, and here they were, only a short drive from Curbar Edge. They decided that there was no better time than now to visit the scene.

There were quite a few cars in the car park at the southern end of the edge, but they managed to find a spot to leave Martin's car, and then set off on foot towards the top of the crag. Before they reached the top, there was an opportunity to descend to the base of the edge down a rough track. They took this and were soon walking along the bottom of the crag through a minefield of boulders and millstones. In three hundred yards they came across their first climber. It was a slim young woman of about thirty. She was wearing jeans and a T-shirt. She had no helmet. She was climbing alone.